Taylor's Father

A LOVE STORY

NEW YORK TIMES BESTSELLING AUTHOR
PENELOPE WARD

Chapter 1

BLAIR

I looked down at the photo of his gorgeous, angular face. *This can't be real.* It was the handsome guy from the lobby, the same one I specifically remembered admiring when I checked into this place. Big and strong. Almost reminded me of a Viking. He had tatted arms and gorgeous, dark brown hair that fell over his eyes a little. It was mostly families or couples here at Midnight Key Resort. I'd assumed he was married, or maybe someone's hot dad—he'd looked old enough to have kids.

Yet I'd just found him on the hookup app I'd joined.

After staring at his photo for far too long, I moved on to the details of his profile.

Tate, 36

I'm not good at describing what I'm looking for. Sometimes we don't really know what we need until we find it. But I guess if I'm on this particular app, you can guess what I might be interested in for now. Anything more would be

*an unexpected but welcome bonus. Just trying
to keep it real.*

Hmm... I appreciated his honesty. Rather than trying too hard to write something witty, he'd written what he felt and what most people were probably thinking. I had to respect that.

Thirty-freaking-six.

Okay, so he was *a lot* older than me. It didn't matter, though. In fact, that sort of turned me on. Being with an older man was always a fantasy of mine, one I never thought I'd have the opportunity to entertain. Tate looked a bit younger than thirty-six, though. I would've put him in his early thirties, maybe.

I felt guilty that I'd lied about my age on my profile. But my first instinct when setting up this account was to not give any true personal details. Yes, that was ironic considering I'd just appreciated the fact that he seemed honest.

Without thinking it through much longer, I swiped right. Almost instantly, a message came on the screen.

It's a match.

Oh my God.

What now?

The room spun a little as adrenaline coursed through me. Actually, maybe that was the one margarita I'd had in months going to my head. Both the margarita and this vacation had been badly needed. Up until recently, when I was dumped, I'd had the same boyfriend since I was fifteen. So, this was the first time in my life I'd ever installed a hookup app. What better time, I supposed, than while on vacation alone at a resort, courtesy of my best friend, Taylor, who had footed the bill. His family owned the place.

A notification sounded.

Hot Lobby Viking Guy had sent me a message. *Gah!*

My heart began to race, but I wasn't ready to click on it, for some reason.

I slurped the last of my margarita, desperate for some liquid courage. I'd managed to finagle that drink from the twenty-four-hour bar downstairs with my fake ID. Not wanting to get kicked out of this beautiful place, I didn't plan on whipping out my fake ID every day while here, though. But the bartender on duty when I'd ventured downstairs this morning looked gullible, so I decided to take a chance. Just because I'd gotten lucky this morning didn't mean it would happen again. Not sure why I ever thought it was a good idea to start my day with alcohol, but here we were.

At nineteen—almost twenty—I was likely the youngest person on vacation alone at this resort. The teenagers closest to my age were generally traveling with their families. I didn't really fit in and had wondered if I might be the only single person here. Though apparently, I wasn't, unless Tate was lying about his status. It seemed like chancing it on this app was my only opportunity to meet someone, since it matched people by proximity. And leaving the premises down here in Key West wasn't an option, since I didn't know the area and didn't have a car. I also didn't want to leave the safety of this all-inclusive, secure place.

Maybe it wasn't exactly what I would have picked for myself, but it was an incredible gift from Taylor, my guy best friend whom I'd first met at sleepaway camp when I was a preteen. While we didn't see each other aside from those weeks at camp, we'd bonded over the course of several summers and also kept in touch online. Eventually, we both became camp counselors together when we turned sixteen. I'd been in a relationship with Daniel since I was fifteen, so nothing romantic ever came of my time with Taylor during those summers. We were true friends, though, and Taylor felt like a brother to me. He'd recently met a girl, right before my breakup with Daniel. So even if we'd had those feelings for each other, the timing was never right. And that was just as well, because Taylor was someone I hoped to have in my life forever. My experience with guys had proven that being in a relationship was one way to ensure you eventually lost the person you cared about. So I was glad Taylor seemed happy with his new girlfriend, and I knew our friendship would withstand the test of time.

After my terrible breakup with Daniel, the last thing I wanted was to get into another relationship. But Daniel breaking my heart had opened the door for me to explore my sexuality. I'd previously resigned myself to only ever being with one guy, but I'd always been curious what it would be like to be with someone else—someone new and exciting. Maybe a little older and mysterious. Maybe that was asking for trouble, but I couldn't quell this itch inside of me right now.

Yet I was still stalling when it came to clicking on the message. I stared down at Tate's photo again. In it, he was leaning against a truck, dressed in a fitted, charcoal gray shirt with his inked forearms crossed. His blue eyes shined. He was an unattainable type of gorgeous. Why this guy needed an app to meet women was beyond me. Surely all he'd have to do was go to a bar, and women would flock to him. But maybe he didn't want to deal with all that, and the app was just easier.

Since I'd never used a hookup app before, it had taken me a while to create my profile. I'd selected a fake name—Delores—and made myself ten years older, twenty-nine. Maybe that was a bit much, but it was too late to change it now, at least as far as Hot Lobby Viking Guy was concerned. In retrospect, I probably could've picked a more age-appropriate name—okay, *a lot* more age appropriate. I didn't know anyone under the age of seventy named Delores.

I'd said I was willing to meet men within a one-mile radius, and the app had shown me three options. Two were men in their sixties, so I immediately rejected them. (I hadn't set an age limit, but that was taking it too far.) The last one, though, was Hot Lobby Viking Guy, whose message was currently burning a hole in my phone. And he had a name now. *Tate*. That seemed to fit him.

Am I really gonna do this?

I stared at his image a little longer before biting the bullet. I remembered being unable to take my eyes off him the day I'd checked in. He was stunning, his slight dark beard peppered with a few hints of gray. But I hadn't seen him again since that first day. I might've convinced myself I'd imagined him were it not for today.

After I closed my eyes for a moment, I clicked.

Tate: Is it really you? I haven't seen you since check-in.

He remembered me?

I typed.

Delores: You remember me?

A few seconds later, he responded.

Tate: I saw you looking over at me in the lobby a few days ago, but I haven't seen you since. How is that possible? This place isn't that big. Where did you disappear to?

He had to mention that I'd been checking him out that day? Even if it was true, it sucks that he noticed.

Delores: Apparently, it's big enough if we haven't run into each other since.

Tate: I have to admit, I'm relieved.

Delores: Why is that?

Tate: I thought you were a lot younger. When I saw you were 29 on the profile, it was an easy swipe.

Crap. Guilt set in as I typed.

Delores: I guess that makes us seven years apart.

Or seventeen. Details.

Tate: Are you here at Midnight Key alone? I assumed you were with someone.

Delores: All by my lonesome. How about you?

Tate: I'm here alone as well.

Bracing myself, I decided to make the first move.

Delores: Do you want to meet up?

Tate: Absolutely. Where would you like to meet?

Shit was getting real. This guy could easily overpower me, and I had to look out for my safety, at least until I got to know him.

Delores: The kiddie pool.

Tate: LOL. The kiddie pool?

Delores: Yup. I have no idea who you are. So I'd prefer a safe place.

Tate: Ah. OK then. Smart. Can't fault you for that. Kiddie pool it is.

Delores: Want to say half an hour?

Tate: Sounds good to me. See you then.

Holy crap. This is really happening.

BLAIR

Not wanting to seem too eager, I decided to show up at the kiddie pool five minutes late. Wearing a black mesh cover-up over my pink bikini, I walked slowly toward where I was supposed to be meeting Tate.

Goose bumps formed on my arms as I spotted the brawny hottie sitting on one of the chairs typically occupied by parents looking on as their kids swam. He hadn't noticed me yet, so I took a moment to admire him from afar while also attempting to calm my nerves. Next to him on a small table were an assortment of drinks. He was wearing shades, but there was no mistaking him. His was a body you didn't forget. Maybe it was a little ridiculous that I'd had him meet me here. It had seemed like a good idea at the time, but now it felt kind of odd.

I walked toward him.

Tate stood when he saw me approaching.

His mouth curved into a smile. "Hey..."

"Hi." I blew out a nervous breath.

"Tate." He held out his large hand. "Good to officially meet you."

"Doris." I nodded. "Same."

He had a firm grip, and my skin prickled as I imagined feeling that hand elsewhere.

"I brought you something to drink." He gestured to the table.

"Looks like you brought more than one thing."

"Well, I didn't know what you liked. So we have a daiquiri, an iced coffee, a hot coffee, and a lemonade." He shrugged.

That was kind of adorable. "So thoughtful of you. I'll take the iced coffee. It's that time of afternoon where I get a headache if I don't have more caffeine."

"Same. I think I'll take the hot."

I nodded, but this guy didn't need any more hot. He was pretty much as hot as they came.

He handed me the iced coffee.

"Thanks." I took a sip.

After a moment of silence, he tilted his head. "What's your *real* name, Doris?"

Heat rose to my face. "Excuse me?"

"You just introduced yourself as *Doris*. But your profile name is Delores."

Shit. I'd been so mesmerized I'd forgotten the damn name I'd chosen. *Fuck my life.*

I surrendered. "It's not my real name. But I prefer to keep my real name to myself, if that's okay."

His expression turned serious. "I have no problem with that. But it would've been nice to know you were using a fake name from the get-go."

I nodded, actually quite annoyed with myself. "Well, now you know." I cleared my throat.

He cocked his head. "Out of all the names, why did you pick Delores?"

I feigned confusion. "What's wrong with it?"

"It sounds like someone's grandmother."

I chuckled. "Look, I just didn't want to give my real name to a stranger. I didn't spend all that much time thinking about it. For some reason, it was the first name that came to mind."

"Why is that so scary? It's just a first name. Not like I could look you up without your last name."

He took off his shades, and for a moment I got lost in the blue of his eyes that were glowing in the sun. Holy shit, this guy was hot—and a little intimidating.

"I've never done this before," I confessed.

"Done *what* before?"

"Met someone on a hookup app. I only downloaded it today."

His eyes narrowed. "What made you start here at the resort?"

"This was supposed to be an exciting vacation. But so far, it's just been...peaceful at best. I wanted to have at least one good story when I got home. I've already wasted a few days. So I figured it was time to start making memories."

He smirked. "*Making memories* sounds a bit too wholesome, considering what that app is normally used for."

"Well, I know." I rolled my eyes. "Are you a regular on there or..."

"Not at all." He shook his head. "I've only used it one other time. I, like you, found myself getting a little antsy here and was looking for some fun." He raised his chin. "Why are you on vacation by yourself?"

"I might ask the same of you. I assumed you were someone's dad."

"Ouch." He nearly spit out his coffee. "Did you just call me old?"

"You're not old, but you do give hot-dad vibes." I felt myself blush.

"Hopefully you mean a dad with *very young* kids."

"Yes." I smiled. "Of course."

"You know..." He scratched his chin. "Come to think of it, up close, you look *a lot* younger than twenty-nine. If your name is fake, who's to say you're not lying to me about your age, too?"

A rush of adrenaline hit. "I just have good genes."

Tate bit his bottom lip. "You're dangerous, Doris-Delores. I probably shouldn't be here at this...*kiddie pool* with you." He gestured toward the children splashing in the water. "I'm starting to worry you should be swimming with them instead of fucking around with me." He sipped his coffee. "I'm thinking I should let you go. Thanks anyway." He nodded and turned to walk away.

What the hell?

That's it?

He wasn't even going to say goodbye? *Who does that?*

"Wait," I called.

He turned. "Yes?"

"I'm nineteen," I blurted.

His eyes widened. "Jesus. I knew you were younger. But *that* young?"

"So what?" I crossed my arms. "I'm legal."

"Barely."

"And you?" I raised a brow. "Are you really thirty-six?"

"Yes." He drew in his brows. "Why would I lie about that?"

"I don't know. How do I know you're not *forty*-six?"

"Do I *look* forty-six?"

"No, but…" I looked down at my feet.

"You're just trying to distract from the fact that you're a liar. The way you really know I'm thirty-six is simple: *I'm not a liar.*"

"Okay, look." I blew a breath up into my hair. "It wasn't right of me to lie about my age. But I was trying to have a little fun, protect my identity, and…I didn't want to be typecast."

"How can I possibly typecast someone who picks a name fit for an eighty-year-old and matches it to an eighteen-year-old's face?"

My eyes widened. "Now I look *eighteen*?"

"You could pass for it."

"Well, if you knew I looked young, why did you meet me?"

"I guess I hoped your age was correct and you just had young genes or something."

"But you said you noticed me when we first got here. Why were you checking me out if I'm too young for you?"

He shook his head. "You're a real pill, you know that? And I *wasn't* checking you out. But I did notice *you* ogling me." His eyes fell to my chest.

"Like you're doing right now?" I asked. "Looking down at my boobs?"

He gritted his teeth. "Have a good rest of your day, Delores."

Then he walked away—again.

Oh my God. Did that just happen? And of course, he looked just as good from the back as he did from the front.

Not only did I feel like a fool for getting caught in a lie, but I had just blown a date with the hottest man I'd ever laid eyes on. *Yes, I'm pathetic.* Even after *all* that, I still wanted to sleep with him.

As I walked back toward the hotel, I called Taylor.

"Hey. How's it going in paradise?" he said in greeting.

"I just did the dumbest thing." I rolled my eyes.

"What?" he asked, though he was already laughing.

I told him the story of my app-date fuckup.

"Why the hell would you pick that name?"

"It rhymes with clitoris?" I chuckled. "Who the hell knows! You know I have problems making small decisions. It takes me forever to pick what I want to eat at restaurants. It was the first name that came to mind."

"You figured the name would offset lying about your age?"

"It wasn't even that calculated. Just a dumb, spur-of-the-moment decision."

"Well, I guess you live, you learn, right?"

"You're not gonna scold me and warn me to be careful?"

"Hell no. You deserve to have some fun. But yes, be careful about who you're dealing with. Don't go anywhere alone with anyone. You made the right decision meeting that guy out by the pool."

"Okay, but if you're looking to hook up with someone, how do you do that in public? At some point, you have to be alone with them."

"Well, at least get to know him first. Make sure he's not a serial killer. Get a vibe for the type of person he is as best you can. Maybe run a background check or something. I don't know. Just don't rush into anything."

"Pretty sure I won't be meeting anyone else. It's slim pickings here, and I won't leave the resort. So no need to worry about any of that." I sighed. "Anyway…what are you up to tonight?"

"Juliana and I are going to the movies."

"Fun. Have a good time. I'm gonna see if I can jump on one of the excursions this afternoon or something. I need a distraction."

"Good idea. The trip will be over before you know it, so you should make the best of it. Don't turn into a mope because of one bad experience. That would defeat the whole purpose of my gift, which was to make sure you forget all about that clown ex of yours."

"I know. Thank you. It's been an amazing vacation so far, even if I've had my moments. It's given me a lot of time to clear my head. I'll never forget you gifting this experience to me."

"Okay." He sighed. "Be careful. Stop trolling older men. And call me if you need to."

"Will do, my friend. Thanks for listening."

After we hung up, I went to the front desk and inquired as to which excursions had open spots late this afternoon or early evening.

There was a spot open on the five o'clock helmet-diving adventure, so I signed up for that.

After returning to my room to freshen up, I walked down to the pier where the boat was located at a few minutes before five. I met the driver, Pete. He was really nice and told me there was only one other person signed up. So, we were just waiting on them before leaving the dock.

In the meantime, he and I got to talking about what to expect. I was a little nervous. The idea of being that far underwater, weighed down by a heavy helmet, got my catastrophic mind churning.

Just as Pete asked me where I was from, a deep voice called from behind me. "Don't believe anything she says."

I froze and turned to find my apparent diving partner: *Tate.*

Chapter 3

BLAIR

"Are you the other diver? I should leave." I sighed.

Tate grinned. "No, by all means, stay."

"Is this your daddy?" Pete chuckled.

"She fucking wishes," Tate said.

I glared at him, and he smirked, seeming all too amused by this coincidence.

As awkward as it was, I had to appreciate the universe's sense of humor. And secretly, I'd been regretting how things went earlier and welcomed the chance to prove to Tate that I wasn't just some silly little liar. This was my opportunity to turn his impression of me around.

The instructor got us suited into lifejackets before the boat took off.

"Now is probably not a good time to mention that I get seasick," I yelled over the motor.

"There's a lot you keep under wraps until inopportune moments," Tate shouted. "What made you go helmet diving if you have a tendency to get seasick?"

"I wanted to challenge myself. That, and it was the only available excursion. I was sort of looking for a distraction after a botched hookup with some old dude earlier."

"You shouldn't be hooking up with older men who want to take advantage of you anyway."

"You're basically warning me against men like yourself?"

"Yeah." He nodded. "I am."

"That's great." I chuckled.

"What the hell are you doing here alone anyway?" he asked.

"I'm nineteen, not twelve."

"That's beside the point. Most people go on vacation with a group."

I narrowed my eyes. "Why are *you* here alone?"

"I needed to get away and reevaluate my life. This isn't about excursions or adventure for me. It's about taking time off from the daily grind to figure out my next move."

I tilted my head. "And you came to the conclusion that a one-night stand with *me* was the answer?"

"That was a moment of weakness and boredom, and thankfully, in the end I used the right head when determining what to do with you, which was walk the fuck away."

I rolled my eyes.

He crossed his arms. "I told you why I was here... Now you have to tell me why *you're* here."

"I just went through a bad breakup and needed to get away from the scene of the crime."

"Pretty expensive getaway."

"A friend gifted me the trip."

"That sounds like a nice friend you got there."

"I needed to get as far away from home as possible for a week."

"Where's home?" he asked.

"Western Massachusetts. You?"

"Texas right now," he said. "Has being away helped you?"

"I think it has, actually."

"But you found yourself feeling lonely earlier?"

I looked into his eyes. "*Lonely* isn't exactly the right word for what I was feeling when I went on the app."

"I see." He grinned mischievously. "Well, probably wasn't a good idea looking for a solution to *loneliness* on a hookup app."

"Yeah, it's a good thing the old man I chose turned out to be a fuddy duddy," I teased.

Tate shook his head. "Who uses words like *fuddy duddy* at your age? You're not very cool, Doris-Delores."

I laughed, and he smiled. Tate's white teeth gleamed, his eyes almost glowing beneath his baseball cap. I sighed. The hat really worked for him. But almost anything would look good on that chiseled face.

I can't believe how close I came to having it between my legs. My mind was not a team player. *Stop it, Blair. He's not into you, and you have to get over it.*

The boat stilled, and Pete turned to face us. "Okay, folks. Given that it's just the two of you, I'm gonna suggest that you stick together down there and try to put your bickering aside long enough to enjoy the dive."

"This should be interesting," I muttered.

He then geared us up, placing the gigantic helmets over our heads.

"I'm a little scared," I told Tate.

"Well, you're lucky I've done this many times before. Stick with me, and you'll be fine."

"You guys have underwater mics built in to the helmets so you can communicate," Pete said.

"Oh joy." I rolled my eyes. While I was pretending to be annoyed, I was certainly grateful that I wasn't doing this alone.

My pulse raced as I looked down into the great unknown. As I lowered myself into the water, the helmet felt overwhelming. But once the water helped manage its weight, things got better. By the time we'd reached the bottom, I'd begun to forget my worries as dozens of colorful fish surrounded us. It was unlike anything I'd experienced before.

"Oh my God. This is so freaking amazing." My voice sounded kind of robotic under here.

"It is," Tate agreed, his tone muffled. "Gets me every time."

"Clearly there are plenty of fish in the sea, Tate. You don't have to resort to picking up women you deem too young."

"Sadly, I still find you the prettiest."

Well, well, well. Could you see someone blush under water? "Are you actually complimenting me?"

"You're a lot of things, Doris-Delores, but unattractive ain't one of 'em. And I'm positive I don't need to tell you that."

I waded over to the reef. When I turned, I found Tate right behind me, smiling beneath his helmet. We were surrounded by colorful fish that wove in and out of the space between us.

One of them swam over to Tate and looked like it was trying to kiss him through his helmet. It wouldn't leave him alone.

"What the fuck?" He laughed.

"She likes you. She has poor judgment, like me. She'll find out soon enough that you're a curmudgeon."

He spat. "Oh my God. It's aiming for my mouth. Imagine if there was no barrier?"

"She would've been the only living being in your mouth today." I winked.

"You got a fresh *mouth* on you, Doris-Delores. Trust me, I did you a favor."

"Well, the joke's on you, since you accidentally ended up on a date with me anyway."

"A date? Hardly. What...are we out for seafood?"

"Don't say that too loudly in front of them." I looked around. "This is the most unusual but awesome date I've ever been on."

He groaned. "Not a date, but okay."

What an ass.

We were just inches apart, and his gaze moved down to my breasts briefly before meeting my eyes once again. Perhaps all was not lost.

By the time the dive was over, I had butterflies swarming in my belly for this man. Apparently, I was willing to forgive his rudeness from earlier. Also, somehow, I wasn't even nauseated on the boat ride back, just aroused. Was that the secret to combatting an upset stomach?

Droplets of water glistened on his perfectly sculpted arms. My eyes feasted on the colorful tattoos covering them. The stubble on his chiseled jaw was also a little wet, enough for me to imagine other things that might cause it to look that way. I was sick in the head to be thirsting after a man who'd humiliated me earlier today.

When I looked up at him, I could see that he'd been watching me watching him with a slight look of amusement. I promptly turned away and continued to ruminate. Was his reaction down at the kiddie pool warranted, though? Had I deserved it for lying about my age? Probably. The more I thought about it, the worse I felt. That seemed more serious than giving a fake name. Maybe if I'd been honest from the beginning, he might've given things a shot, despite our age difference.

After we stepped off the boat, I decided to clear the air.

I pulled in a deep breath. "That was fun."

"Indeed, it was, Doris-Delores."

"I feel a little wobbly now, though, like I'm still experiencing the motion of the boat." I held my arms out to balance myself.

He placed his hand on the small of my back. "You okay?" The contact sent a shiver down my spine.

"Yeah," I breathed. As we walked along the beach toward the main building, I said, "I want to apologize."

He stopped for a moment. "For what?"

"For lying about my age. That wasn't fair to you. You should have the right to make an informed decision about who you hook up with. I'm sorry to have put you in that position."

"No skin off my back, Doris-Delores. It's all good." He sighed, looking up at the sky for a moment. "Actually, today has been the most enjoyable day of my trip thus far. I have you to thank for that. Even if none of it was expected."

"The rest of your trip must've been pretty miserable." I winked.

"No, but nothing made me smile until today. So…"

My heart felt like it skipped a beat. "Well, I'm glad to have made you smile, if nothing else. Obviously, I'd been hoping to make you more than smile. But that's not in the cards for us."

I immediately felt dumb. With this guy, I couldn't stop myself from saying what was on my mind.

But then he surprised me. "What are you doing for the rest of the evening?"

Hope surged in my chest. "Going back to my room to swipe right on the sixty-five-year-old I passed up for you."

Tate's expression darkened. "Not while I'm here, you're not."

My eyes widened. "Oh really?"

"I feel sort of responsible for you, now that I know you're alone and don't have the best judgment."

My brows drew in. "I don't need a father."

"What *do* you need?"

"Something you signed up for but then refused."

"If only what I'd signed up for was real."

"I'm *very* real. I think you've determined that after several sneak peeks at my cleavage," I cracked.

He muttered something unintelligible and looked down at his feet. "I have a kid your age, Doris-Delores."

My stomach sank. "You're married?"

"No." He looked up. "Never married."

"You have only one child?"

"Yes."

Not sure what compelled me, but I reached into my wallet and took my license out. I faced it toward him to show my birthdate but made sure to cover all my other information.

"Okay, so you're really nineteen. Why are you showing me this?"

"I wanted to make sure you knew I wasn't any younger than nineteen."

"Well, I sure as fuck hope not, because then I might have to ask if your parents know where you are." He shook his head. "But nineteen is young enough. So proving you're nineteen isn't any help."

"I'm almost twenty. As you might've noticed, my birthday is next month. So, basically twenty."

He shook his head. "Still nineteen."

I blew out a frustrated breath. "Funny you think nineteen is so young. My mother was nineteen when she married my father. In my family, nineteen is not considered young. And someone your age should know it's not a number that determines whether someone is mature, but their character."

"You lied on a hookup app and had me meet you at the kiddie pool. Pretty sure your character age is about fifteen." He winked, clearly trying to get a rise out of me.

"And you're a grumpy old man who can't get over a girl coming into her own, who's just trying to have some fun on vacation. So I'd say you're about sixty-five."

"Sixty-five. Just like your Plan B." He smirked.

As tough as Tate seemed, I sensed he was softening toward me, even if our bickering held strong.

Leave now.

Let him chase you.

But what if he doesn't?

That would be my luck.

"Well...have a nice life, Tate." I put one foot in front of the other and began walking away.

A few seconds later, he said, "Wait."

Bingo. I stopped, turned, and batted my lashes. "Yes?"

"Have dinner with me." He paused. "*Just* dinner."

"What else would there be?"

"Nothing. But I don't want to be alone and would appreciate the company."

"Dinner with you... Why? So you can hand me a children's menu and taunt me?"

"Come on." He grinned. "I'll buy you a Shirley Temple."

My mouth fell open. "A Shirley Temple! Well, now it's just too tempting to turn down. Sounds like a salacious night ahead."

"Meet you in the lobby in a half hour?"

There was no way I wanted to spend the night alone, either. Having dinner with Tate was an easy yes—as easy as I would've been if he'd gone along with our original hookup plan.

"Well..." I sighed dramatically, pretending to hesitantly concede. "That would be okay, I guess."

"Great." He grinned. "See you then."

Feeling like I was walking on air, I rushed to my room because I knew I'd need extra time to do myself up. Not only did I want to look as mature as possible tonight, I wanted Tate to eat his heart out for having reduced me to some silly kid playing games. While much of my behavior on this trip had been immature, it wasn't a reflection of who I was. I'd spent most of my life overly cautious and overly loyal, and it had gotten me nowhere.

It was time to have some fun.

Chapter 4

BLAIR

Operation Eat Your Heart Out, Tate was in full force.

I'd put on the sexiest dress I'd brought, the highest heels, and a push-up bra. I'd blown my hair out and styled it for volume. I'd also painted my lips red and applied the darkest shade of mascara that brought out the blue in my eyes.

As I checked myself in the mirror, I had to admit: I looked hot. And older. *Older* was definitely what I was going for under the current circumstances.

Tate's reaction when he spotted me approaching in the lobby was exactly what I'd hoped for. Actually, with the way his jaw dropped, it was *better* than I'd hoped for. Naturally, he looked amazing, dressed in dark jeans and a form-fitting black Henley, rolled up at the sleeves to taunt me with those sexy forearms. The sight of him seriously did things to me. And his smell? It was a mix of leather, musk, and vanilla. I wanted to drown in it.

He cleared his throat as he took me in. "Well, if you'd dressed like this when we first met, I might've believed the lie about your age."

"Amazing what some makeup can do for a fresh face like mine, huh?"

"You look nice, but you don't need it."

"Just *nice* is how I look?"

"You look hot, and you know it." He gritted his teeth. "Don't think I don't know what you're doing, Doris-Delores."

"It's called having a little fun." I winked. "You should try it sometime."

"Having fun includes trying to give me a heart attack?"

I shrugged. "I like messing with you."

"You're very good at it." His eyes locked with mine for a few seconds. "Shall we head to dinner?"

I raised my chin. "Absolutely."

The outdoor restaurant was beautiful at night, lit up everywhere with little white lights. I realized I'd been so preoccupied with Tate from the moment of our first meet-up that I hadn't eaten all day. My stomach growled.

The waitress set some menus down in front of us. "Can I get you guys anything to drink?"

"I'll have a Sam Adams," Tate said before gesturing toward me. "She's not of age."

My shoulders slumped. "You always have to point that out." I glared at him before turning to the waitress. "We're celebrating my dad's fiftieth birthday tonight."

Her eyes widened. "Wow..." she said to him. "You look great for fifty!"

"Thanks," he muttered, shooting daggers at me.

"I'll take a Coke, please," I said.

"Coming right up."

I shut my menu. "You're no fun, Tate, you know that? I *had* planned to use my fake ID before you thwarted it."

"You're bonkers and reckless enough as it is. I don't need you under the influence on top of everything."

"I think you're afraid I'll end up on top of *you* if our inhibitions are compromised. Is it that you don't want me to have fun, or you don't want me to impair my judgment because *you* can't be sure of your own intentions tonight?"

His jaw tightened.

"I thought so…"

"You don't know what you're talking about. It really *is* just as simple as you're underage, and I'm not in the mood to get in trouble for ordering a drink for a minor."

"You didn't have to order it. I would've ordered it myself. And *minor* is a harsh word for someone who's a legal adult." I shrugged. "So, I'm not the drinking age—in this country. Big deal. Age is just a number."

"If it's just a number, why did you feel the need to lie about it?" He sat back, crossing his gorgeous arms as he awaited my answer.

I had to admit, he'd stumped me. Why *did* I feel like I had to lie? I wasn't ashamed of my age.

"I was trying to create an alter ego, I guess, one who was separate from the sadness I'm trying to escape by coming here. Adjusting my age was merely a consequence of that. In retrospect, I should've been honest, but I can't help that you have a hang-up about how old you are compared to me."

"You said you were twenty-nine, which would still be a little young for me, believe it or not. There's a world of difference between twenty-nine and nineteen. You may not realize it now, but you *will* in retrospect."

"Or I might think back to the time I met a handsome older man at a resort and we wasted a few good days because he was hung up on a number, even though he was attracted to me and every part of him besides his brain was on board. That man had a problem with letting loose."

Tate cleared his throat. "And just how often do *you* let loose, Doris-Delores?"

"Actually...believe it or not, almost never. That's always been my problem. I've taken life way too seriously and given way too much of myself to one person, who ended up throwing me away. I'll never do that again."

He nodded. "When did this breakup happen?"

"Three months ago."

"You wanna talk about it?"

"Maybe later. Not now. I don't want to ruin my dinner."

He smiled sympathetically. "Fair enough."

After a moment, I asked, "When are you leaving?"

"Saturday. You?"

"Same, actually."

Three days.

It wasn't long enough.

The waitress returned to the table. "A beer for you..." She placed the bottle in front of Tate before setting down my glass. "And your Coke." She looked between us. "Have you guys decided what you want to eat?"

"We haven't even looked at the menu," I admitted. "Dad can't figure out what he really wants. Actually, he *knows* what he wants, but he's not sure if he should go there."

"It's your birthday!" the waitress encouraged. "You should splurge."

"That's what I said." I snorted.

"Let me guess…" the waitress added. "It's the lobster alfredo."

"He's afraid-o, yeah." I laughed.

Tate's jaw ticked.

"Okay, well, I'll give you guys a few more minutes to decide," she said before she disappeared again.

Tate leaned in and spoke low. "You're such a brat."

"If you treat me like a brat, I'll act like one."

He flashed me a devilish grin, and I got the sense that he was letting his guard down. *Please, let that be.* Little by little, maybe I could turn things in my direction if I played my cards right.

"What are you in the mood for?" I asked a moment later, perusing the menu.

"That's a loaded question," he said, still looking at me and not the menu.

"Are you hinting at something, Tate? Because that would contradict a lot of what you say."

"What I *want* tonight and what I will allow are two very different things."

My nipples stiffened. *He wants me. Slow and steady,* I reminded myself.

I forced myself to look at the menu for a minute. When I looked up at him again, I caught him staring at my chest.

"My eyes are up here, Tate."

"Actually, your tits are pretty far up there, too. Not sure what you stuffed that dress with, but they did *not* look like that earlier."

"You've become *very* familiar with them, haven't you?"

He reached for his drink and downed some beer. I watched the way his lips sucked on the bottle, feeling the muscles between my legs tighten.

A moment later, the waitress showed up again.

She flipped a page of her notepad. "Are we ready to order now?"

Since I hadn't been paying enough attention to the menu, I looked down and picked the first thing that met my eyes. "I'll have the swordfish."

She scribbled and turned to Tate. "And you?"

He closed his menu. "And I'll have the prime rib, please."

"Coming right up." She collected our menus and left.

Tate took a sip of his beer then slammed the glass down on the table. "The swordfish...fitting."

I tilted my head. "Why is that?"

"Because it's the big fish that eats everything and spits it out."

I was about to say, "I don't spit," but my instincts told me that was taking it too far. I needed a different strategy, since my smart mouth didn't seem to be getting me where I wanted to go. Perhaps I needed a demure approach.

Once the food arrived, Tate and I had a rather nice meal together, and we even managed to stop busting each other's balls long enough to eat.

I licked my lips as I finished the last bit of fish. "That was very good."

His eyes moved from my mouth to my chest and back. "Best meal I've had so far."

"You haven't eaten here before tonight?" I asked.

"I was referring to the company, not the restaurant."

I squinted playfully. "You starting to like me or something?"

"It was *never* about not liking you."

His eyes widened as he spotted the piece of cake coming toward him, along with three singing members of the restaurant staff. Earlier, I'd pretended to go to the bathroom and asked the waitress if she'd bring a piece of cake to our table for my "dad's" birthday. It was a big milestone, after all.

"What the fuck?" Tate muttered, looking like he was ready to kill me.

I covered my mouth in laughter.

After they sang happy birthday, the waitress shouted, "Can you believe he's fifty?"

Gasps rang out around us. Tate actually turned red. This had been well worth it, just to see the expression on his face.

After the crowd left us, he shook his head. "Thanks for that."

"Of course. I couldn't let this special day go by."

"My fake birthday?"

"Well, that's what *they* think. But in reality, we're celebrating our first official dinner date."

He arched a brow. "You think this is a date, huh?"

"Isn't it?"

"The jury is still out."

"What's the holdup?" I dragged my tongue along my bottom lip as his eyes followed the motion.

He cleared his throat. "There's *more* than one holdup."

"Like..."

"Like the fact that you're young enough to actually be my daughter."

"Aren't we over that yet?"

"Even if I were, which I'm not, there's the fact that you're a liar. And age aside, nothing good can come from messing around with someone, given that we only have a few days left here."

"You seemed to think hooking up with me was a *great* idea at one point."

"That was before I got to know you."

"Wow. I should be so flattered," I said sarcastically. "So I've done nothing but turn you off?"

"Just the opposite. That's the problem."

"Then you're just holding back because you think I'm immature?" When he didn't immediately answer, I crossed my arms. "What about me has screamed immature besides the initial lie? You're proving that you still don't know me."

"Okay." He leaned in, resting his chin on his hand. "Tell me who you are."

I took a deep breath. "I'm studying to become a nurse because I want nothing more than to help people, to hold their hands during the most vulnerable times in life. I can't think of a better profession in order to make a difference in this world on a daily basis. My parents married young because my mother got pregnant with me, but they've been married ever since and have really grown to love each other. They've taught me what I want in a relationship, mutual respect and true love. I thought I'd found that with my high school sweetheart, and I had my entire life planned with him until the day he broke up with me. Then my world came crashing down."

Tate frowned. "Why did he break up with you?"

"He decided we both needed to experience being with other people and experience the world before we could decide whether we were right for each other. Pretty sure that's code for 'I want to fuck other people.'"

He nodded. "And you felt differently?"

"Doesn't matter what I felt. I told him the right person for me would never want time apart. He'd proven he wasn't the one. And I'm grateful he showed me that now and not later. In that sense, he did me a favor. But I also lost my trust in people, to a certain extent, and in my own judgment."

"You said it happened three months ago, but it seems like everything is still raw."

"It is, but I'm finally at the point where I want to meet someone new."

"You're looking for a relationship?"

"Not at this time, no. I'm definitely not looking for anything serious for a while."

"That's smart. I don't think you should rush into anything. In a sense, your ex was right that you need to experience the world before being tied down."

"That's why I'm here." We stared at each other in silence for several seconds before I said, "Any other questions?"

He nodded. "I have lots. So many I don't really know where to begin."

I tapped the table. "Well, keep 'em coming."

"What's your real name?"

"I would prefer not to divulge that yet."

His forehead wrinkled. "Why not?"

"I just think it's more fun if we don't know each other's names. Believe it or not, I don't want to know your last name, because in this day and age, you can find out everything about people online. I'd probably be googling you forever. Keeping it to first names makes things cleaner once we leave here."

"You haven't even told me your first name, though."

"You haven't earned it."

He rolled his eyes. "Anyway...you're talking like something's gonna happen here."

"I'm going on instinct." I winked.

"I wouldn't bet on it." Tate shook his head.

"Don't be an ass."

"I'm only trying to protect you," he said, not a hint of jest in his expression.

"Are you done with your questions?" I crossed my arms.

"No."

"What do you want to know now?" I chewed on my lip.

Tate rubbed his chin. "Why did you swipe on me?"

"Because I find you attractive, even if you might be too old for me. You remind me of a Viking."

He narrowed his eyes. "A Viking..."

"Yeah. Maybe it's your hair or the beard, or just how generally big you are. A combination of everything. I'm not sure. But it's a positive thing. In fact, you're so attractive, I just assumed you're not the type of guy looking for more than a good time anyway. And that's the level of non-commitment I need right now. I can't afford to truly like anyone at this point."

He chuckled. "So you think I'm attractive and unlikeable. Got it."

"More like unattainable. That's probably a better word. I was shocked to see you on the app, to be honest, since I had this preconceived notion that you were someone's hot dad or husband. But once I realized you were looking to hook up, I assumed you were a player."

"Did you expect that I would take advantage of you without question?"

"That's what I'd signed up for, wasn't it? Not like that app is very discreet about its users' intentions."

"Don't you think you should be more careful than hooking up with strangers at a resort?"

"Are you seriously lecturing me when you were doing the same thing?"

"We're just having a discussion. It's not a lecture."

"Why do I need to be careful of you?"

"Because I'm a lot bigger and stronger than you are. What if I were a bad person?"

"The bigger and stronger thing was kind of the point."

"Fuck," he muttered. His face reddened again.

I'd made this powerful man blush more times than I could count tonight.

"My turn." Smirking, I turned the tables on him. "Why did you swipe on me?"

"Because you're beautiful, and I was feeling lonely. It was impulsive."

"You really recognized me right away?"

He nodded.

"So you *knew* I was the girl you saw checking you out and assumed I'd be interested?"

"Maybe." He sighed. "I fooled myself into thinking you might actually be twenty-nine, that maybe my eyes had been tricking me that first day. Then I saw you up close and suspected otherwise again. It was your fake name that gave you away, though."

"But after everything, you're still attracted to me..."

"It's human nature. I can't help that I'm physically attracted to you, even if you're too young for me."

I rested on my forearms. "In a way, does it make me *more* attractive since you think I'm forbidden because I'm too young for you?"

He shifted in his seat but didn't answer my question.

"Did I just make you nervous?"

"You've made me nervous from the moment I met you, Doris-Delores."

"Because you don't want to want me?"

"You'd be correct about that." He began tensely shredding a napkin.

I looked to my left and froze at the sight of the waitress giving me a funny look. I realized she might've heard our conversation and was probably wondering why I was calling my fifty-year-old "father" out on "wanting me."

Ugh.

I leaned in and whispered, "It might be time to leave."

Chapter 5

TATE

Warning bells had been going off all night, but I kept ignoring them. I had no desire to leave this girl and go back to being alone again. I just didn't know what the fuck to do with her. All I knew for sure was what I *couldn't* do with her. That list seemed to be endless. But damn, I was having fun.

As we walked from the restaurant back toward the main building, I turned to her. "Where to, DD?"

She raised a brow. "DD?"

"Doris-Delores…"

"Oh." She laughed. "You mean, you're not ditching me?"

"My better judgment is nowhere to be found at the moment."

Her eyes lit up. "Did I see something about a Wednesday late-night dessert bar?"

Yes. Good. Whatever we did tonight, it needed to be in public, so the dessert bar was perfect.

"Yeah, it usually starts at ten."

"Usually? You've been already, huh?"

Many times over the years. I wasn't about to admit my family owned this place. Not that I was ashamed, but I'd never lived off my parents' wealth, and telling her the owners were my folks would give her the wrong idea about me.

"I heard someone talking about it," I explained.

"Oh, okay. Let's check it out."

I nodded. "I think it's this way." I led her down a hallway to where I knew they set up the dessert bar. I also needed to continue walking in front of her because I couldn't seem to stop staring at her pert little ass, which was torture. I hadn't felt this feral over someone since I was a damn teenager myself, and I needed to get my freaking dick in check before I made a mistake I'd regret. But she made me feel young and carefree, and that was addicting as all hell.

She squealed in delight when she spied the giant chocolate fountain, and I had to smile. The fountain *was* pretty cool, and it reminded me of coming here as a kid when my grandparents had owned the place, before they'd passed it on to my mother and father.

The resort had been renovated multiple times, but the dessert bar was always a staple. I hadn't been back here for several years, but now I needed a dose of the nostalgia and peace it had once brought me. Though *peace* wasn't likely on the menu as long as I was with DD. *Invigorated* was a better word to describe the way I'd felt since the moment she entered my periphery.

"This is too good to be true," she said as she plated some strawberries.

I couldn't have said it better as I once again found myself standing behind her, with my eyes planted on her tight bottom. I supposed this was better than constantly getting caught sneaking peeks at her breasts. I'd been pretty shameless about that, convincing myself it was okay so long as I looked and didn't touch.

She made herself a plate of strawberries with a huge dollop of chocolate sauce in the middle.

"You're not gonna get anything?" she asked.

She seemed to have serious concerns about my lack of interest in the dessert.

"I'm full from that cake," I explained.

"Oh yeah. Almost forgot about the cake. But I had some of that, too. I don't understand how anyone could refuse strawberries and chocolate. I don't care how full you are."

I shrugged. Refusing *her* was a lot harder than the damn strawberries.

We found a table and sat down. Then things took a turn I wasn't sure I'd recover from.

Doris-Delores looked straight at me as she dipped a strawberry into the chocolate sauce. A moment after she sank her teeth into it, chocolate dripped down her chest into her cleavage. I might have thought it was accidental were it not for the mischievous grin on her face.

Blatant torture at its finest.

"You think you're funny, huh?"

"Whoopsie." She laughed.

My lips tingled. There was nothing I wanted more than to lick it off her, and I wasn't sure what that said about me. But I was pretty sure the definition of hell was watching that chocolate drip down her skin and *not* being able to lick it off. My mouth watered as my pants grew tighter. The longer I spent with her, the less I could trust myself. Yet the guilt over my weakness was also starting to wane in favor of allowing myself to appreciate her company and see where this went.

I knew where it *wouldn't* go: my bed. I'd already made up my mind that, come hell or high water, I wasn't going to sleep with her. But I enjoyed being around her. I could do that, right?

In the spirit of *enjoyment*, I reached out my finger. Her eyes went wide.

"May I?" I asked.

She swallowed. "Yeah."

I swiped the line of chocolate from her cleavage up to her neck and licked my finger. Her eyes followed my movements.

"Wow," she breathed.

I licked my lips. "What's that?"

"There might be hope after all."

I chuckled. "Don't get too excited."

She lowered her eyes to my crotch. "You're telling *me* not to get excited? I feel like the bulge in your pants says differently."

"The bulge you speak of is the normal state of things. You can't take credit for it."

Her eyes filled with excitement. "Well, excuse me."

She dipped another strawberry into some chocolate, then reached toward my mouth.

I opened and took a bite, catching some of the chocolate with my hand. Her feeding me was erotic as hell, and I was delusional if I thought this situation was going to end well. I needed to figure out how to get away from her, but I couldn't imagine it. She was a dick magnet. Though it wasn't *just* physical anymore. There were other reasons I was seriously attracted to her. She was funny, charismatic, and refreshingly honest. Well, despite lying about her age and name. Other than that, her honesty was refreshing.

"I'm enjoying your company," I confessed.

"I'm enjoying yours, too." She smiled.

"I know I've been toeing the line with you, but nothing more can happen beyond just hanging out, okay?"

"You feel the need to announce that for the umpteenth time after you practically licked chocolate off my body?"

"That's precisely *why* I needed to announce it again. I don't want you to have the wrong idea."

"Oh sure," she huffed. "Because it's *me* who's confused. You just stuck your finger between my tits and licked it."

She had a point. My jaw tightened.

"Right." I cleared my throat. "That's what I meant. I've been pushing it, and I need to stop."

"I heard you the first time. It sounds more like you're trying to convince *yourself* of something you don't really believe." She stood. "If it would make things easier for you, I can go back to my room. We don't need to see each other again."

My dick was the first to scream in protest.

"I don't want that," I said, placing my hand on her arm until she sat back down.

I realized *I* was the confused one here. I wasn't making sense. Everything I did contradicted what I'd been saying. That was a direct reflection of the war going on between my mind and my body. I wasn't sure what that said about me, but I suspected the news wasn't good.

She pushed her plate aside. "You don't think I can see through you, Tate?"

"Why don't you tell me what you see?"

"You're no different than I am. You're a boy trapped inside a rugged man's body. You want to let loose, have fun with me—every part of you but your conscience. Your brain is telling you that you're too old for me, but you know we're not all that incompatible. You're just as lost as I am, just as lonely as I was before we met." Her mouth curved into a smile. "But we're not lonely anymore, are we?"

God, it was like she could see inside my head. She'd perfectly articulated the scrambled mess I'd been dealing with. I felt anything but lonely around her. And it'd been a long time since I could say that.

She crossed her legs. "Tell me more about you, Tate."

"What do you want to know?"

"Anything you're willing to share."

My first thought was to go back to when I was her age. Coincidentally, that's when my life had turned upside down.

"When I was nineteen, I was playing football in college. I had real potential for a professional career, but then I tore my ACL and never got to the point where I could play again."

Her smile faded. "I'm sorry. That must have been so hard."

"It was. My whole life plan had been centered on football. I didn't know what to do. So, while I wasn't in goodenough shape to play anymore, I *was* able to get a waiver for my injury in order to join the military. It was the perfect escape from my failure and also a way I could channel my energy into something useful. I still had so much drive inside me, which I could use to help make the world a better, safer place. At least that's the way I looked at it back then."

"Wow." Her expression was thoughtful. "That's brave. I admire you for that."

"I wasn't as noble as you might think. There's a big missing piece to the story." I paused. "Two years before that, when I was seventeen, my girlfriend had given birth to our son. He was born while my high school football career was in full swing. My ex felt like I hadn't given her the attention she needed while she was pregnant, though I'd tried my hardest. So much was happening at once. I struggled to keep my grades up so I wouldn't lose my chance to play football in college, and then, there I was, also a brand-new father who had no clue what he was doing."

"That's a whole lot to have to go through at that age."

I nodded. "She and I broke up shortly after she gave birth, and she slowly shut me out of our son's life, even though that wasn't what I wanted. I was scared. Scared of failure. Scared he'd grow up to hate me. So when everything went to hell with my injury, joining the military was a convenient way to escape it all."

Her eyes widened. "How long did you serve?"

"Only six years, but long enough to almost completely miss my son's childhood. My ex's new boyfriend, and eventually husband, became the only father he really knew." I closed my eyes a moment. "In retrospect, I can see that I was suffering from serious depression. Depressed about my football career ending. Depressed about not feeling worthy of being my son's father. But then things got even worse." I hesitated.

She placed her hand on my arm. "It's okay. Take your time."

"There was an accident. We lost two guys in a convoy I was leading." I stopped for a moment to gather my emotions. "While it wasn't directly my fault, I still blamed myself."

"Oh my God." She squeezed my arm.

I placed my hand over hers. "After that, my brain never felt right. I couldn't focus, and that began to be a liability. They honorably discharged me due to PTSD."

"I'm so sorry," she said, her eyes pained.

I nodded. "I think it worked out for the best. I needed to go home and face everything I'd been running from."

She looked away. "I feel stupid now."

"What do you mean?"

"I feel dumb for thinking you and I were not all that different. Because what you went through? I can't imagine it. I've had such a charmed life."

"I don't mean to make it sound like things have always been tough for me. I consider myself pretty lucky. I mean, I'm here, right? I'm healthy. There are much harder things to go through than what I did."

"How is your relationship with your son now?"

Everything in me tensed. "It hasn't been easy. He's never quite gotten over me not being around in those early years. His mother badmouthed me a lot. And a couple of years after I returned home, I left town again, which certainly didn't help. I'd convinced myself he was better off without me. But I know now that isn't true."

"Where did you go?"

"I took a job in Texas. A friend who'd also left the military wanted me to start a home-building business with him. I became a licensed contractor, and we did really well. But in retrospect, moving away was the wrong decision. I told myself that if I could just make lots of money and grow a business, I could make my son proud, maybe build a legacy to pass down. And that would make up for all the time lost. But all he ever needed was my time. He needed me to stick around and tough it out, despite his disdain for me. So moving away for that job meant I'd fucked up again. He and I still have a very strained relationship."

"It's never too late," she assured me. "You seem to think I'm really young, right? Well, you mentioned I was your son's age. So he's still young enough that you have plenty of time to make things right."

I chuckled. "That's a convenient way of twisting things around. Thank you for trying to make me feel better."

"You've had a lot of loss over the past decade. I hope the next ten years bring you nothing but joy."

"Why thank you, Doris-Delores." I reached over to the corner of her mouth to remove a spot of chocolate with my thumb. "Tell me more about *your* plans for the next decade."

"Well…" She exhaled. "I still have a year and a half left of school. It's an associate degree in nursing. I'd love to start saving for a house after I graduate. I'm fortunate that because I'm an only child, my parents are able to help me pay for my education, so I don't have a lot of debt. I greatly appreciate them for that, and I don't take it for granted. I plan to pay them back by being wise with my money so I can help take care of *them* someday, if they ever need it. Honestly, besides being the best damn nurse I can be, I don't have a lot of firm plans for myself. I want to work hard, but not too hard. And someday, way down the line, I'd like to have a couple of children. I think I want to be happy and healthy more than anything."

I nodded. "That's a very wise outlook, because you know, in the end, that's all there is, health and happiness."

"I may be young, but I do realize that. I've watched my grandparents struggle as they've gotten older."

I couldn't help but grin. "You come across like you want to be bad, but I fear you're a good girl with your head on straight."

She shot me a look. "Why can't I be both? Why can't I have my head on straight and also want to have reckless sex with an older man on vacation?"

Fuck. Why did she have to be so damn direct? Moreover, why the fuck was she making sense? I'd only had one drink, so I knew I wasn't delusional.

I started to sweat. "Why do you want to have sex with older men?"

"I didn't say I want to have sex with older men. I only want to have sex with one older man."

"Why me?"

"From the moment I saw you, I was attracted to you. Nothing that's happened since we met makes me regret swiping right. Because now I know you're a decent person, too. And that makes you even more attractive."

A decent person wouldn't have been imagining her kneeling in front of me with my cock down her throat. A decent man wouldn't be imagining licking chocolate off her naked body. A decent man wouldn't be planning to jerk off in the shower tonight to visions of her in order to relieve this frustration.

I cleared my throat. "I think you're heartbroken over your breakup, and you're looking for someone who seems the total opposite of that kid who hurt you."

She shrugged. "Maybe on a subconscious level. But why is that a bad thing? I'm not trying to prove anything to him, but yes, maybe what attracts me to you is the fact that you're unlike anyone I've been with. That's exciting to me."

"You've been with guys besides him?"

"No. He's the only guy I've ever been with sexually."

Just as inexperienced as I feared. But damn. How I wished I could show her what it was like to be properly fucked.

"So you want the second guy you've ever been with to be some dude you met on a hookup app who's seventeen years older than you?"

"You might have been that in the first minutes we met, but I don't see you as just *some guy* anymore. I mean, we've known each other a whole day." She winked. "Feels longer, though, doesn't it?"

"For someone whose real name I don't even know, I have to say... I do feel like I've known you for a while."

She batted her lashes. "Is this the dramatic part of our story where I tell you my real name?"

"Only if you want to, Doris-Delores." My eyes fell to her breasts once again.

"A reminder that my eyes are up here, Tate."

"You want me to touch you, but you don't want me to look at you? Looking is a lot safer than touching."

"Actually, I like it when you look at me. I just also like calling you out on your weakness."

"Exactly why you shouldn't trust me."

"As much as you warn me against you, I *do* trust you. I've done everything to try to push myself on you, and yet you remain protective and responsible—much to my chagrin. You might just be the most responsible man I know."

I sucked in a breath and admitted a hard truth. "A responsible person wouldn't be struggling with whether to protect you or eat you."

Chapter 6

BLAIR

The next morning, I woke up happier than I'd been in a long time.

The prospect of seeing Tate again filled me with anticipation. It was a wonder I'd gotten any sleep.

His words from last night still replayed in my head over and over.

"A responsible person wouldn't be struggling with whether to protect you or eat you."

God, I hoped he ultimately chose the latter.

We hadn't even exchanged phone numbers, so I was pleased to see a message come through the dating app from him.

Tate: I'm heading down to breakfast in a few. Care to join me?

Blair: Only if you order me four different kinds of beverages to choose from. BTW, it's never too early for an espresso martini.

Tate: You're about two years too early.

I laughed as I typed.

Blair: Very funny.

Tate: See you in a few?

Blair: Maybe...

Tate: Brat.

Blair: You like that about me.

Tate: You're not wrong.

My mouth hurt from smiling.

When I got downstairs, I saw Tate before he saw me. He sat at a table with a huge pile of food spread before him. How did this man look even more hot today? He wore his baseball hat backward, which was absolutely my weakness. The way pieces of his hair poked out the sides? Scrumptious. Every look he'd rocked was sexier than the last.

I walked over to where he was sitting. "Hey, you."

He gave me a once-over, and his eyes filled with something that seemed a hell of a lot like desire as he appraised the floral sundress I wore, the top of which was held up by two skimpy strings. My current look wasn't as dramatic as last night's, though. Today I had gone for fresh-faced and sassy.

"Well, hello." He smiled. "How did you sleep?"

"Like a baby..."

"No comment."

"You'd better not." I took the seat across from him. "How did *you* sleep?"

"Best sleep I've had in a while, actually."

"Must have been the company you kept the night before."

"I did have an amazing time with you last night." Tate smiled.

He seemed genuine, and I felt myself blush. "Likewise." I gestured to the food. "Hungry much?"

There were eggs, bacon, a huge stack of pancakes, home fries, and fruit.

"All of this is for both of us. Have you seen that buffet line? I waited for like twenty minutes. Didn't want you to have to do the same."

"Well, I guess I win for being fashionably late. Thank you." I grinned. "Between the variety of drinks the first time we met and this private buffet, I'm starting to think this is your thing—hoarding food."

He gestured to the plates. "Eat up."

How I wish I could.

For some reason, I wasn't all that hungry—at least for food. But it was amusing to watch this big, strong man devour his breakfast.

"What are your plans today?" I asked as he munched.

"Depends on whether a certain girl wants to hang out with me."

"I wasn't gonna be presumptuous. You're the one who's been resistant."

"Only to certain things and for your own good," he clarified. "I'm not resistant to your company in the least. I quite like it."

"So what's another safe activity we can do so you don't have to feel like a creeper?"

Tate stopped chewing for a moment. "I was thinking maybe we could go kayaking, if you're up for it."

My mouth curved into a smile. "I would love that, actually."

In truth, I could take or leave kayaking. But any activity where I'd be in close proximity to Tate today was fine by me.

"Cool. I already booked it."

"Now *you're* the one being presumptuous."

"Maybe, yeah." He winked before stuffing a big piece of pancake into his mouth.

Never thought I could be jealous of a pancake, but here we were.

I reached my fork across the table and began eating off his plate. As I leaned forward, I accidentally rested my foot on top of his at one point. To my surprise, he didn't move it away. The contact sent a rush of desire through me.

I popped a piece of pineapple into my mouth. "Do anything interesting when you got back to your room last night?"

"Not particularly." He chewed.

"After what you said about contemplating eating me, I think you might be lying."

He stopped mid-bite and shook his head. "Even if I did do what you're implying, I wouldn't admit it."

"I'm pretty sure you just did."

"What are you talking about?"

"Your face is red. You're fidgeting. The signs are all there."

I strategically selected a banana, holding it firmly in my hand as I slowly peeled it and took a big bite. Tate's eyes remained fixed on me the entire time. "It was the only way *I* could sleep," I added.

He nearly choked on his coffee.

"What you said riled me up," I told him.

"Some things can remain private." He glared. "You know?"

"So, you don't want to know about my soothing Epsom salt foot soak?"

Tate reached across the table, grabbed my banana, and took a *frustrated* bite.

After breakfast, I went back to my room to change for our kayaking adventure. Then I met Tate in the lobby, and we walked together down to the pier, where the rented kayak awaited us.

"Have you ever been kayaking before?" he asked.

"Yes. We rent a summer home on a lake."

"Ah, nice."

I climbed in first as he got in behind me.

He put a hand on my shoulder. "You okay leading the way?"

"Why not?"

"Just making sure."

As we took off, I was highly aware of his big feet at my back.

"I'm surprised you didn't insist on sitting in front," I said. "You know, considering how controlling you normally are."

"How else would I get to look at you?"

I stopped paddling for a moment. "Are you flirting with me, Tate?"

"I think that's obvious by now, Doris-Delores."

Goose bumps covered my skin. If all else failed and nothing transpired between us by the end of this trip, I sure as hell was having fun flirting with this man.

We paddled quietly for several minutes. The glistening water was as calm as the sky was blue today. We couldn't have asked for better weather.

I sighed. "God, it's so peaceful out here. It feels like we're the only ones in the world."

The low rumble of his voice vibrated against my back. "Strangely, that's kind of how it's felt since the moment I met you."

I felt my eyes widen. "Is that a compliment?"

"It is."

We settled into a blissful calm after that, but about half an hour later, we were out in the middle of the ocean when something suddenly jumped at us from the water. Everything after happened in quick succession. I jerked away, which nearly sent us toppling over. I couldn't tell you how, but Tate swung his arm out to the side and somehow managed to get us back on track.

My heart raced as I got my bearings again. "What the hell was that? Did you see it jump out of the water?"

"Yeah. Not sure what the fuck it was. It was alive, though. Noticed it right before you almost took us out."

"Thank you for steadying the boat." I panted.

"It was instinct."

A shiver moved all the way through my body.

"You okay?" He placed a hand on my back. "You're good. I've got you."

"Thanks. Just a little rattled."

Tate rubbed my back. I closed my eyes for a moment, relishing the feel of his hand against my skin.

"Wanna turn around and go back?" he asked.

I cleared my throat. "Yeah. Let's do that."

Twenty-five minutes later, Tate and I safely made it back to land without further incident.

"What's next on the agenda?" I joked after we returned to the resort. "Anything else we can do where I almost get us killed?"

He scoffed. "We would've been fine with our lifejackets."

"Not if that freakish sea monster jumped out of the ocean again and got us."

Tate's eyes sparkled. "I wouldn't have let anything happen to you."

"You'd risk your life when you haven't even known me two days?"

"I would not have to think twice about saving you."

I playfully knocked my elbow into his. "I liked when you rubbed my back earlier. It made almost dying worth it."

Tate shook his head and smiled. "You're something else, Doris-Delores."

Once inside the hotel, we stood in the lobby staring at each other.

"What's next? I don't want to go back to my room yet," I confessed. "Can we sit for a bit?"

He nodded. "Yeah. Sure."

We meandered over to a café just outside the lobby. He ordered two iced lattes, and we took them over to a seating area.

After my first sip, I sighed. "I have no desire to go home. This trip is going by way too fast."

"Tell me what you're heading back to that makes you not want to leave this place," he said. "What does your day-to-day life look like?"

I took another long sip of my coffee. "Nothing that brings me joy, to be honest. Lots of school work. An apartment that reminds me of my ex, which in turn reminds me of the fact that I wasn't enough for someone I thought the world of."

Tate shook his head. "He did you a favor."

I raised a brow. "You think?"

"You don't need to be tied down at your age. You'll find out eventually that there was a reason it happened. It left room for something bigger and better."

"Bigger and better is sitting right here, but doesn't want me, either," I teased. Well, maybe I was half serious. I couldn't help but feel a bit self-conscious about Tate's continued resistance. Despite our age difference, hadn't I proven myself by now?

There wasn't even a hint of amusement on Tate's face after that comment. "It's not about not wanting you." His jaw tightened. "I want you *very* badly."

"Say that again."

He looked into my eyes and repeated, "I want you very fucking badly."

"Even better when you add the expletive." I smiled, but then it faded.

"What's wrong?" he asked.

"You're sending me mixed messages."

"I know that." He frowned. "It's a reflection of the confusion I feel."

"You're physically attracted to me. And you think I'm nice, even mature for nineteen-almost-twenty. But you've still written me off because of my age."

He nodded. "There might be some truth to that."

"I'm not asking for a relationship with you, Tate. I just want to make some memories while we're here, to experience something I never have. Something thrilling with someone I feel a true connection with. It will give me something to think about when I'm old and gray—you know, the present time for you."

He broke out into laughter. "You little wiseass."

I stirred around the ice in my cup. "Okay, but the truth is, even if we never hook up?" I grinned. "I'm still having the time of my life, and I'm grateful to have crossed paths with you."

"Well, good." He smiled. "Right back at you, DD."

I stood suddenly. "What are we doing next?"

"Your choice," he said.

Yes. I knew *just* the thing.

Chapter 7

TATE

As his hands slid down her back, I wondered how much more of this torture I could take.

Doris-Delores had chosen a couples' massage for our afternoon activity. There were a few problems with this.

One: We weren't a couple, and this activity made it seem like we were to anyone observing.

Two: She'd specifically requested a male massage therapist; pretty sure that was to fuck with me.

And three: Seeing her splayed out on a table half-naked next to me was not helping the situation below my waist. Pretty sure this was all part of her plan to slowly kill me on this vacation.

Just when I'd thought I couldn't be any more turned on, she decided to take her top off, displaying a generous amount of side boob pressed against the table. Only her bottom was covered by the white towel as she lay on her stomach. I had the same situation going on, with only a towel covering my ass. I caught her looking at me with that naughty grin on her face. She knew exactly what she was doing when she'd booked this torture disguised as a massage.

The spa area opened up to the ocean, only partially shielded by linen curtains that blew in the breeze. I tried to concentrate on the sounds of the water versus what was happening next to me, because any time my eyes veered to the side, I only got more pissed off.

Needless to say, this massage wasn't all that relaxing.

"So, are you guys on your honeymoon?" the woman working on me asked.

"No." I groaned. "We just met, actually."

"He's trying to resist me," Doris-Delores added gleefully. "He's thrilled that another man is touching me so he doesn't have to."

The dude massaging her chuckled, as did the woman working on me.

"I see," my massage therapist said. "Interesting dynamic."

With every stroke of the guy's hands on her skin, I felt more territorial. And even though it sounded fucking obsessive, if *I* couldn't touch her, I didn't want anyone to. Not even like this.

It didn't help that the guy was tall and pretty good-looking. He was also closer to her age.

Fuck.

She closed her eyes, seeming to really enjoy her massage. That was the point of this, wasn't it? Except I was too busy monitoring what was happening to the right of me.

She moaned, and I felt it in my dick. She opened her eyes and promptly caught me looking at her. She flashed an impish grin, proving once again how much she enjoyed torturing me.

When he moved to work lower on her back, I gulped. Her skin looked so damn smooth. My hands ached to touch her like that. He applied pressure, circling his thumbs against her spine as I continued to watch like a hawk. I couldn't help myself. I was just as transfixed as I was on alert.

After the torture session, er, massage, was finally over, we exited the spa together.

She let out a long breath. "That was so relaxing."

"I'm glad it was relaxing for you." I groaned.

She blinked innocently. "You didn't find it relaxing?"

"No, I didn't find having to lie there for an hour while some guy got to rub his hands down every inch of your body relaxing."

"You could've stopped it at any time."

"Really?" I cocked my head. "And how exactly would I have done that?"

"You could've admitted that you wished you were the one touching me. I would've ended it early to put you out of your misery."

I gritted my teeth. "It wasn't just that. I didn't like watching someone else take advantage of you. No way a guy in that job doesn't get some gratification out of a client like you."

She shrugged. "He seemed pretty professional to me."

"On the outside, sure..." I huffed.

"What other way is there?"

"You don't know what he was thinking." I shook my head. "Men are... We're fucking pigs, okay?"

"Maybe you should speak for yourself, Tate."

"I *am* speaking for myself. I include me in that comment."

"Well, I was pretending it was *you* touching me. So, oink-oink."

Fuck. I shook my head and spoke up at the sky. "You're trouble."

"You're just figuring this out?"

"I'm not letting you choose the next thing we do."

She waved dismissively. "It's your turn anyway."

"My choice is gonna be wild and crazy," I announced.

She leaned in. "Oh, do tell."

Looking around, I lowered my voice. "We're gonna have dinner in the restaurant."

"Ohhhh. I can't believe you'd dare go there," she said facetiously.

"Right?" I chuckled.

"By the way, I just made an executive decision."

"What's that?"

She raised her chin. "I'm not coming on to you anymore."

I narrowed my eyes. "Why? It's kind of fun when you do."

"Yeah, but I need to get some self-respect. If you seriously don't want to be anything more than friends with me, that's your right. I shouldn't be making it harder for you to say no."

"So, what's this new chapter gonna look like for us?" I asked, disappointed—and disappointed in myself for being disappointed.

"We can still have fun," she said. "I'm just not gonna try to tempt you anymore."

Pretty sure all she had to do was breathe, and she'd still be tempting me.

"Okay." I exhaled. "Well, cool then."

Maybe this was a test. I couldn't be sure. In any case, her flirtatiousness had never been the issue. Aside from that guy touching her, it had been nothing but fun. The problem was *my* weakness and desire to bend her over my knee at any given moment.

She sighed. "I still can't believe this is going to be over so soon."

"I can't believe it either. I'm not ready to let you go." I realized immediately that was probably a little too honest. "What's the first thing you're gonna do when you get home?" I asked as we walked toward the elevators.

"Probably laundry."

"That's pretty boring, but makes sense."

She tilted her head. "You?"

"I'm gonna book a trip to see my son. It's been too long. Well, that's right after I pick up my dog from the sitter."

"What kind of dog do you have?"

"German shepherd. Her name is Khloe."

"Aw. That's so sweet. Should I be jealous?"

"Maybe a little. She's my number-one girl." I winked. "Khloe's been through a lot with me."

"That's adorable." She grinned, but circled back. "As for the trip to see your son, it's never too late to make things right. Don't let other people, like your son's mom, make you feel you don't deserve a second chance. You've been trying your best. That's all you can ever do. Even if you made mistakes along the way, you thought you were doing the right thing at the time. And you've learned from your mistakes."

Her words made me feel warm inside. I smiled. "Thanks for the advice. Who's the old one here?"

"I *do* have an old soul," she said. "I've been told that before. I also think sometimes when you haven't been so scarred by life, you can see things more clearly. You've been through a lot of circumstances that might make you question yourself. But from what you've told me, it doesn't seem like anything that happened was really your fault. It just happened—your injury, your high school girlfriend's unplanned pregnancy, the accident when you were in the military. Sure, you could've done things differently when it came to your son, but like you said yourself, his mother shut you out when she got married. Sounds to me like you've been doing the best you can with what you've got."

I shook my head. "Who the hell are you, Doris-Delores? Are you, like, an angel sent to make me feel better about myself?"

"I've been sent from the Kingdom of Blue Balls to save you from yourself."

That cracked me up. "Figures that's where you came from."

She placed her hand on my cheek. Just when I'd closed my eyes to savor her touch, she moved away. "I'm gonna go get showered and change. What time should I meet you for dinner?"

I looked down at my phone. It was five PM. A little early for dinner, but I didn't want to spend too much time away from her. The addiction was real. "Can you be ready in a half hour?"

"Early-bird special, huh? That's age appropriate for you." She winked.

"Actually, wiseass, we can meet for drinks before dinner."

She raised her hands to make quotation marks. "Drinks."

I felt bad for policing her life. "If you decide to use your fake ID tonight, I won't stop you. But I didn't see anything."

"Ohhhh, letting loose, are we, Tate?"

"I didn't say I condone it. I just said I won't snitch on you."

She chuckled and rolled her eyes. "How nice."

I winked. "Go get changed, pain in my ass."

When I got down to the restaurant, I snagged a table and messaged her through the hookup app that I'd be waiting for her.

Fifteen minutes later, and she still hadn't shown up. But unfortunately, someone I recognized did.

Shit. Langley Munson.

Langley's parents were friends with my mother and father. She and her family had frequented the resort over the years. Langley and I used to hook up when we were younger, but I hadn't seen her in ages. My mother had told me she'd gotten divorced and was on the prowl again.

She'd already spotted me, so I couldn't pretend I hadn't seen her.

Langley approached my table. "Well, well, well. How long has it been?"

I cleared my throat. "Langley, good to see you."

"Did you just arrive?" she asked.

"No. I've been here since last weekend. Leaving Saturday, actually."

"Did you come here alone?"

While I hadn't felt alone for a while, the only correct answer was, "I did."

"Well, basically me too. I'm here with my parents. They're around somewhere. I tried to lose them." She laughed.

I looked over her shoulder to see if Doris-Delores had arrived. "How are your parents doing?"

"They're great. They're probably playing around in the casino right now. You know how old people like to gamble."

"Right…" I craned my neck to see behind her.

She pulled up a chair and moved it uncomfortably close to mine. "Do you still come here a lot?" she asked.

"It's been several years, actually."

"How lucky to have run into you, then. This is our first time out this year."

The look in her eyes told me Langley had some ideas for us. I needed to let her know that she shouldn't get her hopes up. My last day here was already accounted for.

"Actually—" I began, but I barely got a word in.

"I mean, seriously!" she interrupted. "What are the chances? Here I was, thinking I'd be lonely on this trip." Sooner than I could blink, she randomly moved in and kissed me on the cheek.

What the hell?

Before I could lean away and break the news to her that I wasn't interested, I discovered Doris-Delores standing nearby. Her expression was sunken, melancholy. I'd never seen this girl sad until now. She must have witnessed Langley throwing herself at me.

My chest tightened. Before I could explain that this wasn't what it looked like, she started walking away.

Without saying goodbye to Langley, I rushed after her.

I vaguely heard Langley behind me. "Where are you going?"

I didn't bother turning around, instead focusing on nothing but the girl who had made my entire day earlier with her kind and reassuring words, only to be humiliated by this misunderstanding.

"DD, stop! That wasn't what it looked like at all." I grabbed her arm, but she turned and whipped it away from me.

"It doesn't matter. Nothing is going to happen between us, so you might as well fuck a woman your own age before you go home," she spewed.

"I'm not gonna be fucking her. She's someone I knew when I was younger. She just happens to be here with her parents. I'd only run into her a couple of minutes before you showed up. Her kissing me on the cheek was unexpected and uncalled for. I have no interest in her whatsoever." I wrapped my hands around her face and looked deeply into her eyes. "I promise you. That's the truth."

Her eyes glistened. "What's the point of explaining? You don't owe me anything. Soon you'll never see me again. Why don't you go wet your whistle and get it out of your system with this age-appropriate woman who clearly wants you?"

"Because you're all I can think about," I blurted.

I surprised myself with that admission, but it was the damn truth. After that fiasco, I owed this girl a hell of a lot more than a proper explanation.

Her breathing had quickened the moment I put my hands on her. *Fuck*. She was starving. And I'd been denying her. She'd been an amazing travel partner, putting in the time to get to know me, and I'd given her nothing. But perhaps most ridiculous was my attempt to convince myself that what I was about to do was for *her* benefit when I was the one dying.

Fuck it.

Chapter 8

BLAIR

As Tate's face inched toward mine, I lost the ability to breathe. *Is this really happening?* Within seconds, his mouth was on mine. He growled as he pushed me against a wall and not so gently shoved his tongue down my throat. I couldn't open for him fast enough. The way he guided my face with his hands on my cheeks, controlling every aspect of the kiss, told me exactly what I needed to know about how he'd be in bed.

As he groaned down my throat again, I met the vibration with a whimper, dragging my fingernails through his thick hair. *Oh, how long I've waited to run my fingers through his damn hair.* This kiss was more than I'd hoped for. My heart pounding, I felt frenzied, feral, wanting to climb him like a damn tree. He was so delicious, sweet yet somehow masculine. But if he thought this kiss was going to satiate me, he was sorely mistaken. If I'd thought I was addicted before, it was going to be so much worse now.

"Tate..." I muttered, not even sure what I was supposed to be saying.

"Don't fucking say my name like that. I can't take it," he said over my lips.

"Taaaaate..." I repeated, taunting him, pulling his hair and opening my mouth wider.

Pressing my body against his, I could feel his hardness through his pants. He pulled back, covering his mouth with his hand.

"Why'd you stop?" I breathed.

He rubbed his finger along his bottom lip. "Because I'm this close to carrying you to my fucking room."

"So?" I panted.

He glared.

I tucked my hair behind my ear and exhaled. "Okay..."

He ran a hand through his tousled mane. "Can we go and have a nice dinner?"

"You want me to forget that you just dragged me down a hallway and mauled my face?"

"It would be great if you could, yeah, at least for the moment."

"Okay. I can forget the kiss." I paused. "But not the way you stuck your tongue down my throat."

Tate groaned.

"You're gonna pretend like you didn't want that?" I asked.

He gritted his teeth. "You're not getting it. I wanted it more than you could *ever* imagine. The problem is that I want a hell of a lot more right now. So I need to come up for air, give my dick a damn chance to calm down."

"Okay. Whatever you want. I told you I wouldn't be initiating anything anymore. And I'm sticking to it. You going off the deep end and kissing me won't change that."

"Good." He sucked in a breath. "I'm sorry I practically attacked you just now. The way you reacted when I touched your face, it made me...*really* want to kiss you. So, I did. And I don't regret it."

"I don't either." I sighed. "I wish you'd do it again."

He turned and began walking back toward the restaurant. I followed.

When we returned to the dining area, the woman he'd been speaking with earlier was still there, as if she'd been waiting for him. My stomach sank.

She came right up to us. "Where did you go?" she asked.

He looked at me. "I needed to get her."

She turned to me. "And who is this?"

"She's my travel companion," Tate said matter-of-factly.

"Oh..." She blinked. "You said you came alone. I just assum—"

"I did come here alone," he interjected. "But then she and I met. You never gave me a chance to elaborate."

"I see." She looked me up and down. "Okay. Well, it's...nice to meet you. I'm Langley."

It was time.

"I'm Blair," I answered.

Tate turned to me, his eyes widening. "Blair?"

Grinning, I repeated, "Blair."

His mouth curved into a smile as our gazes locked. We entered our own world while Langley stood there and watched.

"Well...you two have a good night, then," she said awkwardly.

"Take care, Langley," Tate said, never taking his eyes off me.

After she walked away, he rubbed my cheek with the back of his fingers. "Blair. That's really your name?"

I nodded. "You earned it."

"I did?"

"When you told her I was your travel companion and didn't try to act like you didn't know me."

His smile faded. "Why would I *ever* do that?"

"Because you think I'm too young."

"I might think you're too young for me, but I'm not ashamed of you, Blair. I am ashamed of *me* for not being able to stay away from you when I know that would be the right thing to do, given the circumstances." He paused. "Thank you for telling me your name. It's so fucking nice to meet you, Blair." He smiled. "I can't stop saying it."

"Nice to officially meet you, too."

"Such a beautiful name that matches your beautiful face."

A woman's voice interrupted us. "I see father and daughter have returned," she said tauntingly.

I turned to find the waitress who'd caught us talking inappropriately the night I'd lied about my "dad's" fiftieth birthday. *Whoops.*

"Want to go to the other restaurant?" Tate suggested.

"Let's," I promptly agreed. "This one has bad juju."

Once Tate and I got situated at the other place, we had a wonderful dinner, our best together so far. Maybe because I'd finally given him my real first name, I found myself opening up to him even more easily. I'd told him a bit about growing up in Western Massachusetts as an only child. I went into more detail about my failed relationship with Daniel and even relayed the story of losing my virginity. Tate also told me how he'd lost his. To my surprise, it was to his son's mother when he was sixteen. He admitted to going a little crazy after they broke up, since he'd only been with the one girl. That was sort of how I felt at the present moment, having only been with Daniel.

But what began with me being horny and bored on this trip had turned into something completely different. I didn't want just anyone anymore. I wanted Tate. Only Tate. I couldn't imagine wanting anyone else for a very long time. I'd always compare my attraction to the way I was feeling right now. How do you go back to boys when you've fallen for a full-fledged man?

As we lingered over dessert, the restaurant staff began shutting things down, which was our cue to leave. Who knew how long we'd have stayed here talking if we weren't forced to vacate? I suspected Tate was happy to have a safe public place to be with me given his loss of control earlier.

"Can we go down by the water?" I asked as he paid the bill.

"Yeah. A walk sounds perfect," he said as he stood from the table.

Only, a *walk* wasn't exactly what I had in mind.

Chapter 9

BLAIR

We'd just gotten down to the shoreline. There didn't seem to be anyone else around, so this was ideal. Throwing caution to the wind, I slipped out of my dress, leaving me in my bra and underwear.

Tate's eyes went wide. "What the hell are you doing?"

"What does it *look* like I'm doing?"

He looked around. "You can't just take off your clothes."

"Why not? There's no one else nearby. I want to go for a swim."

I turned my back toward him, unsnapping my bra and letting it fall to the sand.

Pausing for a moment, I contemplated whether to remove my thong but decided to leave the Tate torture at topless.

He watched as I ran into the ocean, lifting my arms toward the dark night sky and screaming in glee once I hit the water.

I stopped when submerged to just above my chest and turned to face him. Rather than begging him to come in, I simply bobbed up and down, patiently hoping Tate would loosen up a little and decide to join me.

For several minutes, he just stood there in place, rigid, with his arms crossed.

What a hardass.

But then, I finally saw him undo his pants and kick them off. He lifted his shirt over his head, and even from afar, I could make out the ripples in his abs. I'd only gotten quick glimpses of his bare body during the massage, and he'd been mostly on his stomach, but his carved back wasn't for the weak, either.

He stalked toward the water, and I swallowed the lump in my throat. Excitement raced through me.

Tate dove into the water and swam toward me until we faced each other.

"Well, hello there." I smiled. "What made you change your mind?"

"I was afraid you'd get eaten by a shark if I wasn't here to protect you."

"Seriously?"

"No." He shook his head. "*I'm* the shark, actually."

"Oh. I like the sound of that." I winked. "Sharks bite, don't they?"

"Sometimes," he muttered, his eyes falling to my lips. "Hmmmmm..."

He looked up at the purple-hued sky for a moment. "I really want to kiss you again, but I told myself I wouldn't."

"Well, that's dumb." I scoffed. "No one's life will be saved by you depriving yourself, Tate. You're depriving both of us." I splashed him playfully.

To my surprise, he splashed me back with greater force.

We broke out into laughter and a frenzy of splashing until we were both thoroughly drenched.

When we finally stopped, I reached up and ran my fingers through his wet mane. Tate's eyes fluttered closed as he bent his head back and let out a muffled groan.

And then I felt it.

The most excruciating pain in my left leg.

"Ow!"

Tate moved back suddenly. "What happened?"

"I just got stung by something!" Panic filled me. "Oh no. There are venomous jellyfish in this ocean. I remember reading about it before I came here."

"Fuck. Where do you feel it? Your leg?"

"Near my ankle." I felt dizzy.

Tate sprang into action. "Let's get you out of here." He lifted me, and I immediately covered my bare breasts with my hands.

I felt light as a feather in his arms. Tate carried me to shore, and I reached for my dress, quickly slipping it over my head with my back facing him, while balanced on one leg. The sting felt worse now. Adrenaline coursed through me as my mind jumped to the worst-case scenario.

Then I remembered something. "I think you need to pee on it," I told him.

His mouth fell open. "Say what?"

"Pee on my leg, where the jellyfish stung me. I saw somewhere that the pee can help deactivate it."

He blinked and repeated, "What?"

"Please? I'm really scared."

"We need to go back to the main building," he said.

"We're too far. What if this kills me in the meantime? I think you need to pee on it *now*." I pointed to the spot. "It's this area right here, just above my ankle. Urine is a natural sterilizer."

"Shit." He exhaled. "All right...uh..."

Tate slipped his massive dick out of his boxer briefs. After a fleeting look that I knew might haunt me for decades, I turned away so as not to make him uncomfortable as he aimed at my ankle. The next thing I knew, I felt the warmth of his urine on my leg. I tried not to look back at it, instead focusing on the feel of the liquid, imagining that it was thwarting any potential for disaster.

When he finished, I opened my eyes to find Tate tucking himself back into his boxers. "How does it feel now?" he asked.

"The same. Just colder now that it's not being doused in warm pee."

Tate reached for his phone and scrolled. "Okay. It says here that urinating on a jellyfish sting is a myth." He looked over at me. "What made you think that was a good idea?"

"I saw it on *Friends*. Chandler peed on Monica after she got stung by a jellyfish, and she felt better after."

"*Friends*?" He narrowed his eyes. "And you take that as science?"

"I thought there was truth to it." I threw up my hands. "I swear I heard the same thing somewhere else. I just can't remember where."

He returned his gaze to his phone. "This medical article from a trusted source says saltwater is the best thing for it. We probably should've just stayed in the ocean."

"So I can get stung again?" I countered. "No, thank you! I'm done with that water for the rest of the trip."

"Let me look at it." He sat next to me on the sand, turning on his phone flashlight and aiming it at my leg. "It says to remove the tentacles. But I don't see anything. Next step is to keep rinsing with saltwater." He stood and offered me his hand. "Come with me down to the shore."

We sat on the sand at the water line. Tate spent the next several minutes cupping saltwater in his hands and pouring it repeatedly on my stung leg.

As the minutes went by, I began to feel better and more confident that I wasn't heading toward impending death.

"I think it feels better," I announced.

"Yeah?" His worried expression lessened.

I nodded.

He placed his hand on my thigh. "I'm sorry that happened to you, beautiful."

"It's okay." I shrugged. "Thank you for peeing on me anyway."

"Anytime."

"Really?" I laughed.

"No."

I winked. "At least now I can say I got some action on this trip. I mean, how much kinkier does it get than a hot man peeing on you?"

He chuckled. "Whipping out my dick and urinating on you was not on my bingo card tonight."

After a half hour, my leg felt exponentially better, so we went for a stroll along the beach.

Tate took my hand in his, threading his fingers through mine. "Is this okay?"

"Of course."

It felt good to hold his hand. For the past two days, I'd been angling for any sort of contact, and this simple act sent shivers through my body.

Hand in hand, we walked silently along the shore. The waves crashed under the dark night sky. I tried to just enjoy the moment, but the idea that this would all be ending soon continued to put a damper on my mood.

"Are you gonna regret not sleeping with me?" I asked.

"I might," he answered. "I'll probably always wonder. But it would only make things harder if we did."

"You're right," I agreed, proud of myself for resisting the chance at an innuendo.

He stopped and faced me. "I have never had more fun in my life than these past two days. And that's no exaggeration."

"I feel the same, but considering you've lived a lot longer than me, that's a *huge* compliment."

He laughed. "Blair..." he whispered.

"You've been saying my name a lot since you discovered it."

"I'm just so happy you told me."

"Well, I certainly don't tire of hearing you say my name, Tate."

"Blair," he murmured again. "I want to kiss you so fucking badly."

Rather than wait for him to determine that was a bad idea, I reached forward on my toes, took his face in my hands, and did what he'd done to me earlier.

"Fuck," he whispered over my lips. He circled his tongue over mine in slow, firm strokes.

The ache beneath my panties grew as I imagined what that tongue would feel like between my legs. As our bodies pressed together, I felt like an animal in heat, unable to get close enough to him. And I could feel his cock threatening to burst through the crotch of his pants. I wanted to reach down and cup it in my hand, but didn't want to put him in the position to reject me. He'd made up his mind about not going any further than this, and I needed to respect that, just like he'd chosen to respect me.

Still, I confessed, "I want you so badly."

He leaned his forehead against mine. "You have no idea how much I want to fuck you, Blair. My decision has nothing to do with a lack of desire. I want to do things to you that you can't even imagine. Believe me, I *have* imagined it all."

Arousal pooled between my legs. "Is that what you do when you go back to your room at night? Imagine what you could actually be doing if you stopped being chicken?"

He groaned. "What happened to your vow to stop taunting me?"

"You pressed your cock against me. That's what happened. All bets are off now."

He slid his hands down my back. "Probably shouldn't have done that." He stopped short of touching my ass and took me by the hand, leading me over to a spot on the sand.

We sat together, looking up at the bright moon.

"Life is funny, isn't it?" I said. "Out of all the people in the world, we met each other here, both alone and craving companionship."

He took my hand again, looping his fingers through mine. "I definitely don't believe in accidents."

"You think someone up there orchestrated this? Got inside my head, ordered me to get buzzed off of one margarita and go on that app so I could meet you?"

Tate turned to me and smiled, his eyes sparkling in the moonlight. "I can't tell you how it happened, but it feels like I was meant to have this experience with you. You've breathed new life into me."

Looking out at the waves, I sighed. "This would be a nice way to end, wouldn't it?"

"What do you mean?" he asked.

"Our story. Rather than sticking it out for another sexually torturous day and enduring a sad goodbye... It would be nice if after everything, we could just snap our fingers right now and disappear without having to experience discomfort. We could both go back to our respective homes unscathed."

He blinked, seeming perplexed by my sudden wish for *less* time. "You'd really want that, rather than spending one more day together?"

"I'm not sure. I'm getting attached to you. Might be better to rip the Band-Aid off sooner rather than later."

I wasn't sure if I believed my words or was just curious about his reaction. But it did make some sense not to prolong the agony.

"Okay." He squeezed my hand. "Well, we'll have to agree to disagree then, because I wouldn't be happy at all if our time together ended right now."

"You like me." I grinned.

"I do," he said softly, bringing my hand to his mouth and kissing it. "God help me, I do."

That seemed like a great note to leave on, so I let go of his hand, got up, and started to walk back toward the building.

He stood. "Where are you going?"

I walked backward. "In the spirit of quitting while I'm ahead...it's late. I should go back to my room. I think the longer we stay up together, the more trouble you might almost get yourself into with me. So I'm trying to spare you."

"I promise to be good, if you want to hang out more."

"Well, *I* can't promise to be good, so..." I shrugged. "I'd better go."

I waved, then turned and sauntered off. While leaving him was the last thing I wanted, I needed to keep him wanting more.

Shortly after I got to my room, the phone on the nightstand rang. It had never rung before, so it startled me.

"Hello?"

"Hey..." Tate's voice sounded gravelly.

"I never realized you could just call my room."

"Yeah. That's what we used to do in the olden days."

I laughed. "How did you know my number?"

"You told me your room number. And that's all you need. It's free to call from room to room within the resort."

"Nice. I didn't realize that." I cleared my throat. "What's up?"

Tate hesitated. "Did I upset you tonight?"

"No, of course not. Why do you think that?"

"You left me so suddenly. I didn't think our night was over yet."

His bedroom voice felt like a massage to my soul. I lay back on the bed and made myself comfortable.

I wound my index finger around the phone cord. "Didn't we have enough excitement for one evening?"

"Maybe I'm getting a little addicted to you," he said. "It wasn't enough time."

I sighed. "Like I said earlier, every additional moment we spend together is going to make things more difficult. Just trying to do my part to make things easier, I guess."

"How's your leg? Still okay?"

"Feels perfectly fine now. I think I'm gonna live, no thanks to your golden shower."

"Good."

I felt the low vibration of his laughter all through my body.

When he stopped, I could hear him breathing on the line. His breathing alone was enough to make me want to stick my hand down my panties. I couldn't take much more of this need for him. It was literally making me crazy. I'd never been so damn horny in my entire life.

"I've thought of you every night when I do it," he finally said.

It took me a few moments to realize what he was referring to.

Oh, God. I swallowed. "Oh yeah?"

"You were trying to get me to admit that, but I was too ashamed, because I still somehow feel like it's wrong to think of you sexually. But the truth is... I fucking think of you that way all the damn time."

"Why would you be ashamed of something so natural, Tate? We can't help how we feel in that regard."

"I don't have an answer for that, except to say that even when I try *not* to think of you, it doesn't work. It's like you're etched in my brain."

"I think that's because you haven't satisfied the itch. It probably won't ever go away as long as we're physically around each other. But you've already closed the door on anything happening." I paused for a long moment. "You should do it right now...over the phone."

"You want me to jerk off while you listen?"

"Not just listen. I'll join you." I bit my bottom lip.

He hissed. "I don't know..."

"You won't be touching me. How much damage can virtual mutual masturbation cause?"

He said nothing.

I lay farther back and rubbed my legs along the sheets. "You mean to tell me you didn't have sex on the mind when you called me just now?"

"Not gonna deny that. I've been thinking about sex all night."

"Well, we have that in common." I paused. "What would you do if I showed up at your room right now, Tate?"

"Please don't," he said, his voice strained. "Seriously. Don't."

"Okay. I'll stay right here if this is where you want me..."

His breathing changed, becoming labored and heavy. I could hear the rustling of sheets.

"Are you doing it right now?" I asked.

"Yes," he breathed.

Desire shot through me. I slipped my hand beneath my panties and began to rub myself. "Me, too."

"Good..." he murmured.

I let out a long exhale. "What are you thinking about?"

"I'm thinking of your ass in that thong tonight. Picturing you bent over."

"I definitely would've bent over for you."

"Don't say that." He groaned. "I want to be inside you so badly."

"Not more than I want you inside me."

"Stick your fingers inside and pretend it's me," he demanded.

"Only one finger, right?" I teased.

"You're such a brat." He chuckled. "But since you asked...as many as you can fit."

"Well, okay then," I whispered.

"Only you can make me laugh in a moment of heat." He sighed.

Several seconds passed with us just breathing.

"I bet you're so wet," he rasped.

"I am."

"I wish I could taste it. Are you spreading your legs?"

"Yes. Wide open for you."

"Imagine my mouth on your pussy."

"I'd dig my nails into your hair and push your face into me."

"Good." He exhaled. "I'd lick you dry."

My muscles contracted. I nearly came at those words.

"I wish you could taste how turned on I am, Tate. How much *you* turn me on."

This little phone exchange was the most arousing thing I'd ever experienced. I was certainly far more turned on than I'd ever been during sex with Daniel.

"I'd give *anything* to taste you right now, Blair."

Spurred on by this sudden change in Tate, I felt my climax building.

"I think I'm gonna come," I announced.

"Holy shit." He groaned.

As the muscles between my legs pulsed, I heard him coming right along with me.

And then...euphoria. As I came down from my orgasm, it felt nearly overwhelming—and painful, like I might die if I never got to experience truly being with him.

Despite how amazing it was, this phone sex had done nothing to tame the need inside of me. I lay limp, captivated by a man who wasn't even in the room with me. And I realized the worst had already happened.

In a sense, Tate *was* inside of me. He owned my heart and soul after only a couple of days.

Chapter 10

TATE

I woke up on Friday morning more eager to see Blair than ever. And not just because last night had been freaking amazing. I would've been this excited to see her even if she hadn't been responsible for the most mind-blowing orgasm I'd had in ages.

This was our last day together. The clock was ticking, and I had no time to waste.

As I hopped out of bed, I decided to go down to Blair's room to see what she wanted to do for breakfast. I got myself dressed and opened the door to my hotel room, only to find a piece of paper at my feet. At first, I assumed it was one of those *Do Not Disturb* signs that you hang on your door, but upon further inspection, I realized it was an envelope.

I picked it up and opened it.

My heart sank as I discovered a letter from Blair.

Tate,

Don't hate me for doing this. But when I woke up this morning, I realized just how much I'm dreading leaving you. Our intimate moment over the phone last night only made it worse.

So, I checked out early this morning.

I want you to know that this time with you has changed me for the better. I'll always wish you'd taken a risk, so we could've experienced being together at least once. But I understand your hesitancy, and it's not fair for me to continue to tempt you into something your conscience has been fighting so hard.

I will always think of you when I look up at the moon—just like we did together last night on the beach.

And please don't blame yourself for not doing everything perfectly in the past. Today and every day is a new day.

Love,

Blair

The paper shook in my hand.

What the fuck?

She's gone?

I read the letter at least two more times, my hand trembling.

This couldn't be true. *I'll never see her again?* I'd planned to give her my number before she left, in case she ever needed me. Maybe I'd have gotten her last name, though she would've had to trust that I wouldn't spend the rest of my life stalking her.

Sadness consumed me. I couldn't believe she thought leaving without a proper goodbye was the answer.

Should I race to the airport?

My heart pounded.

Think.

Think.

This wasn't a decision she'd made lightly.

I had to respect her wishes, as painful as that was.

Still, I stormed down the hall to the elevator and went to her room—just in case. Perhaps there was a tiny chance she hadn't left yet.

I knocked.

There was no answer.

My stomach knotted. But I still hadn't accepted it yet.

I raced down to the lobby and looked around. No sign of her. I also checked the two restaurants. No Blair.

I asked the front desk if someone named Blair had checked out, and while they said no, it wasn't a requirement to stop by the desk when you were leaving, so that wasn't necessarily encouraging.

After searching the resort inside and out, I had no choice but to try to accept that Blair had left.

She's gone.

My profound sadness was much worse than I'd anticipated feeling when we parted ways. This felt more like having my heart ripped out. It was unlike anything I'd ever experienced.

I returned to my room and lay back on my bed to read her letter a couple more times, then I closed my eyes as I drowned in regret.

I felt completely helpless, with no way to contact her. Visitor information was private, though I probably could've finagled her contact information from our business office. My family did own the place. But if Blair didn't want me to know her last name, if she'd chosen to end things this way, what good would obtaining that information do? She could've left me her number or her last name in that damn letter. But she didn't, and I wouldn't violate her privacy.

As the minutes passed, I felt more and more empty inside, the regret overwhelming. I should've slept with her, should've given her the experience she'd asked me for and that I'd wanted with every fiber of my being. Why had I been so damn scared? Yes, she was young, but she was still a freaking adult. I knew her well enough to see that now—now that she was gone and the choice to act on it had disappeared. Perhaps my hesitancy was what made her decide I wasn't worthy of a goodbye, let alone her last name or number.

I finally went downstairs just before the breakfast buffet ended. Not that I had an appetite, but I needed to do something other than wallow in my room. I arrived just as they were getting ready to clear it, grabbing the last bagel and a banana. But when I spotted Langley sitting with her parents, I decided to take the food back upstairs after all. The last thing I needed was to make miserable small talk while I was feeling like shit.

Before I could make my escape, though, Langley came toward me.

"You're alone again." She smiled.

"Yeah."

"What happened to your...friend?"

"She left." I swallowed, the words leaving a bitter taste in my mouth.

"That's too bad." She tilted her head. "Wasn't she a bit young for you? Looked like someone's daughter."

"She's almost twenty and mature for her age."

I had to laugh at myself, now using the same justifications Blair had used with me—that I'd ignored, always insisting she was still a teenager.

Langley rolled her eyes. "You know, all you men are the same."

My eyes widened. "What's that supposed to mean?"

"Only interested in one thing."

"I'm not sure that's any of your business. And you don't need to lump all men together, either. Sometimes we just want companionship and chemistry. That doesn't always come in the same boring, predictable, age-appropriate package."

She grimaced. "Are you calling me boring?"

"Of course not. Just saying you shouldn't be so quick to judge other people's choices. My comment had nothing to do with you."

She hung her head. "I'm sorry. You're right. My ex left me for a younger woman, and I think I might be a little traumatized by that."

I relaxed my shoulders and forced myself to take a breath. "Damn. I'm sorry. That certainly explains your reaction."

Langley glanced back over at her parents. "I thought this vacation would do me good, but it's only made me sadder. I have so many great memories here. And seeing you… It really brought a lot of them to the forefront." She looked down. "Those days are gone. I know that. But my time here reminds me that I've wasted so many years of my life."

While I felt bad for her, I didn't have the headspace to handle this conversation properly right now. But before I could apologize and say goodbye, she continued.

"And I guess I was a little let down that you weren't interested in me."

I nodded, trying to be sympathetic. "Don't take it personally. Please."

She shrugged. "Okay."

"Look, I have to run…" I told her. "Keep your head up. Things will get better in time. You just need to ride out the storm."

I wasn't sure I believed my own advice, but I figured I'd try to leave her on a positive note, even if it was bullshit. I did wish her the best.

"Take care, Langley."

"Bye," she murmured as I walked away.

Back upstairs, I sat on the edge of my bed and forced myself to eat the bagel. I hadn't even gotten coffee. I knew my head wasn't screwed on straight if I'd forgotten something I was usually addicted to. *Addicted.* That's how I felt right now. Like I was having withdrawals from Blair.

What a depressing fucking day this was going to be. I wondered if I should just check out early myself, since every damn corner of this place would now remind me of Blair—all the things we did and all the things we *didn't* do.

My cell phone rang, and my heart leaped until I remembered Blair never had my number. It was my mother.

"Hey, Mom," I droned.

"Hi, honey. You still at Midnight Key?"

"Yeah." I sighed. "For now. I was supposed to be here until tomorrow, but now I'm not so sure. Might take off early."

"Why is that?"

I tugged at my hair. "I don't really wanna get into it."

"Terry Munson told me her daughter ran into you there."

Shit. Big mouth Langley.

I lay back on the bed and sighed. "She did, did she?"

"Yes."

My mother fell silent, and I knew she was holding back.

I rolled my eyes. "What else did she tell you?"

"She said you were quite cozy with someone half your age."

I shook my head. "She should mind her own business."

"So it's true?"

"I did meet someone who's younger, yeah. A sweet person who deserves better than to be reduced to her age. Nothing happened between us, if that's what you're getting at. It was mostly innocent. We had fun together. That was all. She got my mind off my troubles for a bit. And now she's checked out. The story ends there."

That did pretty much sum it up, even if the reality was much more complex in my mind.

"How old was she?"

"Almost twenty." *There I go again.*

"Well, you know I was around that age when I met your father," Mom said. "But people don't settle down so young these days. If she were the right person for you, though, I wouldn't discourage it just because she's young."

That didn't make me feel any better about my decisions. I shook my head. "It doesn't matter anyway."

"Are you going through some kind of midlife crisis?"

I had to laugh at that. "I'm not mid-life, Mom."

"Not yet, at least." She paused. "Anyway, what's wrong with Langley? She's always liked you."

Langley was the furthest thing from what I wanted.

"There's nothing wrong with her. I'm just not interested."

"You've always been picky."

"There's nothing wrong with being selective."

"Have you been in touch with Taylor?"

"No, but I plan to call him when I get home. If you speak to him, don't mention that I'm here. I don't want him to get the wrong idea and think I chose to come to the Keys rather than visit him. I just needed to clear my head before I came home."

"I haven't mentioned it," she said.

Staring up at the ceiling, I murmured, "I'm long overdue to visit him, even if he doesn't want to see me."

"You have to stop worrying about whether or not he *wants* to see you," she scolded. "He just *thinks* he doesn't want to see you—or more likely, he pretends not to want to see you. But he's starving for that connection with his dad."

I ran my hand through my hair. "I hope you're right."

"You, my son, sound like you got run over by a truck."

That was exactly how I felt. "I'll be all right. Don't worry about me, okay?"

"Well, I hope you can have a good time on your last day there. Your father and I toyed with the idea of showing up and surprising you but decided against it."

"You should've," I said, even if I wasn't sure I meant it.

My parents still technically owned the resort, but they rarely visited, having delegated most of the operations to employees of my father's company. If they'd shown up, they would've rattled more than one person here. Normally it was nice to spend time with them, but I couldn't imagine how I'd have handled that while I was hanging out with Blair. She'd commanded all of my attention.

"Maybe next time," she said. "And maybe one day we can all meet there with Taylor. He doesn't get to enjoy it enough."

"That'd be amazing." I gazed out at the sun peeking through my window. "Anyway, Mom, I better let you go. Thank you for checking in, even if you were just trying to be a buttinsky based on gossip you heard."

She chose not to respond to that. "Love you, my son."

"Love you, Mom. Tell Dad I said hello."

After she hung up, I tossed my phone and rubbed my temples, considering again whether to just get the hell out of here.

Then there was a knock on my door.

Who the fuck is that?

Not giving a shit about anything, I opened without checking the peephole and nearly fell back at the sight of her.

I blinked, suddenly coming back from the dead as I whispered, "Blair…"

"Oh my God, are you okay?" she asked, her eyes wide.

"No," I growled. "I'm not fucking okay. I thought you left. I was fucking mourning you."

Her face reddened. "I never left."

"What the hell?"

"I never left," she repeated as she entered the room.

I turned away for a moment and paced, stunned into silence. But as I took a moment to breathe, my anger transformed into joy. She was really still here. I needed to appreciate the second chance I'd been given.

My breath sped up as I faced her. "I don't understand why you did that, but I'm not sure I give a damn."

Her face turned redder. "It was an April Fool's prank."

My eyes widened. "Are you fucking kidding me?"

I realized it was, in fact, April first. I didn't know whether to laugh or cry.

She shook her head and looked down at her feet. "I feel so bad. I shouldn't have done that to you."

My emotions lurched back to being pissed as I raised my voice. "No shit, you shouldn't have done it."

"You look really upset. I didn't mean for it to play out like this. I left the note super early, and I planned not to let so much time go by. But you must have gotten up earlier than I thought, and I fell back asleep for a bit. I'm sorry you're upset. It was stupid." Blair's voice shook as she started to cry. "Do you hate me?"

"Hate you?" I shook my head and laughed. "No... I'm too fucking happy to see you to hate you. My emotions are just all over the place right now."

She nodded and wiped her eyes, still looking guilty. "In truth, it wasn't just about April first."

"Oh yeah?"

"I wanted you to understand what you gave up." She inched closer. "How did it feel to think we'd never see each other again?"

I stared at her, eyes wide, my thoughts bouncing around like pinballs. "With the exception of the way I handled fatherhood, I've never regretted anything more."

"Regretted what? You didn't do anything."

"Exactly."

She placed her hand on my chest. "It was wrong of me to let you think I'd left, though. I'm sorry for toying with your emotions."

"I'll live." My breathing finally started to slow.

She placed her hand on my face and searched my eyes. "You really do care about me. I know that now."

I pressed my body against hers, a fire igniting at the feel of her breasts against my chest. My eyes burned into hers.

"I think I deserve to be punished," she murmured.

"You fucking minx." I gritted my teeth. "You're gonna drive me to the madhouse."

She pushed her tits more firmly against me, her eyes brimming with desire. I instantly hardened, somehow knowing I wasn't coming back from this.

"Everyone has a breaking point, Blair."

"Do they?"

I nodded. "Welcome to mine."

Wrapping my hand around her waist, I yanked her into a searing kiss. I just hoped she'd forgive me for what I was about to do.

Chapter 11

BLAIR

My body felt like it had been engulfed in flames.

Tate's hands were around my ass, squeezing as our tongues moved against each other. I couldn't taste him fast enough, couldn't explore his body with my hands fast enough, couldn't have him inside me fast enough. I *needed* him.

"Please fuck me," I begged. There was no time to beat around the bush.

Tate spoke over my mouth. "I wish I could stop this—"

"I'm grateful you can't." I raked my hands through his hair, my panties already drenched. I'd never imagined being with a man so muscular, so strong. My arousal had reached a level I didn't think humanly possible. "Don't stop, Tate, I need you."

"You need *me*?" He laughed against my mouth. "I fucking need *you*."

I wrapped my arms around his neck and attempted to climb him. Tate carried me over to the wall, and as my back pressed against it, a zap of adrenaline hit.

He paused for a moment and looked into my eyes. "I don't know how to be gentle. I'm afraid I'm too much for you."

"I don't *want* you to be gentle right now. I want you to fuck me as hard as you want. I want you to do everything to me."

"Fuck," he muttered as he kissed down my throat. "When I thought you were gone, I was goddamn miserable."

Bending my head back, I panted. "I would never have left you without saying goodbye."

He buried his face in my neck. "I need to feel your pussy wrapped around my cock at least once before I die."

"I'm counting on more than once."

Tate carried me over to the bed and toppled us onto the mattress.

He hovered over me as a piece of hair fell over his forehead. I took a moment to bask in the sight of his strong, tattooed arms locking me in.

"Blair, look at me."

My heart pounding, I reached up to move the hair away from his beautiful eyes so I could stare into them.

"I've never wanted a single person on this Earth as much as I want you right now," he said.

"That makes two of us."

His eyes brimmed with desire. "Are you *sure* you want this?"

"Yes."

He nodded, and I knew he'd conceded, his longing tangible enough to cut with a knife. I'd never seen Tate like this and had thought I never would. My leaving had done a real number on him. That's what I'd hoped for, even if my actions had bordered on cruel. But this? It was far more than I imagined.

The look in his eyes turned as vulnerable as it was hungry. "I want to feel how wet you are. Can I touch you?"

"Please," I urged, dying for his hands on me.

Tate slipped his hand under my skirt. He shoved my panties to the side and stroked a finger inside of me. "Holy shit," he muttered. "What the fuck, Blair?" He added another finger, pumping in and out slowly, his breaths turning shakier with each movement. "I can't believe how wet you are."

"Now you know what you do to me," I said. "I've been wet almost every moment we've been together. Being around you makes me so freaking horny."

He groaned. "I've wanted to fuck you from the moment I saw you, even if it felt wrong. I can't help it. You're so incredibly beautiful." He slid his fingers deeper and closed his eyes. "Absolute perfection."

"Don't make me wait any more," I whispered, tightening my muscles around his fingers, feeling ready to come.

"I won't make you wait, baby." He shook his head. "I'm done trying to fight this."

I gripped his sides, my fingernails digging into his skin. "You'd better be."

He withdrew his fingers slowly before thrusting them inside me again. "And *you'd* better not fucking leave without saying goodbye."

We were so close to the end that, in a sense, every minute together now felt like a goodbye. I tried to shake that thought from my mind as Tate rose from the bed and left me for a moment. Cold air replaced the warmth of his body. I panicked until I realized what he was probably doing. The brief separation, though, felt excruciating. How was I supposed to deal with separating from him permanently in less than twenty-four hours? I didn't want him on the other side of the bed, let alone the country. I saw him reach into the side-table drawer.

He placed the condom beside him on the bed before he knelt over me again. As he unzipped his jeans, I licked my lips in anticipation. He lowered his pants and boxer briefs, his cock springing out, wet at the crown. Tate was absolutely huge. I bit my bottom lip as he ripped open the condom wrapper. He sheathed his thick shaft, and as he squeezed the tip, I felt my heartbeat between my legs.

He looked up at me. "I need to taste you first, okay?"

Barely able to speak, I dragged my tongue across my bottom lip and nodded, bracing for what was to come.

Tate slid my underwear down and spread my legs. Just the heat of his erratic breaths drove me mad as he got into position. A couple of seconds later, I felt the sweet heat of his mouth on my clit.

"Oh, God." My eyes rolled back. When he pressed more firmly, I thought I might leave my body. "Oh...my..."

He applied just the right amount of pressure, licking and sucking. The sensation of his hot mouth on me, his tongue exploring me—it was unlike anything I'd felt before. And I knew it was only the tip of the iceberg.

Tate must have used his entire face to pleasure me, as I felt his beard scratching me in an exquisite way. *Holy hell.* He kept muttering indecipherable words. I tightened my muscles to keep from coming on the spot with each whisper against my sensitive skin, each stroke of his tongue. I certainly wanted to hold out for what was next, and didn't want to deprive myself of the full experience by coming too soon.

"I can't wait any longer," he finally murmured when he came up for air. "I need to fuck you."

The sight of my arousal on his mouth was just about the most erotic thing, and when he lowered himself to kiss me, I tasted myself on his lips. I tugged on his hair. "I need you inside me, Tate."

He hovered over me, locking me in with his knees. "What you're giving me right now is the most amazing gift. You're my fucking dream, Blair. Don't ever forget that."

All I could manage was, "Thank you."

It might've sounded stupid and desperate, but I was so thankful that he'd finally let his inhibitions go enough to give me what I'd been yearning for. This was as much a gift to me as he seemed to think it was for him.

"I should be thanking *you*." His eyes glistened. "I don't deserve you."

I reached up and rubbed his chin. "Yes, you do."

Then I felt the burn of his girthy cock entering me. He groaned in the back of his throat as he sank into me.

I let out a shriek of pleasure.

"Fuck, Blair. This is so..." His words trailed off.

He muttered something as he began to move in and out. His words were slurred, yet I knew what he was trying to say. I felt the same indescribable bliss as our bodies became one.

"I know, Tate. I know."

He stopped moving for a moment and shut his eyes. "You feel even better than I imagined. I need to control myself," he breathed. "Give me a second."

Tate tightened his abs. I loved how out of control he seemed, even if I hoped he didn't lose it, because I was nowhere ready for this to end. Quite frankly, I needed him to fuck me harder.

When he'd regained his composure, Tate started slowly, thrusting his hips with controlled movements. And I bucked to meet each and every one of them. But then he began to pound into me, faster, harder. The headboard banged against the wall.

Yes. This was exactly what I wanted, what I'd imagined in my wildest dreams. Actually, it surpassed all of that. I couldn't get enough. "Fuck me harder," I begged, my nails digging into his back.

"I'm afraid to fuck you the way I really want to."

But despite what he said, Tate did slam his body against mine with greater force, the weight of him overpowering as he more fully let go. I'd never felt so turned on and out of control during sex. Perhaps because I'd never been with an actual man.

Tate once again slowed down and began kissing my neck. I grabbed his ass, guiding his movements. Then he devoured my mouth as I wrapped my legs around him.

He thrust again, balls deep, and I felt his body shake.

"Fuck," he grunted. "I'm gonna—"

"Come..." I begged, finishing his sentence as I felt my own orgasm rush through me. I opened my mouth in a silent scream, the muscles of my vagina tightening at the feel of his heat filling me through the condom.

"Oh shit..." he rasped against my neck as he pumped into me over and over, his groans echoing through the room.

We continued to rock back and forth as we came down from that bliss together. When he looked into my eyes, I once again felt immense gratitude.

"Thank you," I whispered.

Chapter 12

TATE

Is she kidding? She's thanking me again?

"I told you. *I'm* the one who should be thanking *you*, beautiful." I carefully pulled out, placing a soft kiss on her forehead.

"Where are you going?" she asked as I got up.

"Condom..." I muttered before hopping off the bed.

She looked alarmed. As if I wanted to leave her right now...

I rushed to the bathroom, discarding the condom and quickly returning to the bed, not wanting to waste precious seconds with her.

Blair reached for me, bringing me into a kiss, her body pressed against mine. My cock began to stiffen. *How the hell?* I'd never been so easily aroused. *And I'm supposed to leave this girl in less than a day?*

When Blair pulled back, she smiled. "Look at that."

"What?"

"The worst has happened, and we're both still in one piece. The sky hasn't fallen. The world hasn't ended." She pointed her finger at my chest. "You were worried for nothing, big guy."

If only it were that simple.

"While I'd love to believe that, I'm not so sure we'll make it through this unscathed. You really think you're not gonna be more hurt after we leave each other now?" I studied her a moment. "Don't get me wrong. It was worth it. But we've made things *a lot* harder, even if you don't realize it yet, Blair."

Her eyes filled with mischief. "I plan to make things hard again."

"It won't be very difficult." I chuckled. "Trust me." My dick twitched.

Her smile faded. "Seriously, though, you don't regret it, do you?"

"Fuck, no. I can't regret something that made me feel better than I have in a very long time. But separating will be more difficult now. That's all I'm saying."

"Leaving each other is gonna be difficult either way," she said.

"Thanks to your prank earlier, I already have first-hand experience with that. So yes, I agree." I glared.

Her face reddened. "I'm sorry again for doing that to you."

Deep down, I knew guilt over having sex with her would also set in once we left each other. But that wasn't enough to make me regret something that had felt so natural, so mind-numbingly amazing. At least I'd have the memory of it now, even if it tortured me. Nothing was worse than the regret I'd felt when she supposedly left earlier. Now I'd never have to experience that again.

"What do you want to do today?" she asked.

I leaned in and kissed her. "This."

She smiled. "You want to stay in bed?"

I spoke over her mouth. "Pretty much."

She turned away, pressing her ass against my cock. I wrapped my arms around her, pulling her close. A peace came over me as I held her. I wished we had more time together. Even if I wasn't right for her long term, she was happy with me now. We made *each other* happy. That had to mean something.

"The time is passing too fast. Stay here with me an extra day—until Sunday," I said before I could think better of it.

Blair rolled over to face me. "Are you serious?"

I nodded. "It's probably prolonging the agony, but I'm not ready to say goodbye."

"I'd have to stay here with you, because I can't afford another—"

"That's a given, beautiful. Of course I want you to stay with me. No need for two rooms anymore."

"Well, then it's a no-brainer." Beaming, she ran her finger along my chin. "I'll change my flight, and we can make the most of the extra time we have."

My dick was now fully hard and ready to go again. That had to be a record for me. But we'd been so frenzied earlier, I hadn't had an opportunity to appreciate her beautiful body. I'd just been ravenous. "Can I look at you for a little bit?" I asked.

"Of course."

I lowered the bed sheet so I could take my time exploring her. I wanted to burn this moment into my memory, never wanted to forget it. Didn't want to miss a single detail, not a single crevice from head to toe. Her beautiful blue eyes, her upturned nose. The way her bottom lip was slightly bigger than the top one. Her long, dirty blonde hair that lay messily down her back. Her soft skin. Her perfectly pink nipples the size of half-dollars. Her innie belly button. The thin layer of light brown hair that covered her pussy. Her smooth legs. Even her toes were perfect.

"Are you scanning me?" she finally asked.

"If there were a way to do that and keep this sight permanently etched inside my head, I would."

Her smile softened. "Maybe it'll be better over time if you forget, though."

"Never." My chest tightened. "It will never be better to forget you."

"Well, you pointed out how painful it will be when we leave each other, so maybe it would be easier *not* to remember details and just hold on to a vague memory. Maybe it's the details that will make it harder."

"Is that what you're hoping? To forget the details?"

She shook her head. "I don't want to forget you, no. But I think over time, the details *will* inevitably get blurry, whether we want them to or not. All I'm saying is that maybe forgetting will make it easier by default. Almost like a protective mechanism."

The mood had turned more serious than I was ready for, especially considering the incredible time we'd just had. Then she solidified the change in vibe.

Blair cleared her throat. "I'm just gonna ask this once, okay? I'm not gonna make it a thing. And I'm *not* gonna pressure you."

I swallowed. "Okay…"

"Do you think there's a chance you and I could ever work out?" Her voice shook. "You know, if we did keep in touch?" Her face turned red, a true reflection of her feelings for me. The stakes were high, because no matter how I answered, I was bound to hurt her.

I looked away for a moment as dread filled me. Even though her question had thrown me for a loop, it shouldn't have surprised me. I desperately wanted that fantasy, too, but I knew with every fiber of my being that I wasn't good for her in the long term. The more time Blair and I spent together, the sooner she'd figure that out. She hadn't even started her life yet. I'd already ruined the lives of several people, from my son's mother, to my son, to the men whose deaths I'd been responsible for when I was deployed. No way in hell was I going to ruin Blair's life, too. That left me with no choice but to hold strong.

I finally found the words. "I would love the opportunity to explore this beyond the resort, to keep in touch and not to lose you." My stomach knotted as I hesitated. "But I don't think that would benefit you, Blair—for so many reasons. Once we start down that path, it will be too late to turn back. So I think it's better for you if we end things when our trip is over."

She nodded as if she'd been expecting that answer. "You think it's better for *me*… But what about you?"

"I told you, I don't deserve you."

"But you'd *want* to be with me, if it weren't for worrying about how it would affect my life?"

Fuck yes. There was no debating that. But I had to think carefully about how to respond. I couldn't lead her on. She'd try to convince me she'd be okay with seeing where this went. It was too big of a risk, and I didn't trust that I couldn't be swayed with the way I felt right now.

"The answer is complicated," I said. "But whether I would *want* to be with you is irrelevant, okay? It doesn't change anything."

"All right." She sighed deeply, sadness on her face. "I'm not gonna push. I'm gonna choose to enjoy the remaining time we have."

I brushed the back of my hand along her cheek. "I already feel myself getting way too addicted to you. And addictions generally need to be broken before they consume us."

She moved in closer and whispered over my lips, "Well, then, if we're on borrowed time, we'd better stop wasting it talking."

My dick grew fully erect within seconds. I had the libido of a teenager suddenly. And I recognized the irony.

Blair raked her fingers through my hair. "I can't get enough of you, Tate."

"How do you want me this time?"

She blushed. "I want you to take me from behind."

Shit.

She somehow knew that's what I wanted to try. That position had always been my weakness. But with her? Her beautiful ass for the taking? I wasn't sure my damn heart could handle it.

I kissed her hard before flipping her over. Blair promptly got on her hands and knees, sticking her gorgeous ass up in the air.

Fuck.

I couldn't help rubbing my shaft along the slit of her ass for a few seconds of skin-to-skin contact. But before I could give in to the reckless urge to sink inside her bare, I hurried over to grab another condom. I couldn't slide it over my dick fast enough.

I jerked myself a few times as she swayed her gorgeous ass from side to side, a silent invitation. While I hadn't given in to the urge to slip inside her raw, I *would* indulge another desire. I lowered my face and devoured her from behind. Blair gasped as my wet mouth found her flesh. She moaned as I alternated between tonguing her ass and her pussy, my cock dripping with excitement.

Once I'd had my fill, I took a moment to appreciate her ass before I entered her. "You're so ready for me, aren't you?"

"Yes," she mewled.

I dug my fingertips into her ass cheeks. "Such a good girl." *Fuck.* Now I was playing into the age dynamics? I was losing my damn mind.

"Fuck me, Tate. I can't wait any longer."

Without further ado, I sank inside of her, the tight pull of her opening nearly too much to take. I shut my eyes to compose myself before beginning to move in and out of her. "Your ass…is exquisite," I panted as I thrust.

She bucked her hips backward. "I love the way you fill me."

"I fucking *love* filling you." I grabbed her hair and bunched it into a ponytail, using it as leverage.

What started as slow and controlled now graduated into harder, skin-slapping movements. I'd aimed to be gentle, but that just wasn't possible with how crazy she made me.

"You're so deep," she breathed, always knowing what to say to take things up a notch.

I tugged at her ponytail, bending a moment to kiss her neck as I attempted to stop myself from coming too soon.

"Don't stop," she pleaded.

I lowered my hands to her hips and guided her over me, fucking her with even greater force.

Blair fisted the sheets, hanging on for dear life as the headboard banged against the wall. That would suck for anyone in the next room, but I didn't give a shit about anyone hearing us.

"Oh my God..." she yelled, and then she shrieked.

When I felt her body quake, I tightened my grip on her ass and let myself go, coming even harder than the first time.

As our movements tapered to a slow rhythm, the only sound in the room was our breath.

After I carefully pulled out, I showered her back with kisses as she collapsed onto the mattress, letting out a sigh.

"That was so good, Tate." She sighed again. "So, so good."

Her words filled me with pride. "It was fucking amazing," I agreed. I wanted nothing more than to completely rock her world during the time we had left.

After I returned from disposing of the condom, I kissed her hard before looking over at the time. "We should probably go get you fed so you have energy for round three. It's way past lunch time."

"I need to shower." She rubbed her finger along the scruff of my chin and flashed a wicked grin. "Know anyone who'd want to join me?"

I shook my head and laughed. "You're gonna be the death of me, Blair."

Chapter 13

BLAIR

I couldn't take my eyes off Tate as he stood at the buffet line getting our food. He'd assigned me with holding the table, since the restaurant was pretty crowded.

He looked more handsome than ever today. Though maybe that was psychological because I knew he was *mine*—at least for the next day and a half. The soreness between my legs served as a reminder of that.

I'd be a wreck when this trip was over, yet I was so damn grateful that tonight wouldn't be our last night, as originally planned. I had been thrilled to call to reschedule my flight. One more full day felt like a lifetime after wishing for more time and being certain I'd never get it.

My body tingled as I noted the way Tate's jeans hugged his ass. Now that I knew what he was packing inside those jeans—and how he used it? It was hard to concentrate on anything besides anticipating the next time we could have sex. How many times was too many in one day? I was nowhere near ready to stop after three—we'd had sex in the shower, too.

I laughed as he piled a bunch of food on two plates. That had become his MO, getting a little of everything because he was never sure what I wanted. A warm feeling came over me. It felt so good to be taken care of. But that was chased by a wave of bitterness as I reminded myself that Tate had closed the door on a future for us. While I understood his rationale and respected his decision, it still hurt. But I vowed not to let that dampen the hours we had left.

Tate wore a huge smile as he finally approached our table with the plates. Though despite my resolution, it only amplified my anticipatory anxiety over the impending heartbreak. Taking a deep breath, I squelched the feeling just in time as he sat across from me.

"I'm surprised you didn't just carry the entire buffet back with you," I said as he set the food down.

"Well, we worked up an appetite, didn't we?"

"We absolutely did." My stomach growled as I selected a ham and cheese croissant and took a big bite.

Tate and I had a pleasant lunch until I looked over and noticed the woman he had been talking to the other night. She kept glancing in our direction.

"Looks like your friend can't stop staring at us."

He didn't even bat an eyelash. "Let her look."

"I have to say... I love this version of you who doesn't overthink everything." I tilted my head. "Who did you say she was again?"

"She's a family friend."

Glancing over again, I nodded. "I see."

"She took it upon herself to have her mother call my mom after she saw us, actually." He chuckled.

"What?" I stopped mid-chew. "She told you they were going to call your mother?"

"No." He shook his head. "My mother called me." Tate took a bite of his sandwich and grinned. "She was interested in knowing what I was doing canoodling with a teenager."

My jaw dropped open. "No."

"Yep." He sipped some water. "Well, she didn't say teenager, but Langley's parents told her I was spending time with a *much* younger woman."

I covered my mouth. "I don't know whether to laugh or cry for you."

"At the time of my conversation with my mother this morning, I thought you'd just left and weren't coming back. So I told her that there was nothing to worry about since you were gone."

"Well, pretty sure she'd be shitting a brick now, huh?"

He shook his head. "I told her about you. Your age and everything. She wasn't judging." He shrugged. "My mother is nosy, but ultimately, she accepts the choices I make. She wants me to be happy." He looked into my eyes. "And that's exactly what I am right now."

Feeling my cheeks heat, I asked, "You think she'll call your mother again?"

"I don't give a flying fuck what she does." He took a sip of his water.

"Should I tell *my* mother what I'm up to, so we're even?"

He nearly choked on his drink. "Please don't."

"My father, then?" I arched a brow.

"Yeah, *definitely* don't do that."

"I'm teasing." I chuckled. "Well…I'm pretty open with my mother. I *will* tell her about this someday. Not anytime soon, though. Probably not this decade."

"What will her reaction be?"

"I think she'll warn me to be more careful about who I trust because she doesn't know you. Then she'll double check that I used protection. But in the end, she'll appreciate it as one of life's adventures. My mother is open-minded and wants me to experience life, because she had me too young to do much of that."

"Your father, on the other hand?" Tate coughed. "How would he react?"

"Not good…" I laughed nervously.

Tate's smile dimmed. "That's what I thought."

"He's not a violent man or anything. Truthfully, I don't know exactly how he'd react."

Tate pushed one of the plates aside. "I'd prefer to never find out."

"I think you're sensitive about it because you know how *you'd* feel if the roles were reversed. If you had a daughter…"

"Probably." He shoveled some rice pudding in his mouth. "And that's totally hypocritical, of course."

I tilted my head. "What if your son met an older woman on vacation?"

Tate sighed. "Okay, now this is gonna sound completely wrong…but I don't think I would care as much as I would if it were my daughter meeting an older guy."

"Interesting…" I scraped together a bite with my fork. "But in the end, you need to realize it's not different at all."

"I think we're far past the point where you need to convince me of anything, Blair. Haven't I been loud and clear on where I stand for the rest of this trip? Whether we're wrong or right doesn't fucking matter, now that I've gotten a taste of you." He locked my feet in with his under the table.

After a half hour of mostly watching Tate eat, my arousal had made a comeback. "I think I've had enough of sitting across from you and not on top of you," I murmured.

He threw his napkin aside. "Well, then we should get going…"

Tate and I didn't even make it to the elevator before he backed me against a wall in the resort hallway to kiss me senseless. I lost track of time as our tongues collided, my loins burning with need as his erection grew against me.

When we came up for air, I felt someone watching us. It was the waitress from Tate's "fiftieth birthday" dinner staring us down. He and I looked at each other, laughed, and escaped into the empty elevator.

After the doors closed, Tate again backed me against the wall and took my mouth as we rose to the third floor.

When we got to his room, I dropped to my knees, planning to do something long overdue. I unbuckled his pants and lowered them to get to his underwear.

He shook his head. "You don't have to—"

I cut off his words by taking his cock into my mouth, swirling my tongue around the salty tip before taking him down my throat. I could feel him throbbing.

His groans only encouraged me to take him deeper, pushing the limits of anything I'd ever tried before.

He bunched my hair in his fist. "Blair…this is too much."

I responded with a hum that I was sure vibrated through his shaft.

After a moment, Tate relaxed and guided my face over his cock. "Your mouth feels so fucking good."

I pulled away, looking up at him with a teasing smile. He rolled his eyes up, taking a moment to find his composure. I licked a line down his length as I felt his hand on the back of my head.

"Suck me again," he begged. "Please."

I returned my mouth to his cock, holding onto his shaft while I pumped and sucked, occasionally swiping my tongue over his balls. I loved pleasing him like this and had never been so into giving a blow job.

"Incredible," he rasped.

When I stopped for air, I noticed his head bent back in ecstasy while I jerked his slick cock. Sensing he was on the brink, I wanted nothing more than to put him over the edge.

When I resumed going down on him, I swallowed him as deeply as I could, nearly gagging before sucking faster. As his breathing quickened, I kept up the momentum until I felt him shake.

"I'm gonna...come," he muttered.

Maybe he expected me to stop, but I kept going until I felt his warm, salty cum sliding down my throat. I swallowed it all, something I'd never done before. And who better to experience it with than the most beautiful man I'd had the pleasure of knowing?

"Wow." He panted. "You didn't have to—"

"I wanted to. All of it." I stood and kissed him. "I want to experience everything with you."

"Be careful what you say," he warned.

"I'll do no such thing."

He pulled his pants up, though he didn't bother to buckle them before he scooped me up and carried me over to the bed.

"What are you doing?" I giggled.

"Payback," he said, dropping me onto the mattress.

Tate spread my legs as he removed my pants and slid down my panties. Already so turned on from giving him head, I felt a jolt of electricity between my legs.

He stared at me for a few moments. "I just want to look at you first. I can't get enough of that."

I sensed myself getting wet merely from the way his eyes moved over me. Tate reached out his calloused hand and rubbed his palm along my inner thigh. My clit throbbed as I fisted the sheets, dying to feel his mouth on me; the wait was torture.

He licked his lips before lowering his mouth to my breasts, kissing me through my shirt before he lifted it over my head. He unsnapped my bra and threw it aside. My nipples hardened in anticipation as he took one of them into his mouth and sucked hard. It was the most pleasurable pain.

Finally, he lowered his fingers to my opening.

"Fuck, you're wet, baby." He groaned, thrusting two of his fingers inside of me, causing me to tighten around his hand. "Hear that? So beautiful..." The room filled with the slick sound of my arousal. He shifted position to hover over me on all fours. My entire body buzzed. "How the fuck did I get so lucky?" he murmured.

"I'm the lucky one," I said.

His Adam's apple bobbed as he moved down and lowered his mouth to my swollen bud.

At the first lap of his tongue, I let out an unintelligible sound. He growled as he picked up speed, tasting and licking. Threading my fingers through his silky hair, I pushed his face deeper into me. He fucked me with his tongue as he used his thumb to massage my clit. I bucked my hips, pulling on his hair.

"That's it, baby," he rasped. "Fuck my mouth. Show me how you want it."

My restless legs twitched in an effort to stave off my looming orgasm.

"I've wanted to taste you from the moment I first saw you. I can't believe this is real, and I'm getting to do it for a second time," he murmured, his voice vibrating against my core. "Mmmm... So fucking good." He looked up at me. "You want to come like this, or do you want me inside you?"

As amazing as this was, the answer was a no-brainer. "Inside me..." I exhaled. "Please."

He reached over to the end table and fumbled for a condom. I watched intently as he lowered his pants and sheathed himself, my pussy clamoring with excitement at the sight of his engorged cock.

I gasped as he entered me. *Holy shit*. The intensity of the feeling never ceased to amaze me.

"I can't even believe I'm this damn hard again," he groaned. "God, I fucking love being inside of you."

I quickly realized he'd pushed me too far over the edge. "I'm not gonna last. I need to come now, Tate."

"Let go, baby. I'll come with you," he said as we rocked together.

As my muscles tightened around him, he thrust hard before groaning, the heat of his release warming me through the condom as I swayed my hips to take every bit of his orgasm.

"What are you doing to me? I can't get enough of you," he finally said, head on my shoulder as he pulled out.

When our breathing had returned to normal, Tate and I turned to face each other.

Harsh reality once again hit me. It seemed to come in waves. After tomorrow, Tate would be gone from my life. I hated that thought, but I couldn't let him know how sad it made me. I couldn't risk him distancing himself to try to protect me. I needed him all in until the last second.

"Where did you go?" he asked.

I blinked. "What do you mean?"

"Just now. Where did you go? Your face changed. It was like your body was still here, but you left the room."

I attempted to shake it off. "It's nothing."

His expression softened. "Blair...talk to me."

I forced a smile. "I'm just really happy, and I don't want this trip to end. I understand why we have to part ways and all that. But I think I'm kidding myself a little, thinking I can handle leaving you."

He caressed my face. "We're both stressed, even if we're pretending not to be."

"I keep telling myself just to be grateful for the extra time."

He nodded. "You can experience both gratitude and sadness, you know. I'm grappling with those right now myself. We can't help how we feel." He exhaled. "I know I made a big deal about our age difference in the beginning.

But the truth is, when I'm with you, I don't feel any differ-ent inside than I did when I was your age. It's like I'm *him* again. That's one fucked-up thing about getting older—you still feel young inside. But being with you makes me feel like the person I was when I had my entire life ahead of me, before I fucked a lot of things up. Before I broke." He sighed. "You make me feel whole again."

I ran my finger along his chin. "It's never too late for a new life. I think you had to grow up really fast after every-thing you went through. Maybe you never naturally out-grew him—that person you were at nineteen."

He nodded. "That's an interesting theory."

I looked at him a moment. "Have you ever gotten help for your PTSD?"

Tate's eyes left mine for a moment. He shook his head. "I haven't wanted to see a therapist, but I suppose at some point, maybe I should." He sighed. "It's just so much easier to block it out."

I caressed his hair. "Do you ever talk about it with anyone, though? Like friends or family?"

"Not really." He swallowed.

"Will you talk about it with me?" I whispered.

He paused a moment then nodded.

I waited for him to speak.

"We were stationed in Afghanistan," he said, shifting his body. "In an area that was notorious for ambushes. But we'd received some intel that implied we were safe. So, I made the call to continue with a routine supply run in the area."

He looked away as he continued. "At one point there was some debris on the side of the road that seemed off, so we had a couple of techs check it out, and it turned out to be nothing. That led me to decide that we could safely continue the run." He shut his eyes briefly. "A short time later, an IED blew behind us, hitting one of the trucks in my convoy."

My heart broke for him. I looped my fingers with his. "I'm so sorry."

"I lost two good friends." His eyes glistened. "After that day, I kept having panic attacks because every little thing looked suspicious to me. I wasn't able to function."

"So, they sent you home?"

He nodded. "Basically, yeah. I was discharged." Tate drew in a breath. "I could go into a lot more detail about what I saw, but it's hard for me. I will tell you, though, in the dead of night, those vivid memories come flooding back. In fact, they'd started again at the beginning of this trip. Before you and I met, there was one night I couldn't sleep at all. But since you came into my life, I haven't had a single nightmare. Obviously, distraction works. It's just always temporary."

I squeezed his hand. "Thank you for sharing that with me. I'm glad I could make you feel better, even for just a little while."

He buried his face in my neck and spoke against my skin. "If only I could just escape into you forever, I wouldn't have to face anything."

Chapter 14

TATE

On the morning of our last full day together, I watched Blair sleep as I quietly dreaded tomorrow. At the same time, I also wanted to get it over with. If there were a way to make time stand still, though, I would've frozen right here in this place and spent each and every day living in the moment with this beautiful girl. What a dream that would be. But alas, she needed to live her life. That meant preventing her from getting involved with a man who'd screwed up every important personal relationship he'd ever had.

Her eyes fluttered open. "Whatcha doing?" she asked, her voice groggy.

"Watching you sleep while I still can."

Both our flights left early in the morning tomorrow, so after today, there wouldn't be much time to enjoy anything. Today and tonight would be like one long goodbye. The mere thought made my chest feel hollow.

The sun peeked through the curtains, an invitation to step outside into the world, but all I wanted was to stay in this bed with Blair. And it wasn't only about the sex. That realization was as enlightening as it was unsettling.

She ran her finger along my chest. "If we were a movie, what kind would we be? A comedy? A drama?"

I scratched my chin. "I think we're neither. We're more like...a really good documentary. Because nothing about this experience has been anything less than real for me, an authentic connection. And while there have been funny moments—mostly thanks to you—comedy would be too simple to represent what this feels like. It also wouldn't be a sad story, despite what we'll inevitably experience tomorrow. So, I think documentary is the closest match, a series of moments where two humans forged a connection that neither one will ever forget."

"That's beautiful," she whispered.

"*You're* beautiful." I smiled. "In fact, I hope it doesn't freak you out, but I want to take some photos of you before we leave."

She flashed a mischievous grin. "Naked ones?"

"Believe it or not, no. I just don't ever want to forget you." I shook my head. "I mean, I'll *never* forget you, but I don't want my memory of you to fade at all. I have a feeling I'm gonna get home and wonder if this was all a dream. I want to be able to look at the photos and smile when I'm down."

"Well, then you have to let me do the same. And of course, we'll have to take some together."

"Maybe we can get that angry waitress to be the photographer." I winked.

She laughed. "Why not ask? We've already pissed her off..."

Once we finally managed to get out of bed and down-stairs, Blair and I ate the quickest breakfast we could, not wanting to waste time. We'd have plenty of time to eat af-ter we left each other.

After breakfast, we took a walk on the beach hand in hand, reminiscing about our short trip together as if it had been a lifetime—everything from the first meeting at the kiddie pool to the helmet diving and massage, to the mo-ment I said *fuck it* and we never looked back.

Eventually we found a shady spot under a tree. Blair took an envelope out of her bag and handed it to me.

My eyes widened. "What's this?"

"It's a letter I wrote you. I don't want you to read it until we leave each other, though."

I swallowed the lump in my throat. "You're making me emotional, and I haven't even read it."

"I needed to get some things off my chest that I knew I wouldn't be able to articulate tomorrow morning in the rush of having to leave."

It made me feel horrible that she'd done something like this, and I hadn't written anything.

As if she'd read my mind, she said, "Don't feel like you need to do the same. Truly. It's just something I wanted to do."

I exhaled. "Honestly, I wish I *could* articulate every-thing, but I'm not very good at writing. It would take me all day to organize what I'm feeling into words, and I don't want to waste our time together trying to get my brain to work. I'd prefer to be with you." I looked down at the en-velope again. "I don't understand, though. When did you write this? We've been together the entire time."

"It's not long. I put it together while you were sleeping last night. I had a little insomnia."

"I had no idea you were awake in the middle of the night."

"It was just an hour. After I wrote it, I was able to go back to sleep. I think all of these emotions had been nagging me. Once I got them out, I felt better."

I shook my head. There was so much I wanted to say to her before we parted. Maybe I *could* figure out a way to write it down. Or even better, maybe I could convince her to give me her contact information, though she'd still said she preferred that we not exchange last names.

"Should we take the photos now?" I asked.

She stood and wiped some dirt off her skirt. "Sure."

We picked a spot under some palm trees. The sun wasn't too bright—it was perfect. Blair leaned against the tree as her hair blew around in the gentle breeze. I was sure there was no more beautiful woman in the entire world. I wondered if I'd always believe that or if my opinion was skewed because of the massive fog of lust and admiration currently engulfing me. Maybe there was a stronger word to describe what I was feeling, but I wasn't willing to let my mind go there.

After taking several photos of her with my phone, I switched positions with her so she could take photos of me.

I leaned against the same tree, making various flirtatious faces at her, some downright silly.

"Be serious for a minute, Tate."

I forced my mouth into a more serious expression. That meant letting reality seep in, which was why I'd been avoiding it.

"Now look at me like you're hiding a secret," she said.

I chuckled and did my best to accommodate her request. I couldn't help but think of the secret I *was* hiding. If she only knew it was taking everything in me not to say *fuck it* again and ask her to run away with me. If she only knew how often that crazy idea had been at the tip of my tongue. I doubted she understood how weak I was when it came to her. I'd put up a strong front, explaining all the reasons why continuing this beyond the resort was a bad idea. But the truth? I was hanging on by a thread.

"I'm gonna ask you a question you've asked me before," she said, putting down the phone. "Where did you go?"

Shit.

"It's just a tough day," I admitted. "Well...tomorrow is gonna be tougher."

Blair walked over and wrapped her arms around my neck. I bent to kiss her, then lifted her and spun around. The sun cast a beautiful glow through her blonde hair. Every time I thought I wanted to freeze a particular moment in time, she gave me another that beat the last one. Holding her like this right now had to be the pinnacle.

When the feeling became too strong, I slid her to the ground. "I've had enough time outside. How about you?"

"It's definitely time for *you* to go inside again." She winked.

I'd miss her little innuendos. I'd miss *everything*. If I could've carried her back to the room without making a spectacle, I would've. That was the kind of caveman I felt like right now.

Back in the room, I couldn't get her sundress off fast enough. Looking at her out at the beach had made me ravenous. What the fuck was I supposed to do tomorrow when I could never touch her again? Maybe taking those photos had been a bad idea. They'd only serve to torture me.

She pressed her body against mine, wearing her bra and panties. "I don't want to go anywhere else today, Tate. I want to spend the rest of the day and night here."

"Done," I murmured over her lips. She fumbled with my belt buckle as I removed her bra. Eager to be inside of her, I nearly forgot to grab a condom before I backtracked and rushed over to the end table.

"Can I put it on you?" she asked.

"Sure." I handed her the packet.

Blair took out the rubber and smoothed it over my cock before she bent to take me down her throat for a few seconds. Apparently, that was just a tease because before I could blink, she was back on the bed, spread eagle, inviting me to enter her.

I crawled over her before not so gently thrusting deep inside. I closed my eyes at the pleasure. "How could you be so wet and so tight at the same time?"

"Because you're so damn big..." She chuckled. "You're really perfect, Tate."

My tongue grazed her neck as I moved in and out of her. "I've never met anyone as perfect as you, Blair."

"Fuck me like you've never fucked anyone before," she begged.

"I've never felt like this with anyone," I told her. "Never felt more alive."

She might've thought fucking her like I'd never fucked anyone meant going harder and faster, but what I wanted right now was to go slow and steady, to savor the feeling of being one with her.

I took her hand in mine, locking our fingers together. I fucked her slow and deep, squeezing her hand as I sucked on her neck.

This felt different from all the other times we'd had sex—more intimate. More like making love. I kissed up her neck to her mouth, devouring her lips as we fell into a slow and intense rhythm.

At one point, I pulled almost all the way out and looked into her eyes before thrusting deep into her again. She gasped, never taking her eyes off me.

"You look so damn beautiful with me inside of you," I whispered.

"You make me feel beautiful."

I hoped she meant that. I wanted her to walk away from this experience with nothing but positive memories. In the end, what we remember most about people is how they make us feel. Even when the memories of a face or conversations fade, we always remember when someone made us feel amazing.

She felt impossibly tight around me, though I wondered if she was tense about our impending departure. Whatever the reason, I wasn't going to last. I tightened my abs to stave off my orgasm until I sensed she was close.

"Tate..." she moaned.

I fucking loved when she said my name.

"Come, baby. It's okay."

Her muscles pulsed around me as I thrust into her a final time. We'd had several orgasms together on this trip, but for me, this one was the most intense. I came in what seemed like an endless flow, and I never wanted to pull out of her—ever.

But after a minute, I eased out and went to discard the condom, returning to the warmth of the bed.

"Let's not sleep tonight," she said, wrapping her arms around me.

I nodded. "You read my mind."

Chapter 15

TATE

If I'd had a gun, I would've shot that damn alarm. We hadn't planned on sleeping, but I'd set the alarm just as a precaution. Good thing, too, as Blair and I had dozed off in each other's arms sometime in the middle of the night.

"Oh my God." Her hair was a beautiful mess as she blinked. "We fell asleep."

"Yeah..." I said somberly.

She reached out to touch my face as we stared at each other.

I exhaled. "I thought I could do this, but now that this day is here..."

There were those words again, at the tip of my tongue, ready to beg her to run away with me. I tried to talk to myself.

You can't be selfish.

She needs to live her life.

You have work to do on yourself that you can't involve her in.

A relationship was never part of the deal.

Let her go.

Let her go.

I knew I'd regret not writing her a letter like she had me. There was just no time left. I'd spent every waking moment with her until sleep took us.

"I've got to get downstairs," she said. "My ride is scheduled to come in ten minutes."

Her flight was two hours earlier than mine, and we'd decided to part ways here to spare ourselves the stress of a dramatic airport goodbye.

My heart raced, even as it felt like it was breaking.

Blair rushed around the room to gather her things without making eye contact. When she finally looked at me, I saw tears in her eyes.

Fuck. She didn't want me to see that she was crying.

I felt my own eyes water. It surprised me how little control I had.

She shook her head and looked down. "I don't want you to come downstairs with me, Tate. It's just too hard. Let's end it here."

No.

This can't be it.

I had to act fast. Reaching out my hand, I said, "Give me your phone."

She handed it to me, and I entered my number.

"I know we said this would be the end. But if you *ever* need me, for anything, even just to talk, call me. Please. Okay? Anytime. You don't need to give me your number, and honestly, I wouldn't trust myself with it. But I feel better knowing you have mine, that the ball is in your court.

Even if years go by, I don't care where I am or what I'm doing, I'll always be here for you."

"Okay." She nodded. "That means a lot. And I *will* take you up on that." She let out a breath. "I do feel better having your number. So, thank you."

I tugged at my hair. "Got everything?"

"Everything but you..." She sighed.

Letting out a long, shaky breath, I nodded. "I feel that, baby. I feel that so hard."

When she reached up and kissed me one last time, I realized just how much our emotions impact our bodies. Normally I would've hardened instantly as her body pressed against mine, with the feel of her lips and her taste. But now my entire body felt numb. *Dead inside.* Sadness had overtaken me, paralyzed me. Fuck, my eyes were watering again. I hoped by some miracle she wouldn't notice.

The moment she pulled back, though, she swiped a finger under my eye, catching a tear. "You really do care about me."

I took her hand in mine. "Probably more than you'll ever realize." I pulled her in for one last painful moment, feeling my heart break more with each passing second. Hugging her tighter than I'd ever hugged anyone, I felt her tears on my face. Or were they mine?

She forced herself back and sucked in a breath. "I'm gonna rip the Band-Aid off now."

Sniffling, I nodded as she turned away from me.

And that was it.

I watched as she walked down the hall. It took every ounce of my energy to keep from chasing after her. I had to tighten every muscle in my body to keep myself in place.

Then she was out of sight.

Gone.

In a daze, I closed the door and sat on the edge of my bed with my head in my hands, trying to talk myself off the virtual ledge.

You did the right thing for her.

While I wouldn't have been right for her, I couldn't see how Blair would've been bad for *me* in any way, shape, or form. The only thing I supposed was that having a soon-to-be twenty-year-old girlfriend might've given my son even more reason to despise me. But I would've risked that if I didn't truly believe being with me was harmful to Blair in the long term. Doing the right thing didn't make this any easier, though, and it didn't fill the emptiness inside me. This feeling was completely foreign. It was the first time in my thirty-six years that I'd been heartbroken. *I guess it's never too late.*

I looked over at the bedside table, where I'd placed the letter Blair had written me. It taunted me. I'd thought I would wait to read it until I got home, but I missed her already and wanted to hear her voice again, even if that was just through words on a piece of paper.

Screw it.

I reached for the envelope and stared for a few seconds before opening it.

Her cursive handwriting was just as beautiful as she was.

Dear Tate,

As I write this, you're sleeping right next to me. You look so peaceful, and I'm happy to have contributed to that.

I know you're fighting a lot of demons, but I hope our time together helped quiet them for a bit. I can't begin to understand the pain you've been through. You've lived a life, and I've yet to really begin mine. But this experience will always be a highlight for me. You've taught me a lot in our brief time together.

Among the things I've learned:

It's never too late to make things right. Your determination to reconnect with your son speaks volumes about the type of person you are.

As much as you might disagree, I've also learned that age is just a number. I'd always heard that saying but never realized how true it was until our connection. Maybe you still doubt that, but for me, there wasn't one moment I didn't feel we were on the same level. Maybe that speaks to your immaturity? LOL (Kidding.)

More than anything, you made me feel more beautiful than anyone ever has. I came on this trip so heartbroken and feeling as though I wasn't good enough because I'd been thrown away by the only "love" I'd ever known. But the way you looked at me, the way your body reacted to me, the way you got lost in me, the way you treated me... You made me feel special. And I will carry that confidence throughout my life. I'm so glad Daniel broke up with me, because it allowed me to meet you. I wouldn't change anything.

allowed me to meet you. I wouldn't change any-thing.

Lastly, we've only known one another for a matter of days, but I love you, Tate. I don't think you need to have spent a lifetime with someone to say that. Love isn't measured by time. It's a feeling that you know to be true.

It's okay if you don't love me back in the same way. I just want you to know that I love you, and I always will. It wouldn't surprise me one bit if someday when I'm old and gray and ready to take my last breath, your face is the one that flashes before my eyes. Though you'll be long gone by then. (I hope that made you laugh. If we don't laugh, we'll cry.)

Thank you for the best not-even-week of my life.

Love always,

Blair

Her words left me unable to move. That was so much more than I'd expected. There was no greater ache than words left unsaid, and while she'd spoken her truth, mine now burned a hole in my heart, potentially forever. How had I ever thought it was a good idea to leave myself so powerless? With no way to contact her.

I didn't trust myself. That's why.

I opened my camera roll to look at the photos I'd tak-en of her in the sun. The moment I saw her again, I began to cry. I realized, perhaps for the first time, that I loved her, too. That feeling I'd told myself I'd never felt for a woman before? That was *love*. That's why it had felt so new and indescribable. It transcended explanation and certainly transcended age and logic. At thirty-six years old, I had never been in love until Blair.

I resolved to channel that love into something positive. To be grateful for the experience and allow it to make me a better person, too.

I'd start by working on my relationship with Taylor. But that couldn't happen until I worked on myself. Maybe I'd finally go to therapy and get some real help for my PTSD. Until I believed in myself, I wouldn't be capable of much.

If I could've written down my thoughts, I would've told Blair I hadn't felt capable of any of those things until I met her. Were it not for the renewed energy she'd given me, the love she'd showed me, I might never have been ready to move forward.

That should've gone in a letter to her. Maybe I'd still write it someday, even if just to get the emotions out on paper. But for today, I'd mourn the end of a beautiful but short chapter in my life.

I had about an hour before I had to head to the airport myself, and I knew I'd be a ball of fucking mush until then. I couldn't stop thinking about her, how she hadn't even had breakfast before she left. I hoped she found something good at the airport. I hoped her stomach wasn't as upset as mine and she could actually eat it. I hoped she wasn't still crying.

I hoped she had a fucking amazing life.

Chapter 16

BLAIR

The flight home was uneventful. Well, aside from the storm of emotions battering my heart.

I'd spent the entire plane ride staring at the photos of Tate, torturing myself. I wasn't sure how I was supposed to get over him. But today had to be day one of trying.

I realized getting over him and forgetting him were two different things, though. I'd never be able to *forget* him. I didn't want to. I just needed a way to live without him, to try not to see him every time I closed my eyes at night. I needed to move beyond how amazing it felt to have him inside of me so I could someday allow someone else in—both literally and figuratively. I couldn't imagine anyone measuring up. So maybe another thing I'd have to practice was accepting second best.

I wondered whether Tate had read my letter. I couldn't even remember everything I'd written, just that it had been a purge of my thoughts in the middle of the night. I hoped he wouldn't be shocked when I professed my love. I'd given him my rawest thoughts and taken the risk that he'd accept and cherish them. What was the harm in telling him how I truly felt? It wasn't like my thoughts could cause him to run away. The worst had already happened in that regard.

Back in Massachusetts, my phone rang as I stood waiting at the train platform. My heart leaped, but then I remembered he didn't have my number. *Why the hell didn't I just give it to him?*

At least I had his.

This was Taylor calling.

"Hey," I said in greeting.

"Hey, you," he replied. "How are you doing? You disappeared. I was expecting more updates during the trip. You must be home by now, right?"

"Yeah." I scratched my head. "Um..."

I wasn't sure whether to tell him about Tate. I wondered if it might be better to keep the experience to myself. I didn't want anyone tainting it, trying to convince me that Tate had taken advantage of me. I knew that wasn't true.

"I ended up staying an extra day, so I'm only just now back in Mass."

"Really? I wondered what happened because you slipped off the radar. You weren't online or anything. What made you decide to do that?"

"Wasn't ready to come back to reality. Don't worry." I cleared my throat. "I paid for it," I lied. "It wasn't on your dime. Since you were gracious enough to gift me the week, I could afford to add one extra night."

I hated lying to him, but I wasn't sure he'd understand why I'd let "some guy" pay for another night.

"Well, I wish you had told me. An extra night would've been no skin off my back."

"No." I shook my head. "I've had enough nepotism. You did too much for me already."

"Well, I'm happy to hear you had a good time. I knew you'd like the resort."

"Midnight Key was exactly what I needed, time away to think."

And meet and lose the love of my life in four days.

"So it helped you forget about Daniel?"

Who? I suppressed a chuckle. "Yeah. I'm so refreshed now. Ready to tackle the world." I felt tears in my eyes again.

"That was the goal," he said. "Sometimes all we need is a change of scenery."

Or a life-changing love.

"Yup." I sniffled.

"You got a cold or something?"

"No."

"Where are you now?"

"At the station waiting for my train. I'm so ready to be home."

"Cool. Well, all right. I just wanted to make sure you were alive and well since you dropped off the face of the Earth."

"That was the point, though, wasn't it?"

"Yeah." He laughed. "For sure."

"I'll call you once I'm settled. Thank you again for giving me one of the best weeks of my life."

"Wow. That good, huh?"

I felt myself nodding. *That* good.

That great.

That earth-shatteringly amazing.

"It was," I assured him.

"Anytime you want to go back, just let me know."

"Thank you," I said. Though I knew already that would be too painful. I'd never want to be there again without Tate.

After I hung up, guilt washed over me for not coming clean. Maybe someday I'd tell Taylor exactly how important this trip had been. But this wasn't the time. I wasn't ready.

When I turned again to look at the big board, a notification flashed on the digital screen indicating that my train was delayed.

Crap.

The station was oddly desolate. Annoyed that I couldn't just be home and in my bed, I decided to get myself a treat. After I got a snack from the vending machine, I took it over to a bench, plopping my bag down next to me.

As I took the first bite of the protein bar, I closed my eyes and sighed. Trying to meditate, I kept my eyes closed until the moment I felt it—a whoosh of some sort whipped by me. I opened my eyes to find a man running away— with my bag!

I jumped up. "Help! Help!" I screamed as I ran after him. "He's got my bag!"

I tripped and fell, scraping my knee on the pavement. That gave him just enough of an edge to open some distance between us.

As I looked up, he ran across the train tracks and jumped a fence.

A train was coming, and I was afraid I wouldn't make it if I ran across after him.

I eventually found someone who let me use their phone to call the police. I gave the authorities my parents' number and a vague description of the assailant in case they were able to track down my phone and bag. In the meantime, I wasn't sure when I'd have a phone again or if I'd be able to get the same cell number.

Panic gripped me as I realized everything that meant anything to me now was inside that bag. And by *everything* I meant...Tate. His number was only on my phone. I'd never thought I needed to memorize it because it'd been safely entered into my contacts. Without his last name and number, how would I ever find him? Tate wasn't all that common of a name, but there had to be millions of them.

Even after it was delayed, I missed my original train because I had to stick around and talk to the police.

By the time I boarded a later one, I felt like every ounce of life had been sucked out of me. I stared blankly out the window at the moving trees and buildings. That robber thought he was stealing my physical possessions. He had no clue that he'd also taken my heart.

Four Years Later

Chapter 17

BLAIR

"I can't believe you're getting married." I smiled at my best friend, dressed in a tux.

It was afternoon on the day of Taylor's wedding, and I'd stopped by his apartment to say hello as he was getting ready. I'd brought some of his favorite donuts and a box of takeout coffee from the café.

"I know, right? It's kind of crazy," Taylor said. "Were you able to get a hotel room?"

He was the sweetest. The last thing he should've been concerned about was my hotel room when he had so much going on.

"Yup," I assured him. "I snagged one with the special rate you gave out a few months ago. They told me I got one of the last rooms available."

"Make sure they actually charged you the discounted price," he said through a bite of donut.

"Don't worry about me. You're getting married in a matter of hours. That's all you should be focused on."

He shrugged. "I'm looking forward to hanging at the reception later. It's been too long since we've had a chance to catch up."

I shook my head. "You're gonna be a little busy to hang out much with any one person, you know. Don't worry about giving guests attention. Just enjoy the day before it passes you by."

He laughed. "Okay. You're right." He sighed. "My dad flew into town yesterday."

"I was gonna ask you about that…"

Taylor nodded. "Things have been good with him. He's really made an effort over the past year. Honestly, I was the one holding that relationship back for a long time. I had so much bitterness toward him, but sometimes you just have to force yourself to let it go."

"Part of growing up, right?"

"Exactly," he agreed.

"Have you seen him?"

"Yeah, he came to the rehearsal dinner. He brought a date. She seems nice. He doesn't usually bring women around me, so I don't know if it's new or something serious. He'd never mentioned her before. Just showed up with her. I guess he's bringing her to the wedding, too."

"How does your mom feel about that?"

He shrugged. "There's no bad blood between them anymore. She's fine. They even all sat together last night, which was totally odd but cool."

"Oh wow. Well, that's good. You don't need any family drama right now."

"That's for damn sure." He laughed. "You look nice, by the way."

I looked down at my dress. "It's been a while since I've cleaned up."

He smirked. "Actually, it's a good thing you did. I want you to meet someone later."

Dread filled me. "Uh-oh. You didn't."

"His name is Adam. He works with me. I think you'll like him. He's a good guy."

I cringed. "Please don't tell me you sat me next to him."

"Okay, I won't tell you I did, even if that's the case. It can just be a surprise." He winked.

"Great."

"It was Juliana's idea."

"Well, remind me to strangle her when it's not her wedding day." I exhaled. "Does this guy suspect you're trying to set him up?"

"Kind of. I've talked to him about you a little. But there's no pressure. We just sat you at the same table. If you don't like him, don't talk to him."

"Well, that would be kind of rude, don't you think?"

Before we could discuss it further, the photographer arrived and stole Taylor's attention. Since there wasn't much time left before the ceremony, I went over to the café around the corner for a quiet moment to myself before the chaos. I hadn't been to a wedding in a long time, let alone by myself. Now that I knew Taylor was trying to set me up with someone, I had to be even more prepared to be "on." I wasn't sure I had the energy.

After a half hour, I looked down at my phone and realized I didn't have a whole lot of time to get to the church. So, I forced myself up and tossed the rest of my matcha latte on the way out.

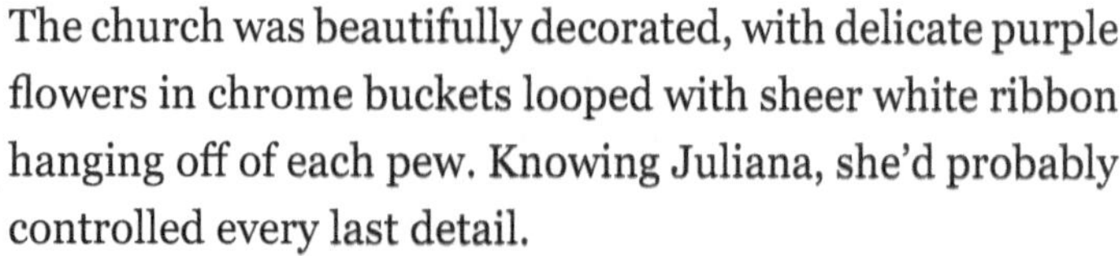

The church was beautifully decorated, with delicate purple flowers in chrome buckets looped with sheer white ribbon hanging off of each pew. Knowing Juliana, she'd probably controlled every last detail.

As I sat in one of the back rows, I turned to find the bridesmaids lining up. Their dresses matched the purple of the flowers, which was darker than lavender, but not too dark. I was suddenly relieved I hadn't worn the purple dress I'd considered, instead having opted for a short pink number that while a little revealing, fit me much better than the purple one. Though now that I'd be meeting that guy Adam at dinner, I wished I'd dressed more conservatively. I didn't need to look too eager, when in fact I wasn't *looking* for anything at the moment at all.

I turned my attention to the front of the church. From this far back, I couldn't see the altar too well, but I had the best view of the bridal party lining up in the foyer. Just beyond the bridesmaids, I got my first glimpse of Juliana.

Chills ran over me as I realized how beautiful she looked. Her dark brown hair was styled into loose curls, half up, half down. Her silk dress had a fitted bodice and large skirt. Sequins sparkled under the lights, and a sheer veil covered her face. I wondered if Taylor would cry when he got a look at her. Words could not describe how happy I was for the two of them.

The joy I felt right now confirmed that I'd never had any real romantic feelings for Taylor. There wasn't an ounce of envy in my body. I felt nothing but happiness for my friend and the beautiful woman who loved him.

As I looked on, Juliana licked her lips. She seemed nervous, as I imagined I would be too in the same situation. Her dad stood next to her and whispered in her ear.

Then the organ began to play, and I watched as each beautiful bridesmaid passed me and headed down the aisle. A couple of them flashed really stiff, fake smiles. One walked super slowly while another sped past. Their flowers were a wonderful mix of purple roses and white peonies.

I felt chills once again as Juliana appeared, arm in arm with her father. Her bouquet was bigger, all lilac roses with no other flowers mixed in. The music changed to the Wedding March, and they began their journey down the aisle. Juliana wore a huge smile, and I turned in my seat as she moved past. I realized maybe this wasn't a great seating choice after all, since I'd wanted to see whether Taylor was crying. From this far back I couldn't tell. Knowing him, though, he probably was.

Once everyone was in place, I struggled to stay focused on the actual ceremony. I'd always found myself very impatient in church, bopping my legs up and down and daydreaming.

I strained my eyes to see the family members up front, as I was curious about Taylor's dad. I'd never seen what he looked like. This was another reason sitting so far back had become a hindrance. Kind of hard to people watch from back here.

I could sort of make out the silhouettes of Taylor's family, though. His mom wore a long, blue dress and had her hair up in a twist. I assumed the guy next to her was her husband, Taylor's stepfather. I'd only ever met them a couple of times.

In the row behind them were a man and a woman I didn't recognize. But I assumed if they were sitting that close to the front, they were family. From the back, the man had the same stature of someone I'd long tried to forget. Well, I'd tried to forget him and remember him in equal measure. Maybe this wedding was making me emotional if I was suddenly seeing Tate in random people. But not many men were that tall and muscular *and* had beautiful, thick hair. My chest hollowed at the reminder of Tate.

I'd tried for years to find him to no avail. But I didn't need those lost photos to remember his face. It still haunted me every day, four years after I'd last had any contact with him. My life might've been so different if I could've found him. *Seriously, Blair? Get a grip.* I forced my attention back to the ceremony.

At one point, the priest called the parents of the bride and groom up to the altar to light candles. The man who reminded me of Tate rose, along with Taylor's mom and stepfather, and all three of them lit the groom's candle. My stomach twisted. *Holy shit. That* guy was Taylor's father!

I recalled Taylor saying once that his dad was "annoyingly good-looking." And now I knew what he meant—at least from the back, because I'd yet to see his face.

With each second that passed, as Taylor's parents stood at the altar, I became more paranoid. It couldn't be, right? I mean, that would be the craziest thing. I frantically opened the program to find the names of those in the bridal party, including the groom's parents.

The Wedding of Taylor Edward Shea and Juliana Elaina Alves

I looked down at the family members listed.

Mother of the Groom: Shayla Lively
Stepfather of the Groom: Stephen Lively
Father of the Groom: Theodore Delaney

I'd always known Taylor had taken his mother's last name. He'd never actually told me his dad's name, and I'd never asked since it was such a sore subject.

Theodore—not Tate.

Phew.

Shit! Looking down at the program, I had missed my chance to see his dad's face as they returned to their seats from the altar.

You'd think my panic would've dissipated after learning his dad's name was Theodore, yet another rush of adrenaline hit as I recalled Tate's struggles with his son. In retrospect, it sounded a hell of a lot like Taylor's struggles with his father. I couldn't believe I'd never connected those two situations, but why would I? Until now, when the back of Taylor's dad's head had triggered me.

The room began to sway. I had no idea how many minutes had passed. I totally missed the vows, stuck in my head trying to work this out, trying to reassure myself that there was no way my theory could be true. Every time I convinced myself I was out of my mind, another frightening hypothesis would hit.

What if Tate had given me a fake name?

But he'd never mentioned anything about his family owning the resort. I knew it was Taylor's grandparents on his father's side who owned Midnight Key. Even when things were rocky with his dad, Taylor had always been close with his grandparents.

Surely Tate would've mentioned it if his parents had owned the resort, right?

What about that woman he knew? *Langley.* I'd never forget her name. Weird that he'd run into someone he knew at the resort...unless maybe *he'd been there before.*

Okay. *Think.* Tate never said his family owned the resort—but he never said they *didn't.* We just never discussed it.

Oh my God.

What if?

I *needed* to see this man's face.

I *needed* to know.

But how?

I didn't want him to see *me.*

There was another entrance to the sanctuary closer to the front. If I snuck out the main entrance behind me right now and reentered through that other door, I'd have the correct angle to see his face.

Though some soloist was singing, I grabbed my purse and tiptoed out of the church. Once outside, I walked around to the side of the large stone structure.

As cars on the main road whizzed by, my heart pounded. Once I turned the corner to the quieter street where the side entrance was located, I could hear my blood rushing in my ears.

When I got to that side door, my pulse picked up yet again, as it was locked.

Fuck!

A brisk wind blew my hair around then lifted my skirt. I nearly gave a passing car a free show.

What now?

For several minutes, I tried the door periodically to see if by some miracle it opened. I felt like a crazy person. I'd just left my best friend's wedding and was now trying to break back into the ceremony from another door because I worried his father might be Tate. It sounded crazy.

And the door wouldn't budge. I had no choice but to go back inside through the main entrance. I'd just have to wait for the family of the groom to make their way down the aisle after the ceremony. Maybe I could move to a seat away from the aisle to make myself less noticeable.

When I returned to the foyer, though, Taylor and Juliana were already standing in a receiving line, along with the entire wedding party and their parents. I must've been outside longer than I'd thought, and the ceremony was over.

My heart lodged in my throat as I stood near the entrance, observing the line. And I felt all the air leave my body as I got my first look at *him*.

Please make it make sense.

Standing next to Taylor's mother was Tate. Definitely *my* Tate. The lost-love-of-my-life Tate. The man I could never get over, the man who still lived in my dreams, was Taylor's father.

He hadn't noticed me yet. There was still time to run. But how would I explain that to Taylor? Didn't matter. I could worry about that later. For now, I needed to leave. But as much as I wanted to flee, my legs were frozen in place. I couldn't take my eyes off him. Tate shook hands with person after person as he nodded and thanked them for coming. When he flashed his beautiful smile, it hurt my heart.

Stop looking at him. You need to leave!

But just as I turned to make my exit, I heard my name.

"Blair!" Taylor shouted.

I pivoted slowly and looked up to find him waving me over. With a lump in my throat, I stepped toward them.

Everything thereafter seemed to happen in slow motion.

Tate's eyes widened, and the color drained from his face the moment he finally noticed me.

This was not the reunion I'd imagined in my dreams. Far from it.

This was a nightmare I'd never imagined possible.

Chapter 18

TATE

What's happening?
What...the fuck...is happening?
That was all I could think as she walked toward me.
Blair.
Lord knows I'd blinked enough times to know I wasn't hallucinating.

After Taylor had called that name, I'd felt a shot of adrenaline zap through my body. And once I realized it was my Blair? I had no words. Everything about this day changed. Everything about my *life* had changed.

How the hell does she know Taylor?

Before I had a chance to consider anything, she stood before me, a look of warning in her eyes. I knew what she was telling me. Even without understanding how on earth we'd gotten here, she and I were on the same page: *Taylor can't fucking know about us.*

I put on the fakest smile I'd ever conjured as my son proceeded to introduce me to the one woman who needed no introduction in my life.

"Dad, this is Blair Moynihan. She's one of my best friends."

Moynihan.

That's one thing I'd wished I'd had all these years—her last name. Knowing it might've changed everything. Knowing it would've meant I could've found her again.

Blair Moynihan.

I offered my hand. "Very nice to meet you, Blair." My eyes burned into hers.

When she gave me her hand, I felt it shaking. I squeezed, a silent reassurance that despite whatever was happening now, it was going to be okay. It had to be. I needed to believe that for my own sanity. I needed her to believe it, too.

She cleared her throat. "It's nice to finally meet Taylor's father."

The receiving line needed to keep moving, but I couldn't seem to release her hand. Even under the worst possible circumstances, I didn't want to let go of her.

But I had to. I reluctantly loosened my grip.

Blair turned to Taylor. "I'll see you at the reception," she said. Then she glanced at me before walking away. It felt like she'd taken my soul with her as she disappeared down the line and eventually out of the church. My eyes followed her until the moment she was gone.

As I faked my way through the remaining introductions, my mind raced. I thought back to what she'd told me when I'd first met her at the resort: a friend had *gifted* her the trip. I'd never asked about that. But now it made total sense. It was my son, who of course didn't have to pay a red cent since his grandparents owned the place.

Why the fuck hadn't that occurred to me? Why hadn't I thought to ask who was footing the bill?

The way her hand had been shaking just now—it haunted me. Had I scared her? Had she come to think badly of me over the years, concluding that I'd taken advantage of her? Or was she just spooked by this cruel coincidence the way I was?

"Tate, are we ready to go?" Leah's voice snapped me out of my thoughts.

The receiving line had disappeared around me. I turned to her, forcing a smile. "Yeah, we are."

Leah and I had just started dating. Things had been going well, better than anything I'd experienced in a long time, so I'd asked Taylor at the rehearsal dinner if it was okay if I brought her as my plus-one. Things had been going well between my son and me—over the past year, in particular. He'd said he was happy I'd met someone and of course I could bring her. So here we were.

Except this night would be a hell of a lot easier now if Leah weren't here. It was going to be difficult enough to act normal in front of Taylor. Now I had to keep my cool around Leah, too, *and* figure out a way to talk to Blair without drawing attention to myself.

As Leah and I drove to the reception, I worried about whether Blair had made it to the reception hall okay. She'd clearly been upset and probably shouldn't have been driving. And I wouldn't blame her if she'd chosen to skip the reception altogether. I doubted either of us would do that to Taylor, though, particularly the father of the groom.

"Are you okay?" Leah asked from the passenger seat.

"Uh-huh." I exhaled.

"You're acting a bit odd."

"Am I?" I let out another breath. "Sorry about that. Might've been something I ate this morning. I'm feeling a little out of sorts, to be honest."

"Well, you'd better pull yourself together. They're going to introduce you at the reception."

My eyes widened. "They are?"

"Didn't you hear the wedding planner giving instructions on what to do when you get to the venue?"

That was laughable. I hadn't even realized there *was* a freaking wedding planner. Was she giving instructions before or after I'd noticed Blair and lost my damn mind? Because everything after that was a blur. Shit, the last thing I needed was to be in any kind of spotlight now.

As I continued the drive, my thoughts returned to Blair. She'd looked so beautiful, exactly the way I remembered her, yet more grown-up and mature—which of course she would be after four fucking years. Standing before her and being unable to hug her, to comfort her when she was shaking, had been awful.

Though, who was I to say she'd even want that? She'd never reached out to me. I'd been sure she would call me at least once, but that assumption was stupid on my part. I'd been deceived by our intense chemistry. That didn't change the reality of the situation. I was never right for her. Yet I was *still* disappointed that she'd never reached out.

The past didn't matter anymore, though. Everything now took a backseat to protecting Taylor, and I was certain Blair agreed with me on that.

Maybe if I'd used my actual name on that trip, she might've figured it out. Tate was a nickname I'd been given in the military. After my discharge, I'd started using it more than Theodore when I met someone new. I wasn't sure Taylor even knew about that name. He'd only ever known me as Theodore or Teddy, as my immediate family called me.

"Earth to Tate!" I heard Leah say.

Fuck. How long had I been ruminating this time? I hadn't even realized we'd pulled up to the reception venue. Pretty dangerous to be driving and not know how the hell you'd gotten there. And I was worried about *Blair* driving? I needed to check myself.

Leah grinned as she removed her seatbelt. "Ready, handsome? It's showtime." Thankfully, she didn't seem to be holding my behavior against me.

I forced a smile. "Yeah."

The moment we entered the venue, I began looking around for Blair. But she was nowhere to be found.

Before I could go into the reception with all the guests, I was ushered over to where the wedding party had congregated behind a partition.

"Where have you been, Teddy?" my mother asked. She smoothed her brown, beaded gown.

"I got a little diverted on the way here," I told her. *By a twist of fate you'd never imagine.*

"You okay, son?" my father asked.

"Yeah," I said, wiping sweat off my forehead.

After about twenty minutes, the wedding planner began lining us up outside the entrance to the reception. Where the hell was Leah? I couldn't remember separating from her, but it must've happened before I got dragged over to join the wedding party. Dread developed in my stomach as I wondered where they'd sat Leah and prayed it wasn't anywhere near Blair. That caused me to sweat even more.

The DJ began announcing us one by one. My heartbeat accelerated as I waited my turn, and I finally entered the hall to cheers I certainly didn't deserve. Waving to the crowd, I made my way to the assigned head table. I was honored that my son had included me in the special placements today. I needed to keep the focus on him and behave accordingly.

I forced myself not to run around in search of Blair just yet, owing Taylor my full attention as he and Juliana were announced. I'd never get this moment back. As my handsome son and his beautiful wife waltzed in, I smiled, beaming with pride, despite my inner turmoil.

Continuing to stay in place, I folded my hands together as I watched their first dance. After, I listened as the best man and maid of honor each gave their toasts. But I was getting more antsy by the minute.

The second that dinner was announced, I found Leah at her assigned table, which thankfully didn't include Blair. After checking in, I told Leah I needed to use the bathroom. Instead, what I actually did was walk around the ballroom for a bit, surveying the space as my gaze moved from table to table. I wondered if Blair had skipped the reception. Once I determined she was nowhere to be found, I actually went toward the bathroom.

Just as I turned the corner into the hallway where the restrooms were, I stopped short at the sight of Blair exiting the ladies' room.

Chapter 19

BLAIR

When I spotted Tate walking toward me, I nearly had a heart attack. It wasn't like I could turn around now.

He looked so damn gorgeous in his tux. My heart ached. Everything ached with the need to touch him, despite what I now knew to be true: I would *never* be able to touch him again.

"Blair..." he murmured before looking over his shoulder.

I shook my head, feeling tears in my eyes. "I don't understand, Tate."

"I don't either, but we need to talk about how we're gonna handle this."

Looking beyond his broad shoulders, I whispered, "Well, we can't do that here."

"Are you staying at the hotel tonight?" he asked.

I nodded. "Yes."

"I'll come to you later...after the wedding is over."

A chill ran down my spine. "I don't know if that's a good idea. What if someone sees us together?"

"I'll be careful," he said. "We have to risk it, because we need to talk."

I knew that was true. There was so much I needed to say to him. So many questions. "Okay." I licked my lips. "Yeah."

"What room are you in?"

I closed my eyes trying to remember. "One thirty-five."

"Okay." He exhaled. "I'll come see you later."

"All right."

Tate looked over his shoulder one last time before he disappeared into the bathroom.

I felt an odd thrill at the prospect of him coming to my room later, though any chance of us being together again had died the moment I'd realized he was Taylor's father.

I needed to remind myself of that, because for a moment I'd gotten lost in the idea of *My Tate*. *My* Tate no longer existed. *My* Tate was an illusion, because he'd been Taylor's father the entire time. *Theodore*. Taylor's fucking father! Why had he given me a fake name? That didn't make any sense considering how much value he'd placed on knowing *my* real name. Tate had told me he wasn't a liar. I'd even told Taylor about him in the years since, referring to him as Tate. Taylor had never seemed to suspect a thing.

Returning to my assigned table, I sat in a daze, unable to think about anything but meeting Tate later.

A voice interrupted my thoughts. "Blair?"

I turned to find a guy around my age smiling at me. "I'm Adam."

This was the person Taylor wanted to set me up with. I'd been hiding in the bathroom since arriving here, so I hadn't seen him. This poor guy had no clue he'd be getting the absolute worst of me tonight.

"Yes." I cleared my throat. "Hi." I took his offered hand. "Very nice to meet you."

So not in the mood for this right now.

"I work with Taylor."

"Yes." I forced a smile. "He mentioned that we'd be sitting together."

"You guys go way back, right?"

"Yeah." I nodded. "Taylor and I were camp counselors together for many years, and we've remained close."

"That's so cool. He's such an awesome guy. I'm very happy for him and Juliana."

"Yeah. Me too. They're perfect together."

An awkward silence filled the space between us as I gulped down all of my water in about ten seconds. *Maybe I should just leave.* I could go to my room now. Taylor might not even notice.

Suddenly the thought of having to make small talk with this poor guy while freaking out about Tate made me ill.

"Excuse me." I stood and left the table.

That was most definitely rude, but I needed some air before I passed out.

Escaping out a side door to a veranda that overlooked Boston in the distance, I took a deep breath.

Truths about this situation continued to bombard me, like the fact that the woman I'd spotted earlier standing next to Taylor's father was actually *Tate's* girlfriend. Taylor had said his dad had just started dating someone. So it was new. Jealousy hit me like a ton of bricks. But I couldn't look at this situation like that. I had to see him as

Taylor's father now, not Tate. I had to get myself to understand that this wasn't a reunion. It was something entirely different, something he and I had to figure out how to handle.

"Blair?"

I turned to find Taylor standing at the entry to the veranda.

"Hey!" I feigned my best smile as my heart accelerated.

He tilted his head. "What are you doing out here?"

I placed my hand on my stomach. "I started to feel a little queasy, believe it or not. Just wanted to get some air."

"Shit. Can I get you some water or anything?"

"No." I waved him off. "Please go enjoy your wedding. Don't worry about me. I'll be absolutely fine after a few minutes."

I didn't like the idea of Taylor paying *any* attention to my behavior tonight, because if he looked closely, he'd figure out that something was very wrong.

"You sure I can't get you anything?"

I shook my head. "No, but how did you know I was out here? You're supposed to be focused on your reception."

"I went over to your table to say hello, and Adam told me you'd left suddenly and gone outside. He thought maybe I'd want to check on you. Said you didn't seem right."

He's correct about that.

"I see." I exhaled. "Well, I'm fine. Truly. Just needed some air."

"Okay. If you say so. You might want to come inside, though, because they're serving dinner, and it'll get cold."

Eating was the last thing I felt like doing right now. "Right." I nodded. "I'll come inside in a sec. Don't worry about me. Please enjoy your night."

"Okay." He waved before heading back inside.

Relief washed over me. It was short-lived, however, once I reentered the venue and locked eyes with Tate. He looked just as preoccupied as I felt. I realized that he, too, had probably seen me leave to come outside. But unlike Taylor, Tate knew *exactly* why I'd needed air.

I forced my eyes away from him. It was hard to look at him and hard *not* to look at him. Hard to realize the pain in his eyes matched my own. Hard to fathom where we were supposed to go from here. I didn't know what he knew about me now. Had Taylor spoken about me, even if Tate hadn't made the connection?

How was I possibly going to handle the weeks to come?

But I had no option to sit this out. I owed Taylor the decency to be present at his wedding. He deserved a beautiful evening without having to worry about me and my "illness."

After returning to my table, I made small talk with Adam, though he had to be getting the vibe that I wasn't interested based on my demeanor. Maybe in another life, a blind date with this guy might've worked. He was cute and seemed nice. But he'd caught me at the worst possible time, so there was just no chance for us.

Tate's presence across the room continued to consume me. And when I caught him looking my direction, I had to stop myself from going to him. Even worse was when his date pulled him by the arm onto the dance floor for a slow song. Another woman's hands on his back as they swayed reminded me of what it felt like to touch him. She looked up at him with the same adoration I remembered feeling. And when he looked over at me as they danced, I was certain he could see the sadness written all over my face.

But there were sparks of goodness as well. I smiled, too, as I noticed Taylor smiling over at Tate. For the first time in his life, Taylor and his father had developed a real relationship. From Taylor's perspective, all must have seemed right in the world tonight with both of his parents here and getting along. And then I noticed Adam dancing with one of the bridesmaids. *Good*. At least I hadn't ruined his night, too.

When the waitstaff began bringing out dessert, I wondered if I'd put in enough time here to make a graceful exit. I'd endured three-quarters of a wedding, so surely it was okay to leave without seeming disrespectful.

I just needed to do it.

Taylor was talking with someone when I came to stand next to him.

"Excuse me," he said to the guy when he noticed me. He turned in my direction. "Are you feeling better?"

I nodded. "I am, but I think I need to go upstairs and rest. I hope you don't mind."

"Of course not. Did you at least eat?"

"I did." I managed a smile. "The food was delicious." *Well, what I tasted of it.*

"Will you be at the brunch tomorrow morning?"

The brunch. I'd nearly forgotten. Accepting that invitation had been a no-brainer before all of this happened.

Now it would be another tense event to endure while trying not to seem like a crazy person.

"I'm gonna try," I told him. "Depends on how I'm feeling in the morning, okay?"

He squeezed my arm. "No pressure. But you should come down and at least make a plate to bring back to your room if you're still feeling crummy."

"Okay." I smiled before reaching out to hug him. "I'm not sure where Juliana is, but please tell her I said goodnight. I'm so happy for you, my friend. This wedding was truly a dream."

"Thank you for being here, Blair. It wouldn't have been the same without you."

"I wouldn't have missed it for the world." I smiled, suddenly drowning in guilt. Never would I have knowingly betrayed my friend.

After saying goodbye, I made my way out of the reception hall. I could finally breathe a little.

But back in my room, the countdown began. When would Tate come to see me tonight? I wished I knew. As it was, I'd spend the remainder of the evening on pins and needles, waiting for a knock on the door.

When I couldn't take the waiting, I decided to take a shower. I needed to relax. I let the warm water rain down on me, still unsure about how much I was going to reveal to Tate. More than anything, I wanted to understand why and how this had happened. Why had he given me a fake name? Was anything real about our time together? One thing I knew for certain: he'd had no idea I was his son's friend at the resort. Like me, Tate would never have knowingly betrayed Taylor.

My tears mixed with the water as the enormity of this night sank in. Perhaps I could get all the emotion out now, rather than in front of Tate.

After my shower, I dressed in what I planned to wear to bed: a T-shirt and soft cotton shorts. There was no reason to try to impress Tate anymore. My wet hair fell down my back, making a damp spot on my shirt.

I'd just sat back down on the bed when a knock on the door scared the bejeezus out of me.

Chapter 20

TATE

Nervous as fuck didn't even begin to describe how I felt as I stood outside Blair's hotel room.

Not only was I petrified of someone catching me with her, I had no idea what I could say that would properly sum up the tornado of emotions inside me. I'd made it through the reception by the skin of my teeth. Leah suspected something was up with me, but I had no idea how to explain it. I'd hardly believe it myself if I wasn't living it. From the moment I'd spotted Blair in that receiving line, my head and my body had been operating on two separate planes.

I looked around again to make sure the hallway was empty.

Then I knocked. I swear I could hear my heart beating.

When Blair opened, I nearly fell back from the sheer impact of seeing her. She had wet hair and wore a T-shirt, like not a moment had passed since our amazing time together at the resort four years ago.

"Come in." She waved, quickly ushering me past the door.

The moment it closed behind us, my nerves settled a notch, because at least no one could see us together now. We were finally alone. That was half the battle tonight.

I took a moment to just look at her as she took a seat on the bed. Earlier I'd thought she looked a bit older than I remembered, but the fresh-faced woman in front of me looked exactly like the Blair I'd known and loved four years ago. So instantly taken by her, I almost forgot what I'd come here for. But when she cleared her throat, I snapped out of it.

"I'm not sure where to begin," I told her, feeling frozen in place, just inside her hotel room.

"I know." She looked down at her feet.

"I've imagined reuniting with you so many ways, but none of them was like this."

Blair looked up at me. "How did this happen, Tate?" Her voice shook. "Or should I say *Theodore...*"

My stomach sank. *Does she think I did this on purpose?*

Her gaze returned to the floor again.

"Blair, look at me." I waited until her eyes met mine. "I was *not* deceiving you. I had no idea you knew my son. Tate *is* my name. When I was in the military, all of my buddies called me Tate, and it stuck after I left. I prefer it to Theodore, which I've never liked. My mother can attest to that. Taylor doesn't know me as Tate because my family calls me Teddy. But Tate is the name I use for myself. It's what I share when I meet someone new."

She shook her head. "I've talked to Taylor about you as Tate, and he never flinched."

My eyes widened. "You've spoken to Taylor about me?"

She nodded.

Blood drained from my face. Not sure why that seemed so shocking. If they were close and she'd had no idea who I was, that made sense.

"He never seemed suspicious," she said.

I exhaled. "That doesn't surprise me. He called me Theodore out of spite for several years..." I swallowed. "But now he calls me Dad." I got a little choked up, thinking about how far Taylor and I had come, only to have our relationship potentially destroyed now. *But maybe it doesn't have to be.*

As if she'd read my mind, Blair shook her head. "He can't know about this."

Relief washed over me. "I agree. I don't plan to tell him, if you don't. There's no reason he has to know."

She hugged her arms, seeming conflicted, which worried me. Could I trust her with this? She had to understand that nothing good could come from him knowing about us.

"I want to make something clear, Blair."

"Okay..."

"Not telling Taylor has nothing to do with feeling ashamed of our time together. It doesn't change what we experienced. It's only because I don't know if *he* can handle it. Taylor's very fragile. He's—"

"You don't have to tell me that," she said, almost defensively. "He's my best friend. And I completely agree that he wouldn't understand." Her eyes watered.

Fuck. I'd never ached to reach out and hold someone more in my life. Now more than ever, though, I needed to stay in my lane. But I still needed answers. After a long moment of silence, I had to ask. "How come you never called me?"

That question had come from the part of me that was still just Tate, not Taylor's father.

She sniffled. "Does that matter now?"

It would always matter to me. Because as much as I'd hoped she wouldn't need to call, I'd also sure as fuck hoped she would. Every damn time the phone rang for the past four years, my heart had filled with hope. I'd been so sure she'd reach out, even if just to say hello.

I looked away, but then back at her. "I always thought I'd hear from you at least once."

She closed her eyes, and a tear finally fell.

"Hey…" I stepped forward, unable to stop myself from wiping the teardrop with my thumb. It took everything in me not to take her in my arms. But that wasn't where we were right now. "What's wrong?" I whispered.

Her voice trembled. "It wasn't my *choice* not to call you."

I narrowed my eyes. "What do you mean?"

She looked up at me. "I was robbed on my way home from that trip. While I was waiting at the train station, someone took the bag that had my phone in it."

It felt like I'd been punched in the chest. "Are you serious?"

Blair nodded. "I was devastated, and it took me a long time to come to terms with it. I filed a police report and constantly checked in with the authorities near where it happened, but they never found my belongings. I lost everything—my wallet, my phone, all my contacts." She wiped her eyes. "But the only thing that mattered was your number and the photos I'd taken." She shook her head. "I lost *you* that day."

I let out a long breath, countless emotions swirling through me. "I can't believe that happened."

"You think I'm lying?"

I shook my head. "Of course not. That's not what I meant. I just assumed you'd chosen not to contact me. I never imagined that you had no choice. That's some really bad luck."

She laughed angrily. "Well, I would say *this* twist of fate is a lot worse than that."

I stopped myself from wiping her tears again and tried to organize my thoughts. "I wished every day that I had gotten your last name," I told her. "But I also thought maybe you didn't want to talk to me because you never called. Through the years, I think I'd sort of accepted it. But now that I know you lost my number…" I shook my head. "It sets me back mentally. I don't know how to feel right now." I exhaled. "Everything I thought I knew about this situation was wrong."

She straightened her back. "After what we found out today, though, none of that matters anymore. Does it?"

I opened my mouth, then closed it. If only it were that simple. "You'll *always* matter to me, Blair. This doesn't change how I feel about you, even if it changes what I can say or do about it." I paced, still trying to sort through all of this. "I have questions."

She crossed her arms as she watched me pace. "Okay…"

"Back when we first met, and you said a friend had gifted you the trip... That was Taylor."

"Yes. It was the only way I could've afforded it."

I nodded. "When you told me that, it struck me as a little weird, but I didn't want to insult you by questioning how you had a friend who could afford it, I guess. But it makes sense now that it was him."

She raised her voice. "Why didn't *you* tell me your family owned the resort? If you had, I would've surely put two and two together."

"I didn't want you to get the wrong idea about me." I threw my hands in the air. "I've never lived off of my parents' money. Never took a dime from them, and I wasn't in the habit of flaunting that connection." I closed my eyes and blew out a breath. "But you're right. I absolutely should've told you, and I regret how I handled it."

Even as I spoke, I wasn't sure those words were true. Because if I'd told her, she would've figured out who I was. And we never would've been together. Even now, I wouldn't change anything about that. Fucked up or not, I'd always cherish the time we had.

Blair's face reddened. "You accused *me* of being deceitful on that trip, yet it seems you were the one keeping the most secrets—not telling me your parents owned the place, giving me your nickname..."

"It *is* my name, just not the one my family uses," I insisted. "Please stop thinking I tried to deceive you." I stopped pacing to look her in the eyes. "I've thought about you every day, Blair."

She turned to me, her expression softening. "I've thought about you, too."

My chest constricted, and once again I had to stop myself from stepping forward to hold her. "Where do we go from here?"

Her face was strained. "I don't think *we* go anywhere."

I knew that made sense, yet the old feelings for her came flooding back. I didn't want to hear it. "This is it?" I finally said. "We're just gonna pretend we don't exist to each other? That doesn't work for me."

"Pretending you don't exist isn't an option," she murmured.

I let out a long breath. "I don't have all the answers tonight. I'm still absorbing this, grappling with the fact that I may have inadvertently sabotaged my relationship with my son by sleeping with one of his best friends." I paused. "But also...seeing you again is a fucking dream come true." I shook my head, nearly overcome with emotion.

Blair blushed and looked away. "Where does your date think you are right now? Is she your girlfriend?"

"Helping my parents with something in their suite." I swallowed. Leah hadn't entered my mind once since I'd come to this hotel room. "She and I only started dating a couple of months ago. She's a good person."

"Well, that's *great*," Blair said almost bitterly. "I'm happy for you."

I stared at her a moment. Something else was going on here. Blair was...different.

"Why are you looking at me like that?" she asked.

"Is everything okay with you? I mean, outside of this situation?"

"I'm fine," she insisted, her blush deepening.

"Where are you living now?" I asked.

"North of Boston. About an hour from here. My parents moved from Western Mass to the Boston area when my father switched jobs, so I followed. I don't live with them, though. The move meant I also now live closer to Taylor." She paused. "He mentioned that his father had moved here, too. You left Texas?"

I nodded. "It was time, yeah. I wanted to be closer to him and the rest of my family. I've been garnering a lot of business here, too."

"You're still doing the home building?" she asked.

"Yeah. But less manual labor up here and more management. It's like starting over in a way, but it was the right decision."

My phone chimed with a text. Leah was wondering why I was taking so long.

Blair looked at my phone. "You need to get back?"

Nodding, I exhaled.

"What does she think you're doing for your parents?"

"I told her my mother needed help with something broken in her room. I didn't want to lie, but..."

"I get it. We have no choice but to lie right now."

I took a deep breath and stepped toward the door, but I wasn't about to make the same mistake twice. "Can I have your number?" I asked, turning back. "I think we need to continue this conversation—maybe when Taylor and Juliana are out of town, so there's no chance of them seeing us together."

To my relief, she nodded and didn't try to convince me that talking was a bad idea. I handed her my phone, and she entered her contact info. I watched as she typed in her last name: Moynihan. Even though Taylor had uttered it once earlier, there was something particularly profound about her finally giving it to me.

I looked down at her name when she returned my phone. "Thank you."

I sent her a text so she'd have my number.

Blair rubbed her arms as her phone chimed. "You'd better go."

No part of me wanted to go back out into the world. I couldn't fathom how I was supposed to just go on with my life after this. But in the end, I forced myself to leave. "Talk to you soon, Blair."

As she nodded, I quietly slipped out her door, making sure to look both ways before walking down the hall. It felt like I was outside of myself as I entered the elevator.

When I returned to my room, Leah was understandably annoyed.

"That took long enough," she said.

"Yeah." I loosened my tie. "Sorry about that."

"I was hoping we could have a little fun before you get out of that tux."

The last thing I wanted right now was sex. I could barely think straight. As shitty as it was, I had to pile an excuse on top of my lie.

"It's been a long day." I sighed. "I'm sorry. I'm beat."

"Okay..." She frowned.

"Gonna get cleaned up for bed," I said, barely able to look her in the eye.

In the shower, I let the water wash over me as I thought about Blair. Something had changed in her— more than just shock about this latest turn of events. She was different. I needed to know what life had been like for her these past four years.

At the age she'd been when I met her, four years was a damn long time. She could've experienced any number of things. Had she fallen in love? Was she a nurse now? She'd mentioned speaking to Taylor about the man she'd met at the resort. Had she told him *everything*? The list of questions in my head seemed endless. And it would likely be a long while before I got the chance to ask.

Chapter 21

TATE

The following morning, Leah and I went down to the first floor where a brunch had been set up for the wedding party and close friends.

Taylor and Juliana had already arrived and seemed to be enjoying themselves. As I looked over at my son conversing with some friends, I realized how lucky I was that Blair and I were on the same page. Even after all this time, I trusted her, trusted that she cared about my son enough not to want to hurt him. You'd think that might have provided me some relief, but my feelings about Blair and about my life in general remained tumultuous.

I couldn't get over her phone being stolen mere hours after we'd left each other. It made my heart hurt, and I realized it was possible to see this situation simultaneously through parallel lenses. One view only wanted to protect Taylor, while the other would always hold a place for Blair, would always mourn the idea that she might've called if she'd had my number. And would certainly mourn the idea that she and I might've had a future together.

That torturous question popped into my mind once again. Would I have done things differently if I could go back in time and know Blair was Taylor's friend? No. I was still certain I wouldn't have changed a thing. If that made me a shitty person, so be it. I couldn't imagine never having known her, never having those precious days together.

Leah and I found a spot to sit, and as I walked back from the buffet, I noticed Blair. I hadn't seen her enter the dining room. She looked more refreshed than last night and wore a floral dress, reminiscent of the ones I remembered her wearing at the resort.

She glanced up at me and then to the plate I'd piled high with food. She shook her head and smiled, which surprised me. I looked down at my plate and realized she must've been thinking that some things never change. Her smile was a bit of nostalgia amidst the chaos of this wedding weekend. I cherished it. Maybe some things *were* still the same.

If no one else had been here, I would've gone straight to her table, shared my food with her, and urged her to tell me everything about her life. The fact that I couldn't felt almost cruel. Instead, I buried the urge and passed her table, finding my seat next to Leah. I'd gotten enough food to feed three people, but my appetite had vanished.

I watched as Blair got up and went to the buffet line. As she stood with her back to me, I admired her beautiful, long blonde hair, recalling how it had felt between my fingers. She was right here, and yet I missed her so much.

As she moved through the line, Taylor walked over to chat with her. I could tell how close they were. My stomach sank, followed by a flash of panic. Had they always been *just* friends, or was there a time when it had been more than that? I couldn't ask Taylor, of course, so the only way I'd ever know was to ask Blair. Not sure why it mattered. Taylor was happily married now. But my curiosity lingered throughout brunch, and I felt like I was going insane. I should've been embarrassed for being jealous of my own son.

"Are you okay?" Leah asked.

If I'd had a nickel for every time she'd had to check on my sanity this weekend...

"Yeah." I sighed. "I'm fine."

"You keep looking over at the buffet table. Did you not get enough food?" She laughed, gesturing to my plate. "I mean... It'll take you three days to eat all that."

"I'm just spacing out." I rubbed my eyes. "Still pretty tired from yesterday."

"Hmm..." she said.

After about ten minutes of trying to eat, I excused myself to go to the bathroom, planning to throw some water on my face and reset. Or that's what I *told* myself. I'd also seen Blair leave a minute earlier and wanted to see if I could steal a moment with her. I hoped for just one more opportunity to talk before we parted ways today. It would be a hell of a lot harder to see her without the wedding excuse.

Blair was nowhere to be found in the hallway outside the dining room. I decided to get some air, and I found her standing just outside the door.

My heart raced as I stepped out. "Hey."

She flinched and looked around. "What are you doing here, Tate?"

"I'm sorry." I looked over my shoulder.

"You need to go back inside."

But I couldn't. "I need to ask you something really quick. Something occurred to me…"

A look of alarm crossed her face. "What?"

"I know you and Taylor are great friends. That's very apparent." I pulled in a breath. "But were you ever more?"

She shook her head. "No. Never. We never had that kind of relationship. Not even once." Blair looked me straight in the eyes, and I knew she was telling the truth.

A long breath escaped me, and I felt a little euphoric, like a cloud of calm had enveloped me after I'd nearly sent myself off the deep end. It was pathetic, really.

"I'm sorry, Blair. Not very mature of me to be focused on my jealousy when we have bigger fish to fry." I placed my hand on my heart. "But I couldn't breathe until I knew."

"It's okay." She nodded. "I get it. I'd want to know the same thing."

"Thank you for understanding."

"There's no playbook for how to react to this situation," she said.

"That's for damn sure."

"You'd better go back inside, Tate, before someone sees us."

I looked over my shoulder again. "You gave me your number. Is it okay if I call you soon?" I shook my head. "I assure you, I don't have an ulterior motive. I just feel like we need to talk. I'm not going to be able to focus until we do."

"I agree that we should talk more, but I need you to give me some time. I'm not at a place in my life where I can easily handle this."

My brows drew in. *What the hell does that mean?* But I couldn't very well force her to keep in contact with me. "Will you promise to let me know when you're ready?"

She nodded. "Yes."

My stomach twisted, but there was nothing else I could do. "I'm going back in now." I exhaled. "Take care of yourself, Blair."

"You, too."

I stepped back inside and started down the hall to the brunch, but my pace slowed as I noticed Taylor walking toward me. I stiffened. How close had I come to getting caught talking to Blair outside? *Jesus.*

"Have you seen my friend Blair?" he asked.

My blood went cold. *Why is he asking me that?*

"No." I cleared my throat. "Why? What's going on?"

"I saw her leave the brunch a while ago, and I wanted to be sure she was okay. She's been acting a little bit strange this whole wedding."

"I see..."

Had he noticed *my* strange behavior? I had to have been just as conspicuous.

He sighed. "When are you heading home?"

"Probably right after brunch."

"It was nice meeting Leah. I was just chatting with her."

I forced a smile. "I'm happy you like her."

"Do you think that's going somewhere serious?" he asked.

"I honestly couldn't tell you." I shook my head.

"Well, she seems great." Taylor smacked my arm.

Leah *was* great. And I'd thought maybe I could learn to be happy again. Yet the only time I was *sure* I'd been happy was with his best friend, Blair. It was so fucked up.

"I appreciate your approval," I told him.

"I know you and Mom have your issues," he said. "But I'm proud of you both for getting along this weekend. It can't be easy being around each other, but it's meant a lot to me."

"Your mother deserves my respect. She did a damn good job raising you to be the man you've become. And I'm happy she and I are cordial now."

"Yeah…" He smiled. "Me too."

"When do you leave for your honeymoon?"

"In a week. We're so psyched. We need a vacation badly. Work's been crazy for Juliana and for me."

"Aruba, right?"

He nodded.

"I hope the trip is everything you want it to be."

"Well, I'll let you know." He smacked my arm again as he walked away. "Make sure you come say goodbye before you leave."

"Of course."

I watched him continue down the hall. I wondered whether Blair had left her spot outside the door or whether he'd find her still standing there. I hated that she would have to look him in the eye and lie again about why she'd been acting strangely.

As I returned to the brunch, I prepared to face Leah. What was supposed to be a quick bathroom trip had turned into a twenty-minute disappearance.

"Sorry I took so long," I said.

"Were you in the bathroom all that time?" she asked.

"Actually, I ran into Taylor, and we had a quick chat."

Her mouth curved into a smile. "Oh, okay. I'm happy you and he are getting along."

"Yeah, so am I."

"What do you wanna do for the rest of the afternoon?" she asked.

I scratched my chin. "Actually, I have a ton of errands. Just some stuff I've been putting off around my new place. Need to go to Home Depot for some supplies. I've got a busy work week, so I won't have much time to deal with that stuff other than today."

She looked at me a moment. "Well, I was hoping we could have some alone time, but if you think that would interrupt your plans..." There was a hint of spite in her voice.

I nodded, but didn't take the bait. I couldn't give her what she needed today. I wanted to be alone to decompress. Every muscle in my body was tight, wrought with stress. "We can catch up tomorrow," I suggested.

She looked away, and I knew I'd messed things up. Not sure I'd be able to come back from what I'd pulled this weekend. But until I could get past all this, I couldn't be the person Leah needed me to be anyway. All I could think about now was Blair.

Chapter 22

TATE

Two weeks after the wedding, I still hadn't heard from Blair, and my relationship with Leah was practically nonexistent. I'd made up one excuse after another to avoid seeing her.

Blair had said she needed time before talking to me. But I'd hoped she'd reach out while Taylor was away so we could safely meet in person. My life felt like it was on hold until I could see her again. One day, since she still hadn't reached out, I decided to do a little investigating.

Investigating is the gentler term for stalking.

Now that I knew her last name, it was easy to find out where she lived. She'd told me she lived about an hour from Boston, and the address I found online corroborated that.

To justify driving to Blair's neighborhood, I did actually wait until I needed to visit a worksite out that way, north of the city, to give an estimate. I hoped this trip could be my way of finding out what her life was like without having to push her for answers. The more I could quietly discover on my own, the better. It would keep me occupied while I waited for her call and also help prepare me mentally.

After my visit to the jobsite, I'd driven by what I assumed was her house three times this afternoon, and so far, I'd seen nothing of interest. There wasn't even a car parked in the driveway, and it didn't seem like anyone was home. Just my luck. Perhaps it was the time of day—the middle of the afternoon. She was probably at work.

Taylor was due back in a few days, so I didn't have all that much time. I had no idea how often he ventured out this way to see her, but if he was in town at all, it would be too risky for me to show up here.

Since there was nothing to see as of now, I decided to grab a quick bite and drive by one more time before I made the half-hour trip home. I'd been renting a house near where Taylor lived until I could find a place to buy.

The next time I returned to Blair's house, there was a car parked in the driveway. Adrenaline pumped through my veins. Was it her car or her significant other's? I had no idea if she lived here alone.

I parked around the corner, but at an angle where I could still see her house—as stalkers do. It was about four PM, and I told myself I'd stay until five. After opening the sandwich I'd bought at a drive-thru, I played some music to pass the time.

Just as I'd begun to worry I might doze off, I jumped at the sight of someone exiting her house. I squinted. It was her. Blair's long blonde hair shifted in the wind, and she held the hand of a little boy. *What the...* I leaned in as she placed him in the backseat of the car and walked around to the driver's side.

As she drove off, I scrambled to turn on the ignition and follow her. I slapped on sunglasses, hoping for a bit of disguise in case I caught up to her and she happened to look in the rearview mirror. She didn't know what kind of truck I drove, though, I reminded myself.

When I spotted her car in front of me on the main road, I took a deep breath in and calmly followed. Maybe she was a nanny dropping this boy off somewhere. I needed to not draw any conclusions. Yet my heart pounded as various possibilities ran through my mind, the most far-fetched of which was unthinkable.

Blair slowed and pulled into a playground, and I continued past and parked in a spot far from the entrance. It had been a beautiful sunny day today, but the late afternoon light had mellowed. From a distance, I watched her help the kid out of the car before she walked with him over to the jungle gym in the middle of the play area.

Well, sitting in a playground parking lot hadn't been on my itinerary today. I needed binoculars so I could get a close-up look. That would've officially sealed the stalker deal, I supposed. The longer I sat here, the more wrong I felt about spying. But now that the kid had further sparked my curiosity, there was no way I could leave.

As I continued to strain my eyes to see them, I realized hanging out in a truck at a playground didn't exactly help someone stay under the radar. It was probably best to go back to my spot around the corner from her house. It wasn't like I was going to confront her at the playground.

And maybe there would be someone *else* there if I returned to her place.

So, I drove back to Blair's house. There was no other car parked in the driveway, but it was after five now; if she had a partner, they might be coming home soon. I needed gas to get home, so I drove to the gas station real quick before returning for one last pass by her house.

As I approached, I noticed her car in the driveway again. *Crap.* I cursed myself for missing the opportunity to see if she'd returned with the little boy or alone. I stopped down the block and leaned my head against the back of my seat, pondering what to do next.

But after a moment, I knew. I *had* to see her. It was now or never. Taylor would be back in a few days, and I needed to take advantage of this opportunity.

I moved my car to park in front of her house, took a deep breath, and walked up to her door. My stomach was in knots, and after I knocked, my heart pounded. It had only ever beaten this way for Blair, whether out of excitement or, as was the case now, fear of the unknown. I hoped she would forgive me for intruding on her privacy.

The door opened, and a look of absolute shock crossed her face. "What are you doing here?" Her voice shook.

This isn't good. "I'm sorry," I said quickly. "I needed to see you. And Taylor is away. So it was the best time to come without him seeing us together."

She swallowed hard. "I told you I needed time before we talked."

"I understand that. But it's been a couple of weeks, and honestly, Blair, this situation is never going to be an easy one. I'm going out of my mind. I'll leave if you really want me to, but…" I lost my train of thought as tears came to her eyes.

She shook her head. "You really shouldn't have come."

What the fuck?

I wanted so badly to ask her whose kid she'd been with today. But I couldn't let her know I'd been following her. As I looked beyond her into the small house, though, it was quiet. "Can I please come in?"

Before she could answer, I heard tiny feet.

He'd come out of nowhere.

I looked down, and my eyes slowly widened as I caught my first glimpse of a face that looked very, very much like mine.

Chapter 23

TATE

Everything began to spin. When I finally lifted my eyes to Blair's again, the look on her face told me everything I needed to know.

Rather than scream like I wanted to, I instead vowed not to do or say *anything* to scare this little boy right now. He didn't deserve that. And I didn't want his first impression of me to be a bad one.

Blair continued to stand there frozen.

"Who's that, Mommy?"

Mommy.

What had been a 99.9-percent certainty now moved to 100 percent.

I knelt, my voice gentle. "I'm a friend of your mom's."

Blair cleared her throat. "Nicholas, sweetheart, go play with your toys for a bit, please." She pointed. "In the living room."

Nicholas.

He wouldn't move. Instead, he clung to her leg as if he was trying to protect her. It pulled at my heartstrings, though at the moment it felt like my heart was hanging out of my chest.

"It's okay. He doesn't have to go anywhere," I spoke softly so as not to scare him, staring at his face in awe.

My face. Or at least the one I'd had when I was his age.

When he let go of her and ran over to a corner in the living room, I stepped inside the house without permission. There was no more handling this situation delicately.

Tugging on my hair, I mouthed to her, "What the fuck?"

Her face reddened. "Tate…"

"He's mine, right?" I asked, my voice choked with emotion.

"Yes," she whispered.

I closed my eyes for a moment to grasp the enormity of that. To grasp the fact that my life would never be the same. Any plan for how to handle Taylor had gone straight out the window.

I finally opened my eyes. "How did this happen? We were safe."

She shook her head. "I don't know. It just *did*."

"I'm so fucking confused right now." I pulled on my hair again and paced.

She followed me. "I've both dreamed about and dreaded this day. Before I knew who you were, I dreamed of finding you and telling you. But then at the wedding, everything changed. That dream became more like a nightmare. And I hadn't figured out what to do yet. But please know I was going to tell you. I would *never* keep this from you."

I turned to her. "This is why you said you needed more time."

Blair nodded. "Before I found you at the wedding, I'd resigned myself to the fact that you'd never know him. I wasn't happy about that, but I'd accepted it." She paused. "This? You being Taylor's father? I don't have a plan for this scenario, Tate."

I still had so many questions. But those could wait. There was only one thing that mattered right now. I walked over to where Nicholas was playing, sat on the couch, and watched him. I soaked in every inch of him as Blair stood in a corner of the room and looked on.

His eyes were like saucers as he focused on adding a block to his structure without the rest toppling over.

Eventually I had to force myself away because there was still so much I needed to ask Blair, and I realized it was probably better to do that while his attention was on the toys.

I walked past Blair and into the kitchen. She followed.

"I need to know everything," I told her, leaning against the counter. "From the very beginning. Tell me what happened after you got back from our trip, how you found out you were pregnant."

"Well, I didn't know I was pregnant right away. There was no reason to think that, because we were safe." She shrugged. "It was a fluke. I didn't know for almost three months. I hadn't felt sick or anything. Just noticed I wasn't getting my period, so I went for a test." She exhaled. "Those first few months after I got home, I was mostly devastated about losing my phone. I spent those days really mad at myself—mad that I'd never asked you for your full name."

She shook her head. "Of course I didn't know the half of it then. I wondered if the stress of losing you had caused me to skip a couple of cycles. It wasn't until the third one I missed that I decided to take a test just to be sure."

I had to force myself to breathe. "You've been out here all this time, raising *my* kid." I let out a long breath. "Blair, this is..."

The right words escaped me. There were *no* words. I didn't know whether to mourn all that was lost or celebrate. Never mind me, though. What about *her*?

"What happened to your plans?" I cried. "School. Did you graduate?"

Her gaze fell to her feet. "I dropped out. I'm only now finishing nursing school. I didn't have that much longer to go, and I joined an online program recently to finish my degree."

My chest constricted. This had impacted her life so profoundly. "After you found out, did you try to find me?"

She nodded. "First, I redownloaded the app, hoping you were still on there, but you must've deleted your account."

"I did." I sighed. "I figured you had my number and wouldn't need the app to reach me."

Blair continued, "I even enlisted Taylor's help to get a roster of names from the resort—people who'd stayed there that week. But there was no Tate."

Shit. Of course there wasn't. "My name wouldn't have been on there anyway, because I didn't pay for my room the normal way. If there's a room open, anyone in my family can take it without having to formally book it. So I wouldn't have been on any official list."

She chuckled. "Because you own the freaking place. If only I'd known that."

"My *parents* own it," I clarified. "And again, I didn't want you to get the wrong idea about me being entitled." My thoughts felt like ping-pong balls. I could hardly contain them long enough to make a connection. "What does Taylor know about Nicholas's father?"

"I told him I'd met an older guy on vacation. And I told him the guy's name was Tate. He never seemed to suspect anything."

I ran my hand through my hair. "Fuck."

"Tate..." Blair murmured.

"Yeah?"

"I'm still processing this, too. I never thought I was keeping anything from Taylor. I didn't know who you were until the wedding. I don't want to be responsible for his pain any more than you do."

I nodded. "I know. We have that in common."

She ran her hands over her arms. "I'm still not sure we should tell him."

For me, this discovery changed everything. I looked into her eyes. "He has a *brother*. He needs to know."

She sighed. "He's close to him already. Nicholas sees Taylor as an uncle. He and Juliana even babysat Nicholas once."

I cringed. "Jesus."

"I know." Blair's eyes welled up again.

I wanted to hug her, but it didn't seem appropriate. *Fuck.* I still felt my heart beating for her. "It'll be okay, Blair. We'll figure it out. Together."

She sniffled. "You really need to consider whether telling Taylor is the right idea before we make any rash decisions."

I wanted to calm her nerves, so I nodded. This was a lot. "We don't have to do anything right away. We have time to figure out the best way to tell him."

"Do you want a paternity test?" she asked.

"I don't need one. He looks exactly the way I did when I was his age."

Blair chewed her lip. "Well, anyway, I haven't…"

"You haven't what?"

She paused. "I haven't *been* with anyone else. So there's no way he could be anyone's but yours."

My eyes widened. "You weren't with anyone else around that time…or you haven't been with anyone *since* me?"

Blair murmured, "Both."

Oh my God. That wrecked me.

"But I would still like you to get a paternity test, just so *you* have it on record," she continued. "It would make me feel better to know you have that certainty."

I nodded. "Yeah. Uh… I'll go to a lab." I paused. "Anything you need. I'm not trying to make your life more difficult."

"I don't need anything from you, Tate. I've been doing just—"

"I know you don't *need* me. You've clearly been handling everything. But I want to be in his life, Blair. And I want to help you financially."

"I don't need it," she insisted.

"It's not up for debate," I pushed back. "Now that I know about my son, I'm not going anywhere. I want to take care of him, even if I have to do it discreetly for a while."

"How long is a while? Do you think there's still a chance we may never tell Taylor?"

The idea of keeping a secret so monumental seemed impossible. But this knowledge could destroy any shred of faith in me he'd mustered. "Moving back to Massachusetts was supposed to be about rebuilding my relationship with him. I can't tell you how things are going to play out, except to say that I do believe we need to tell him."

"I know Taylor. The truth would traumatize him," she reasoned.

Immediately, a vision sprang to mind—Taylor accusing me of preying on Blair, of not being responsible, of abandoning a second child. I prayed the answers would come to me, but right now, I needed to focus on what I could more easily control.

"When can I come back to visit Nicholas?" I asked her.

The kitchen overlooked the living room, where he was still playing. She looked toward him. "I don't know if you should ever come back *here*."

My heart sank until I realized what she was getting at. "This house, you mean."

She nodded. "Taylor could come by on his commute from work. He's been known to do that. I'm not far from his job. He has to pass my exit to get home."

"Okay. Of course." I scratched my chin. "I'll figure something out. Maybe I'll rent a place where we can meet, some place farther out of town."

After a moment, she nodded. "That would work."

Her agreement brought me relief. At least I could see Nicholas while navigating the rest of this mess. "I think we need to keep this to ourselves for a while," I said. "I don't just mean Taylor. I mean other family members, too."

"I haven't told anyone, Tate. I can't imagine explaining the situation."

"I haven't told anyone about us, either," I said. "I don't think we can risk it until Taylor knows. He deserves to be the first."

"I agree."

I moved back toward the living room. "Can I spend some time with him before I have to leave?"

She smiled sadly. "Of course."

"Thanks."

I walked over to where Nicholas was playing. Overwhelmed by a mix of love and sadness over everything I'd missed the past four years, I got down on the ground and helped him finish building a structure with his blocks. One block at a time. *One step at a time*, I told myself. It's not going to be okay overnight, but someday it *will* be okay.

"What about this one?" I asked him. "Can I put it on top?"

He nodded enthusiastically. His huge eyes felt like a window into my soul. Such a beautiful boy. *My* boy. One who would've been fatherless if the original story had been true. Despite everything, I was grateful the situation had played out the way it did. I just needed to figure out how to openly love this son without shattering the other.

Chapter 24

BLAIR

I'd dreamed of the sight before me too many times to count.

It was never my intention to keep Tate from his son. I just hadn't been able to find the man. And even after I'd discovered who he was, I never considered not telling him about Nicholas.

I just wished there was a way for Nicholas to experience the gift of his father without causing turmoil in Taylor's life. Tate shouldn't have to trade one child for another. I'd never forgive myself if all the effort Taylor and Tate had put into their relationship was erased by this revelation. I'd also never understand how fate could've allowed this to happen in the first place.

When Tate stood from where he'd been playing with Nicholas on the floor, I looked away, not wanting him to see how transfixed I'd been. The father clearly still had a hold on me, not just the son.

"Thank you for letting me spend time with him," he said as he returned to the kitchen.

"Of course. I'd never keep you away."

Tate drew in a breath. "I'm gonna get moving on finding a place out of town where we can meet without worrying."

"Okay." I let out a shaky breath.

The idea of going to meet Tate at some hideaway gave me mixed feelings. I knew this was about Nicholas, not Tate and me, but it was sometimes hard to separate my memories from the present.

Tate looked back over at Nicholas, shaking his head. "I can't believe Taylor has babysat him and everything…"

I smiled. "Nicholas loves Uncle Taylor. Taylor has been one of the only males in his life, aside from my dad. He's been supportive since the very beginning when I found out about the pregnancy."

Tate closed his eyes a moment. "That's so beautiful and so fucked up."

"What made you come by today?" I asked.

"It was mostly Taylor not being in town. Knowing he's coming back from his honeymoon soon really lit a fire under my ass. But also…" He hesitated. "I haven't been able to stop thinking about you since the wedding, even if that's wrong." He sighed, looking over at Nicholas. "And now I have even more reason to be careful with you."

Talk about a mixed message. Was he trying to tell me he still had feelings for me, or that he had no intention of crossing the line?

"The moment I realized you were Taylor's father, I closed the door on any hope I might've had for us." I scoffed. "Besides, don't you have a girlfriend?"

Tate turned to me. "Want the truth?"

"Always."

"Leah knows something is up with me. I haven't been able to concentrate on anything—her or otherwise—since the wedding. And that was *before* I knew about my son. She probably thinks I'm cheating on her, since I keep canceling our plans, making excuses. I haven't told her anything." He exhaled. "But things aren't looking good for her and me right now."

"Well, I'm sorry if I disrupted your life."

He shook his head. "I would never change this outcome. If Taylor wasn't my son and you weren't at his wedding, I'd never have known about Nicholas. The idea of never knowing I had another son breaks my heart." Torment filled his eyes. "I can't go back and change those years when Taylor was growing up. But Nicholas is still young enough that he won't remember the time I wasn't around." He took a moment to breathe. "That's why Taylor's gonna have to find out, Blair. I can't be Nicholas's dad in secret. He deserves a hundred percent." He paused, looking pensive. "But I need to strengthen my relationship with Taylor a bit more before we throw this on him. He and I just made it to the top of a mountain after a long and arduous journey. Telling him now would be like pushing him down."

I nodded. Nothing wrong with having a little more time before what would be the most difficult conversation of my life. "There's nothing that matters more to me right now than protecting my friend. I know Nicholas will be fine. *We've* been fine all this time."

Tate turned to look into my eyes. "Thank you."

"For what?"

"For taking care of him when I couldn't. For giving

up your life to do so. For being the amazing mother you shouldn't have had to be so young."

"I might not have been ready for him, but I'm so glad he was born. This is a fucked-up situation, but it's not *his* fault. He's my greatest blessing."

Tate's eyes glistened. "I have so many questions about these past four years, but I'm having a hard time knowing where to start."

I shrugged. "Well, I'm not going anywhere, if you think of them."

Tate's mouth curved into a slight smile. His eyes fell to my lips, and I instinctively licked them. God help me, despite everything, I still wanted him with every fiber of my being. I'd longed for him every day for the past four years. Now I didn't think I'd ever be able to have him again—not if it meant hurting Taylor. I couldn't change Nicholas being Taylor's brother, but I could choose the way I proceeded with his father. And that meant not *proceeding* at all. Unfortunately, that only made me want him more.

"Should you be getting back?" I forced myself to say.

"I don't want to go," he muttered.

"It's getting late," I added. "I need to put him to bed."

"Can I stay until you do?" he asked softly.

How can I say no? "Of course. I have to give him a bath. He won't mind an audience." I smiled. "He loves baths."

Tate grinned. "He does?"

I laughed. "By the time we get done, it usually looks like I took one with him."

He chuckled, and his eyes lingered on mine again. "So much I've missed. It still feels like a dream."

With my emotions rising to the surface, I quickly switched gears, rounding up Nicholas and running his bath. I couldn't let Tate see how much of an effect he had on me.

Tate sat atop the toilet as he watched our son play in the suds.

Our son.

It was the first time I'd referred to Nicholas as anything but *my* son, even just in my head.

I tried to focus on the task at hand but couldn't help looking at Tate from time to time, catching the look of awe on his face as he watched Nicholas splash and squeal with delight.

As I knelt to lather Nicholas, I thought I sensed Tate peeking down my shirt. Or was it my imagination? Either way, I felt my body come alive at the mere idea of his eyes on me. I'd spent the past four years either pregnant or ignoring my own needs in order to keep another human being alive, which didn't leave much time to feel sexy. But Tate's mere presence served as a reminder of what it had felt like to be desired.

Tate began a game where he'd steal some of the bath toys, hide them behind his back, then throw them back into the tub for Nicholas to catch. Nicholas giggled whether he caught them or not.

From the outside, it looked like a simple bath. But it was the beginning of a new normal I had no idea whether I was ready for. Could my heart handle what I had to do when it came to Tate? We had to find a way to be co-parents and nothing more.

Chapter 25

With butterflies in my stomach, I pulled into a parking spot at the aquarium.

Before Tate had left last night, I'd asked if he wanted to join Nicholas and me for an outing today, since it was the last full day we wouldn't have to worry about Taylor spotting us together. Taylor and Juliana were scheduled to return from Aruba tomorrow.

Tate was waiting at the entrance when Nicholas and I approached. His hands were in his pockets as he looked around, seeming to search for us. He hadn't noticed us yet, but the sight of him took my breath away. Tate was always handsome, but he looked hotter than ever in his dark-wash jeans, rugged boots, and a hooded gray sweatshirt rolled up at the sleeves, displaying his sexy tattoo-covered forearms. He wore a baseball cap backward, which had been a weakness even before I'd seen Tate wearing one. But on him? It was still my kryptonite.

He has a girlfriend, I reminded myself. The idea of Tate with another woman still stirred jealousy inside me.

Over the years, I'd often wondered whether he'd gotten married or fallen in love, and I'd always felt jealous. I'd finally mastered the art of blocking the idea, but that was out the window now.

"Hey." Tate beamed when he turned and saw us coming.

I held Nicholas's hand and looked down at him. "You remember Mommy's friend..."

Nicholas nodded.

Tate knelt. "Are you excited to see the fish?"

Nicholas smiled but said nothing, hiding his face behind my leg.

"He's being shy today," I explained.

"That's okay." Tate stood. "He doesn't owe me anything."

The three of us entered the building, and Tate went straight to the counter to purchase our tickets.

Once we were admitted, Nicholas ran ahead. He looked all around, instantly transfixed by the space-like lighting and tanks filled with colorful aquatic species.

Tate and I sped up to keep close to him.

"Is this his first time at an aquarium?" Tate asked.

"Second," I said. "But we haven't been since he was two. I'm sure he barely remembers."

After perusing various displays, Nicholas stopped at a special tank where kids could stick their hands in the water and touch living things. The attendant was really sweet with him, guiding his fingers while Tate and I looked on.

At one point, while we were walking, Nicholas reached for Tate's hand. My eyes widened as Tate looked over at me and smiled. They walked together over to another tank, where Tate knelt to meet Nicholas closer to eye level.

I stood back, watching as Tate rested his arm gently on Nicholas's back while he pointed out various fish. I couldn't hear what they were saying, but I took it all in, feeling grateful. Despite the difficulties that lay ahead, there was no greater gift I could give Nicholas than a relationship with his dad.

After a minute, they came back over to where I was standing. Tate looked confused. "I asked him if he wanted to go see the sharks, but he said no?"

I chuckled. "He's scared of sharks, but he does want to see them. He just wants assurance that they can't get him. He's afraid one of them will jump out somehow."

Tate smiled down at him. "Aw, buddy. You don't have to be scared here. They can't get you through the glass." He knelt. "How about this... I promise to protect you. Will you go see them with me?"

After some hesitancy, Nicholas finally nodded. My son seemed to trust Tate, even if he didn't know his damn name.

When we arrived at the shark tank, Nicholas was shaking a little. Tate lifted him, holding him tightly as they watched the sharks swim by. Minute by minute, Nicholas seemed to relax, with his little arm wrapped around Tate's neck. He even leaned forward to touch the glass, which was pretty brave. My heart nearly burst as I witnessed their bond growing.

Tate put Nicholas down and they walked toward me, hand in hand. "Where to next?" Tate asked.

"We still haven't seen the jellyfish," I suggested.

Tate smirked. "Jellyfish, you say?" Once Nicholas looked away, he leaned close and added, "Should I be prepared to pee on something?"

The contact of his breath put my body on alert.

"Not this time," I told him.

He winked.

It was a brief acknowledgement of where we'd come from. Yet even as we stood here with the product of that time, those days seemed a world away.

We walked together and stopped at the final exhibit, featuring the infamous jellyfish. Per Nicholas's request, Tate lifted him again so he could see better.

But when I looked over, I found Tate not studying the jellyfish, but staring at me. Rather than look away, he offered a smile. I wondered what he was thinking, if any of the feelings he'd had for me in the past had risen to the surface today. I'd battled my own feelings every moment of this aquarium trip.

Nicholas yawned, which was my cue that he'd had enough.

On our way out, one of the workers stopped us as we passed a photo booth with an oceanic backdrop. "Would you guys like a family picture?"

A family picture. That made my heart hurt.

"No." I shook my head before Tate could say anything.

He seemed disappointed, but as much as I'd enjoyed this outing, I wasn't sure I could handle a photo of us as a family. We might never actually be that. And anyway, where would I put it? Not like I could display it at home.

Tate walked us to our car and took the lead in getting Nicholas situated in his car seat. He gave him a big hug. "Thanks for a fun time, buddy."

After he closed the door, he joined me outside the driver's door.

"And thank *you* for today," he said. "For letting me share this experience. It might be the first aquarium trip he'll remember, and he'll know I was here."

"You're so good with him."

"It feels natural, Blair. It's amazing, actually, how easily it's coming to me. I don't remember it being like this with Taylor. I was so much younger then, so unprepared to be a father. I feel ready this time." His eyes brimmed with hope.

"I can relate to being wholly unprepared." I chuckled.

"You'd never know it now." Tate smiled. "He's such a sweet and well-behaved kid, and that's all you. You're a freaking wonderful mother."

I had to smile at that. It felt good to have my efforts acknowledged.

"I'll be in touch," Tate said after a moment. "I'm going to a lab tomorrow to get swabbed."

"Oh, right. Us too, actually. Thank you for doing that."

"Of course. Anything you need. Always."

I was pretty sure there were a few things on my list Tate couldn't give me anymore.

Silence fell between us, although neither of us moved.

Then he reached for me, pulling me into a hug. His warmth engulfed my body, and the intimate contact was almost too much to bear. I could feel his heart beating against my chest, and in that moment, I was nineteen-year-old me again, remembering the reasons I'd gotten into this predicament, the magnetic pull he'd had from the very beginning. I felt so safe in his arms and had no desire to move away.

Just as I was about to force myself back, he hugged me tighter. Surrendering, I relaxed into him, intoxicated by his scent and touch. Being in his arms felt so good. And yet this was innocent. It wasn't a passionate kiss or anything sordid. Just an embrace between two people who had to keep so much inside.

"I wish things were different," he finally whispered.

I knew exactly what he meant.

Chapter 26

TATE

My heart raced as I logged into the portal four days after I'd taken the DNA paternity test. Not sure why I was so nervous. I *knew* what it was going to say. I'd have bet my life on it.

I clicked into the report, and the words appeared in bold, clear as day:

High probability of paternity. 99.9 percent.

I closed my eyes and laughed almost deliriously. Taking a test to confirm this seemed comical. But now any shred of doubt had been removed.

My complete and utter love for that boy washed over me, chased by a desire to make up for lost time so he never remembered me not being his dad. There was only one thing in my life equally as urgent: protecting my relationship with my older son.

Speaking of Taylor, I'd been getting ready to pay him a visit when I got the email about the results. Now I was officially late to his house.

I got into my car and raced three miles to the condo

Taylor had recently rented with his new wife. They'd just returned from their honeymoon a few days ago.

Taylor was outside washing his car when I arrived.

"Hey, dude," I said.

"Hey." He grinned and put the hose down.

"How's it going?" I smacked his shoulder.

"Good. Tons of shit to do since we got back. You know how it is when you go away. You gotta pay for it when you come home."

"How was Aruba?"

He shook his head, a dreamy look on his face. "So freaking nice, man. You should go sometime."

I grinned. "Bet you didn't want to come back."

"I sure as heck didn't." He laughed. He used his hand as a visor as he looked up at me. "How are things with you?"

"Good." I let out a long breath, feeling guilty already.

"Things still going well with Leah?" he asked.

My stomach tightened. I didn't know how to break it to him. Taylor had been happy that I was in a relationship because it brought some stability to my life. I assumed that made him feel like I was more prepared to be the kind of dad he'd always wanted—a father less likely to fuck up again and move away. But I had to be honest with him where I could, since I was still hiding *so* much.

"I don't know if things are going to work out with her," I admitted.

His eyes widened. "Seriously?"

I nodded. "I know that sucks to hear, because you like her."

His face changed. "It's not that. I just feel like you deserve to be happy. I mean, no offense, but you're forty years old. You're not getting any younger."

"Thanks for the reminder."

"Although, some of my friends who saw you at the wedding thought you were, like, early thirties." He rolled his eyes. "One of them said you were hot."

I knew which friend *hadn't* made that comment. I cringed. "Sorry about that."

"It kind of made me want to vomit." Taylor chuckled.

I cringed again. *You have no idea, my poor son.*

"It was cool that so many of my friends got to finally meet you, though."

I gulped, feeling beads of sweat on my forehead. "Yeah. It was great to meet them, too." I cleared my throat, eager to change the subject. "What time does Juliana get home?"

"Right around five. And then we're going out to dinner with my friend Blair. You met her at the wedding, too."

My pulse raced. "Right." I nodded. "I do remember her."

"Blair's one of my best friends. I tried to set her up with my friend Adam that night, but she wasn't feeling well at the wedding. She didn't seem too into him. But he liked her, so I'm inviting him to come along, see if maybe there's a spark tonight now that she's feeling better."

"I see." I swallowed. "Does she know he's going?"

"No." He shook his head. "She's probably not gonna be very happy about the surprise, but I think he'd be good for her if she took the time to get to know him." He paused. "She has a three-year-old son, Nicholas. And Adam's good with kids. He's got a ton of nieces and nephews and didn't seem turned off by the fact that she had a child when I told him."

My chest constricted. I sucked in some air, trying to be inconspicuous. "That's kind of you to look out for her." I paused, cognizant of the fact that I might've been showing too much interest. "Seems like she's important to you. How did you and she meet?"

"We went to Camp Mystic together and then were counselors there, too, for a few summers in a row. Remember how I used to go there every year?"

I nodded. "Of course, I do. Yeah."

"Well, she and I talked a lot during those years. I was struggling with stuff. And she always seemed to make things better."

Stuff. Mostly issues having to do with me, I presumed. "And you never liked her as more than a friend?" I couldn't help but ask, because, well, I needed to know just *how* badly I'd be hurting him.

He shrugged. "She had this boyfriend, Daniel, for a while, and then I met Juliana. She was very loyal to him, even though he ended up doing her dirty." He paused. "I did sort of like her *that way* for a while in the beginning. She probably doesn't realize that. I always thought the world of her, but in retrospect, it's better that we remained friends."

My stomach sank. "What does Juliana make of Blair?"

"You mean, is she jealous?"

"Well, yeah. A male-female friendship like the one you have seems rare."

"She was a little suspect of me having a female best friend at first. I can't blame her. But she and Blair get along well now. Over the years, she's seen the kind of friendship we have."

"That's good."

"Anyway…" he said. "I gotta start getting ready to go out tonight. You want to take a look at the car?"

"Yeah, of course." I gestured for him to lead the way.

My mind whirled as he popped the hood and I helped him change his spark plugs.

Am I making a mistake by waiting to tell him?

Maybe getting closer to him will only make it more of a betrayal.

Who's watching Nicholas while Blair goes out with them tonight?

Would Blair actually like this Adam guy?

How will I handle it when she inevitably gets a boyfriend?

It was a wonder I could focus at all on the task before me.

After we finished the plugs, I closed the hood and turned to Taylor. "Well, that'll do it. Have fun tonight."

"I will. Thanks again for stopping by. I appreciate it." He paused. "Maybe you can work on teaching me how to fix these things myself so I don't have to keep bugging you."

My heart filled with pride. "I'd love to. You just let me know when you have time for some lessons."

"I guess that can be a perk of having you close by again, huh?"

"And to think I thought you'd be annoyed to have me back in town." I winked.

"Bye, Dad." He gave me a quick hug, which I tried not to prolong, though I wanted to.

"Bye." I turned and headed back to my car, still smiling, but also swallowing past a lump in my throat.

Taylor didn't call me Dad all that often, and when he did, it made me emotional—especially now. I was desperate not to return to the way things had been with him in years past.

Guilt hung over me the entire ride home, and it worsened when I pulled up and saw Leah waiting in front of my place. Yet another person I was about to let down. But the situation with her I *could* control.

"Hey," I said as I exited my car.

She smiled. "I just stopped by and knocked before I realized you weren't home. I came by to see if you were interested in grabbing dinner."

Between confirming I was Nicholas's dad, having to lie to Taylor today, and my lingering jealousy over Blair's setup tonight, I had no energy to attempt to give this woman what she deserved. I couldn't spend another second pretending everything was normal. I needed to let her go. I'd been dreading this, but it had to be done.

"Actually, Leah... Do you think we could go inside and talk?"

Her expression dimmed.

She knows.

How could she not with the way I'd been acting lately?

As she followed me inside, I wished this was the toughest talk I'd have to have this year. But it was only the tip of the iceberg.

After the devastation of breaking Leah's heart and ending our relationship, I sat in my living room, staring at the wall for most of the evening. Always one to sense when I was down, my German shepherd, Khloe, stayed right by my side.

"Girlie, I wish you could talk because I'm holding a secret right now that's killing me."

She rested her head on my shoulder.

I rubbed between her ears. "I don't know if you've ever been around kids. I know you're gonna be a sweet girl around Nicholas, though. We need to make sure of it. He needs to fall in love with you, just like I did."

Khloe closed her eyes.

"I know you get excited with new people, but we don't want to scare him away." I smiled. "He's technically your brother."

I paused for a moment, realizing how nuts I sounded. I needed to talk to someone other than Khloe about this before it drove me insane. Someone trustworthy. I wondered how Blair would feel if I told my mother what was going on. Mom was the only person I'd trust with this secret, and I could use her advice about how to handle things with Taylor. She'd been close to him for years, and in many ways, she knew him better than I did.

I realized I'd been dozing on the couch when my phone rang at almost eleven PM. It was Blair. I picked up right away, panic rising. "Blair, is everything okay?"

"Yeah. Everything is fine. I'm sorry if I worried you."

"I wasn't expecting to hear from you tonight, that's all."

"Oh? Why is that?"

I hesitated. "Taylor told me you guys were going out."

"He did?"

"Yeah. I went by his house earlier to help him fix his car. He mentioned that he and Juliana were having dinner with you tonight. I was planning to call you to talk about the DNA results, but I figured I'd catch up with you tomorrow morning. I'm happy you called, though."

"You obviously saw that Nicholas is yours."

I had to laugh. "I saw that he was mine the moment I looked at his face, Blair."

"Yeah." She chuckled. "Thank you for taking the test anyway. It's important to me that you have confirmation."

"My pleasure." I leaned back and kicked up my feet, feeling calmer than I had all day, even if there was no reason for it. I just loved hearing her voice. "Tell me about your night." I took a deep breath to prepare myself. "How was it?"

"I got home a little while ago. It was nice to see them. It was my first time since the wedding."

I tugged at my hair. "Where did you guys go?"

"To Bianco's. Nice Italian restaurant."

It killed me not to ask her about the Adam guy. I'd hoped she would offer that info, but maybe she didn't want to upset me.

"Who was watching Nicholas?" I asked.

"My parents. I try not to impose on them too much, but they're always happy to come hang out with him when I need it. They just left."

"That's nice of them. You have a good relationship with your folks, right?"

"Yep. I'm lucky."

Curiosity consumed me.

Don't say it.

Don't say it.

"How was Adam?" I could taste the bitterness on my tongue.

You're fucking pathetic, Tate.

She was quiet a moment. "How did you know about that?"

"Taylor told me. He said he'd invited a friend he thought would be good for you."

She exhaled. "Well, I didn't know he was going to be there."

"I know. Taylor said he was surprising you."

"I wish he hadn't done that."

"I suspected you might not be thrilled about it...not because of the dude, but just because no one wants to be surprised with a date," I added.

"It wasn't a date."

"Right." I dug for a little more info. "Are you not... interested in dating?"

"It's been a very long time, as I've told you. And I just..." Her words trailed off.

"What?"

"It has to be the right person. It takes a lot for me to leave Nicholas and go out, let alone give a piece of myself to someone when I still feel like I don't have much to give. But I need to force myself to get out there more."

Now I wished I hadn't asked. That thought made me miserable. I tightened my fist. "Taylor seems to think this Adam guy is perfect for you."

"Yeah, well, Taylor doesn't really know what I need right now, even if he means well."

"What *do* you need?" I asked in a low voice.

After a pause, she answered matter-of-factly. "The same thing I needed the night I met you."

My eyes widened. This was the Blair I'd known four years ago—no-holds-barred, unbridled honesty. It was my first taste of the old Blair since we'd reconnected.

My face burned. "You need no-strings sex?"

"What I *don't* need is someone who needs something from me. I don't have anything left to give. And I won't pretend I do."

"But despite that...you have a physical need," I prodded, ready to tear my hair out.

"I'm still human, so yeah. But I'm not about to go on some hookup app at this point in my life. I have to look out for myself more than ever. So, it's a conundrum. Nicholas and I... We have our cocoon. It feels safe, and I'm not ready to venture outside of it."

I want to be in that cocoon.

But I can't.

I fucking can't.

I attempted to change the subject, more for my sake than hers.

"What do your parents know about Nicholas's father?"

"They know as much as Taylor does—that I met an older man named Tate on the trip, that we agreed to remain relatively anonymous when we parted ways, and that I lost my only way of contacting him when my phone was taken. They know I tried to find you and everything."

I shut my eyes. "They must hate me for messing with your life."

221

"Any animosity they might've had toward you disappeared the day they met their grandson. Nicholas has that effect on people. No one questions how he got here anymore."

I smiled. I wanted my mom to know she had another grandson. "I want to ask you something."

"What?"

"How would you feel if I told one person what was going on?"

"Why would you want to do that?" she asked, a hint of alarm in her voice.

"Because I'd really like her take, and she's the only person I can trust."

"Your mom?"

"Yeah. But I won't say anything if you're not okay with it. It's your call."

"Well, if you tell your mother, can I tell mine?"

"Of course. But won't she want to kill me?"

"Kill you for what? Like I said, they know how I met you. And it's not like we ended up in this situation intentionally. Once I found out I was pregnant, I had nothing to hide. I told my parents as much as I knew. They just don't know I've discovered you're Taylor's father."

"Fuck." I blew out a long breath. "All right. Well, yeah, I mean, if I tell my mother, you should be able to tell yours, as long as you can trust her not to say anything."

"I trust her with my life."

"Okay." I nodded. "Same with my mother."

She laughed a little. "Let me know if your mother has any brilliant ideas about how we can handle this."

"Right? I'm desperate for that."

"You won't tell the woman you're seeing?" she asked.

Ugh. I grimaced. "About that..."

"What?"

"I ended things with Leah earlier today."

"You did?"

"I needed to free up my head emotionally, and she needed more than I could give her right now. I need to be alone for a while. That's what's best."

Blair went quiet on the line. I could only imagine what she was thinking.

"Are you still there?" I asked.

"Yeah," she said. "I just...wasn't expecting that."

"Does it make you nervous or something?"

"No, of course not. Why would it make me nervous?"

"I don't know. But you shouldn't worry. My decision to break up with Leah was independent of our situation. I don't intend to cross the line with you, Blair. That would only complicate things more."

"I wasn't implying that you broke up with her because of me. I just said I wasn't expecting it," she said defensively.

"I'm sorry." I rubbed my temples. "I don't even know what I'm fucking saying. Today was just...a lot."

Her tone lightened. "You found out you're indeed the father, like on some old-school Maury Povich episode, lied to your son's face, *and* broke up with your girlfriend in one day. What could possibly be the problem?"

I snorted. "You're too young to remember The Maury Povich Show."

"I've seen clips on social media about the DNA-test episodes."

"Unlike me, who's old enough to have actually watched that show."

"You're old, yeah." She chuckled. "But you look even hotter than you did when we met. Not sure how that's possible."

I shook my head and sank deeper into the couch. "I've been thinking the same about you."

"Oh, now you're a liar?"

My eyes widened. *Does she not realize?* "Why would I lie about that?"

"When you showed up at my house, I was wearing a dirty T-shirt and had my hair in a messy bun… How could I be hotter than you remember?"

I loved the way she'd looked that day. Her hair was up, showcasing her long, beautiful neck. I remember wishing I could take a bite out of it. She also hadn't been wearing a bra. It had been hard not to stare at her, especially during Nicholas's bathtime. I'd spent way too many minutes since then thinking about how damn gorgeous she was.

"You look the same, but even more beautiful," I told her. "That's coming from someone who's looked at the photos of you from the resort often over the past four years."

"You did?" Her voice was barely a whisper.

"Yep. Even though I thought you'd chosen never to contact me again, I still tortured myself with those photos." I hesitated. *Fuck it.* "And that letter you left me… That was…"

"When did you read it?"

"Minutes after you left the resort."

"Minutes? *That* soon?"

"I was a fucking wreck when you left. I needed something. The letter was all I had."

"I can't remember everything I wrote. I just poured out what I was feeling in that moment."

"Everything you said, I felt the same."

"It doesn't matter anymore, though, does it?" she said.

For a few seconds, you could hear a pin drop.

"I don't know how this is gonna play out, Blair. But I'm gonna be here for that boy. That's my focus now." I paused. "Speaking of which, I think I found a place for us to meet."

"Where?"

"In Western Mass. That's where you grew up, right?"

"Yes."

"It's a couple hours' drive from here, but the house has a swing set in the back for him."

"He'll love that."

"Will you mind driving that distance?"

"Nicholas is good in the car, so it should be fine. The farther the better, I think."

"Okay." I nodded. "I can lease the place for a three-month minimum."

"That works."

"Would you be able to meet there this Saturday?" I asked, eager to see them.

Them.

Deep down, I knew this wasn't just about Nicholas.

"Actually, this Saturday I can't. My cousin's thirtieth birthday party is at my aunt's house on Saturday. Nicholas will be coming with me, since there'll be kids his age there."

That was a bummer, but I didn't have much choice.

"How about the following weekend?" she asked.

"That works for me," I said, trying not to let my anxiousness show. I'd have cleared my calendar if I'd had any commitments.

I had to remind myself I was invading a life she'd done a damn good job of building on her own. I wanted to be an asset, not a hindrance or an additional responsibility she had to deal with.

"Okay, weekend after next, then," she said.

"Has Nicholas asked about me since the aquarium?" I braced myself.

"No."

My shoulders slumped. "I need to tell him my name. But Tate would be stupid, right? Since he might mention me to Taylor?"

"We shouldn't take the chance. Especially since Taylor knows my baby daddy's name was Tate. Maybe we just give you a nickname for now."

"Like?"

"I'll think of something."

I chuckled. "That should be interesting."

"I'd better go. It's late. Nicholas gets me up pretty early in the mornings."

"Yeah. Of course. You go. If there's anything I can do before we meet, please let me know."

"We'll be good. But thanks."

Of course they would. Once again, I reminded myself that Blair had done just fine without me all these years. She didn't need me to swoop in, trying to be some goddamn superhero who didn't know his ass from his elbow

when it came to kids. I needed to earn my place as a help-
er. That would take time.

Before I went to bed that night, I pulled up the old
photos of Blair I had stashed away in a special album for
easy access. But this time, I looked at them in a different
light. Never before had I realized she was probably already
pregnant with my baby in these images. My body buzzed.

I was deep into staring when my phone buzzed.

Blair: I've got it.

Tate: Got what?

Blair: The nickname Nicholas can call you.

Tate: What is it?

Blair: Mr. T.

I had to laugh.

Tate: That's funny.

Blair: Why is that funny?

Tate: Mr. T?

Blair: I don't get it.

Tate: The guy from The A-Team?

Blair: The what?

I laughed harder.

Tate: The A-Team. It was a show back in the eighties. And shit, I just realized why the fuck you wouldn't know what that was. I remember my dad watching reruns when I was younger.

Blair: Correct. I have no idea what you're talking about. LOL

Tate: I thought that's why you picked it, but that show was way before your time. Mr. T works, though.

I caught myself smiling like a fool. *"I pity the fool."*—Mr. T used to say that.

I needed to go to sleep, because I was clearly delirious.

Blair texted me one last time.

Blair: Goodnight, Mr. Teabag.

Now *that* was the Blair I remembered.

Chapter 27

BLAIR

"Where are we going, Mommy?"

My son had asked me several times today where we were headed, probably because it was unusual for us to be in the car for so long.

"I told you... We're gonna go meet Mommy's friend again, Mr. T."

Every time I said "Mr. T," I laughed to myself.

Nicholas nodded. "Okay."

I smiled as I looked back at my beautiful boy through the rearview mirror. He was such a mild-mannered child, down for almost anything. He never complained. I sometimes wondered how I'd gotten so lucky. It hadn't been easy being a single mother, but I wouldn't trade this life with him for anything.

"I heard he has a swing set," I added.

Nicholas's eyes lit up. While he loved going to the playground, a swing set was one thing we didn't have at home. Installing one in our yard was on my long list of things to do.

By the time we finally pulled up to the house Tate had rented, I was very ready to get out of the car. It was a small, light blue, one-level home on a tree-lined residential street. I'd grown up in this general area, but I'd never been to this town before. I felt confident about our anonymity here.

Tate was sitting outside on the front steps, waiting for us. As he stood, I was struck by how tall and strong he seemed. Each time I laid eyes on him, I could hardly believe I'd had the pleasure of being with this man. Today he wore black jeans, black boots, and a beige, hooded sweatshirt. I loved his rugged, fall look. Well, I loved *all* of his looks.

"How long have you been waiting out here?" I asked as I exited the car.

"A little bit." He smiled. "I got worried since it's about a half hour after I thought I should expect you. Was there traffic?"

"No." I shrugged. "I'm just a slow and careful driver."

"Well, you have precious cargo. So I understand." Tate scratched his chin. "I forgot to ask if he's okay with dogs."

"He loves them."

"Good. Khloe's inside. If you'd told me he couldn't handle her, I would've figured something out."

I opened the back door, finding Nicholas's eyes groggy. He'd almost fallen asleep before we got here.

Tate joined me and reached out his hand. "Hey, buddy. Do you remember me?"

Nicholas hesitantly took it, but shook his head no. I was pretty sure he was just messing with Tate.

I chuckled. "He's a little tired from the ride. Makes him cranky and shy."

"That's okay. We'll wake you up." Tate winked. "I have snacks."

"Oh good. I'm hungry," I teased.

Tate grinned as our eyes locked. Then he gave me a once-over. I wasn't sure if he'd meant that to be obvious. "Don't worry. I'll feed you, too," he said, a hint of seductiveness in his tone.

Was this my imagination? It was so hard not to flirt with him. That had been the case from the moment I'd met the guy.

Nicholas held my hand as we entered the house. I sensed Tate's presence behind me right before I felt his hand at the small of my back, guiding me inside. It sent a zap of electricity through my starving body.

Tate's German shepherd immediately ran to greet us, her paws scratching against the floor.

"Calm down," Tate said as he grabbed her by the leash. "Nicholas, this is Khloe."

Nicholas reached his little hand out to pet the big dog, who calmed down fairly quickly. Tate smiled as he looked on, still holding Khloe's leash.

After only a few minutes, Khloe seemed used to us being here. She also listened very well to Tate's commands.

"You hungry, little guy?" he asked our boy.

Nicholas nodded eagerly. He was back to his normal, vibrant self now that he'd had a little time out of the car.

Tate waved us farther into the house. "Let's head to the kitchen, then."

My eyes widened when I got a look at the kitchen counter. Tate had laid out dozens of snacks, everything from Cheez-Its to Teddy Grahams to Oreos.

"Oh my God." I laughed. "Did you rob the snack aisle?"

"Hit the market while you were on the road. I never asked you what he likes and didn't want to bother you while you were driving, so I just got a little of everything. I know it's a lot of sugar. But I wanted to impress him the first time. I'll tone it down, eventually."

"Something tells me you won't. That's always been your thing." I winked.

He returned a flirtatious grin.

Yeah. It can't be my imagination.

Tate prepared a plate of snacks for Nicholas and sat across from him at the table, watching him eat like it was a spectator sport. And Nicholas was in his glory as the dog sat at the base of his chair, waiting for the crumbs that would inevitably fall.

When Tate finally pulled his gaze from Nicholas, he turned to me. "What can I get you?"

"Got anything to drink besides juice boxes?"

"I have water, seltzer…wine. Although, I doubt you want to drink at three in the afternoon."

"Look at you offering me alcohol."

"Well, you *are* legal now."

"Seltzer sounds great, actually."

He stood. "I have mandarin orange, lime, strawberry, or grapefruit."

"True to form, you just get them all, huh?" I shrugged. "Surprise me."

Tate walked over to the fridge, opened a can, and poured it into a glass. He handed it to me, and when I sipped, I tasted lime.

"Thank you," I said, fighting the urge to burp after drinking the carbonated beverage too fast.

"Nicholas, what do you want to do after you eat?" Tate asked. "Play on the swings?"

My boy's face turned red. He was back to acting shy again for some reason.

I smiled at Nicholas. "I know one thing he'd *love* to do."

"What's that?" Tate turned to me, his eyes eager.

"I see you have a big truck out there. One of his favorite things is to sit in the driver's seat and pretend to drive. He does it with my dad's truck all the time."

Tate grinned as he turned to Nicholas. "I used to love that, too, when I was your age. Someday I can teach you how to really drive one."

Nicholas smiled. That last part was profound. *Tate plans to be here for all of Nicholas's milestones.*

I wished I could tell Nicholas right now that Tate was his dad. But that would have to wait. The shift from thinking my son would never know his father to knowing he'd always have him around made my heart full, despite what we'd have to endure for Tate to love him openly.

After Nicholas finished his snacks, we went out front where Tate had his gray truck in the driveway. It was a dark, smoky color that suited him well. He let Nicholas sit in the driver's seat and play with the steering wheel and all of the buttons. Nicholas even hit the horn a few too many times, and one of the neighbors walked out to make sure everything was okay. The man's rigid expression softened when he got a look at Nicholas bopping around in the seat. The guy waved and promptly went back inside.

After Nicholas had his fill of the truck, we went around to the backyard. Tate pushed him on the swings until Nicholas tired of it. He eventually wandered off to play in the sandbox while Tate and I stood on the grass a few feet away.

"Was the sandbox here, too?" I asked.

"No." Tate shook his head. "I bought the stuff to build it and came out earlier this week to set it up."

"That was really thoughtful of you."

He shrugged. "It's the least I can do. I have a lot of catching up."

"You shouldn't look at it that way, Tate. It wasn't your choice not to be there for him. You can just start from today, without feeling like you need to work ten times harder to make up for something you didn't know you were missing."

"Thank you for saying that. It's clear that despite my absence all these years, Nicholas doesn't want for anything. He's happy, healthy, and balanced. That's all because of you, mama. I'm so fucking proud of you."

I didn't need his approval, but his words warmed my soul. In his absence, I'd often wondered whether Tate would be proud of the job I was doing raising his son.

He looked over at Nicholas playing. "I failed so badly with Taylor. I can't let anything like that happen with Nicholas."

"It won't. You've grown a lot since then, and things are so much better with you and Taylor."

Tate took a deep breath. "We need to work out how I can help you financially. I'd like to set up a system where I put a certain amount of my salary into an account for Nicholas each week."

I stiffened. "I don't need your money." *Why does that idea make me so uncomfortable?*

"But I *want* to help, even if you don't need it. It's not like you're living in the lap of luxury. Taking care of him is just as much my responsibility as it is yours. You shouldn't have to bear the brunt of it anymore."

With that, I identified the source of my fear. Financial help was a reminder that Nicholas was no longer solely mine. It felt like a loss of power somehow. Yet I needed to get used to it. "You wouldn't try to take him from me, right?"

Tate's brows furrowed as disappointment crossed his face. "Of course not."

"Maybe that was the wrong way to phrase my question. I know you wouldn't *take* him per se." I let out a shaky breath. "But I don't want to give up *any* custody. I don't want him to have to live in two places."

Tate's eyes softened. "Blair, I have no intention of taking him away from the home where he feels safe. I just wanna get to know him and love him. And I want to support you in any way I can. That's really all. I'm not gonna turn this into some kind of competition." His eyes seared into mine. "You have my word."

Nodding, I said, "Okay." I exhaled, feeling a bit foolish. "I'm sorry I went off the rails for a minute there. It just hit me that since we now have DNA proof, he's not legally *all* mine anymore. You have rights, Tate. And it's wrong of me to even ask you to ignore them, but—"

He cut me off. "I would *never* do anything to hurt you or him. Please believe that. I want to be in his life, but not in any way you don't want. Promise you'll trust me."

"I do trust you." I looked down for a moment, trying to gather myself. "I just let my fear get out of hand."

When I looked back up at Tate, he was closer. The fear I'd felt a minute ago transformed into something altogether different. I tried to curb the feelings of longing, but in this moment, I was transported back to that place four years ago, where desire consumed my every breath. Tate cupped my cheek before tracing my face with the back of his fingers. Then he pulled away with a jolt, as if for a moment he'd forgotten our dilemma. He'd forgotten about Taylor. He was just my Tate again. But before I could blink, it was over.

He walked over to Nicholas and joined him at the edge of the sandbox. Goose bumps peppered my skin as I watched them play, still reeling from the brief feel of his fingers against my cheek.

As the sun began to set, the three of us walked back into the house together.

"Can you stay for dinner?" Tate asked, the tension in the air certainly thicker than when I'd first arrived.

I thought it wise to limit the time spent around Tate today, given my inability to avoid feeling things I shouldn't, yet I didn't want to disappoint him after he'd gone to such lengths for Nicholas. And we did need to eat something before getting back on the road.

"We can stay, sure."

"Does he like pasta?"

"Loves it."

"I bought like five kinds." Tate flashed a crooked grin.

"You don't say..."

"What's his favorite?"

"Spaghetti."

"Got that." Tate nodded, seeming pleased with himself. "And what does his mama like?"

God, that was a loaded question. Now probably wasn't the appropriate time to admit I was most hungry for him. "I'll have some of whatever pasta you make."

Nicholas had gotten interested in a train set Tate had set up in the living room.

"Why don't you relax while he plays?" Tate gestured over to the couch. "Can I pour you a glass of wine while I make dinner?"

"Sure, yeah," I said. "That'd be great. I could stand to relax a bit. Just one glass, though, because I have to drive."

"Got it." He nodded. "White, red...rosé?"

"You bought different kinds of wine, too?"

He shrugged. "Didn't know what you liked."

"I like all three, but I'll have red tonight."

"Coming right up."

Red matched my mood. It felt more tumultuous.

I sank into the sofa, feeling like a huge weight had lifted. I hadn't known what to expect with this visit, but it had gone well, despite the tension in the air between Tate and me. From Nicholas's perspective, it had been the perfect day. And I didn't really want to leave either.

Of course, even thinking that was dangerous. But I felt safe around Tate. And I loved that my son got to be with his dad, even if he didn't realize it. One day he would, and days like this would mean even more.

I'd been resting my eyes when Tate's deep voice startled me. "Here you go."

I opened them and took the glass of red. "Thank you."

"My pleasure," he murmured.

When he walked back to the kitchen, I longed for his presence. Even if we couldn't touch each other, I still ached for him, ached for his eyes on me.

I sipped the wine slowly, appreciating the warmth of this humble rental home and, most of all, appreciating the effort Tate had put into this visit. From my seat on the couch, I had a clear view into the kitchen—a clear view of Tate moving around, opening cabinets and drawers as he cooked. There was nothing sexier than a hot man who knew his way around the kitchen. I enjoyed this side of him, yet sadness washed over me. What if someday he met someone? Now I'd have a front-row seat to it. The only good thing about having been estranged from Tate was not witnessing him with other women. Now that was inevitable. I'd dodged a bullet with Leah, but that luck wouldn't last forever.

Khloe, Tate's dog, interrupted my staring as she hopped up on the couch and took the spot next to me.

"Hey, you," I muttered, rubbing between her ears. She closed her eyes.

My gaze traveled back to Tate and the way his jeans hugged his ass as he stood at the stove. A vision of that brawny body hovering over me haunted my memories. My skin tingled. I hated that I couldn't control these sensations.

"Mama, look!" Nicholas called.

He had arranged the trains in a pattern he was apparently quite proud of.

"Wow, honey. You did so good."

A moment later, Tate called us into the kitchen. He'd plated our food and had poured me a glass of seltzer and Nicholas some lemonade.

While Tate had also served himself, rather than eat, he mostly watched Nicholas twirl his pasta and slurp the noodles. Watching a father fall in love with his long-lost son one precious moment at a time was beautiful—truly a gift to me as well.

"This is really good. It's al dente," I said with my mouth full.

"Yeah. My mother always taught me not to overcook it."

"Your mom's Italian, right?"

"Yeah." He grinned. "Taylor must have told you."

"You definitely get your looks from the Italian side."

"Taylor looks like his mom," he pointed out.

"That did nothing to help me figure out your connection to him." I smiled over at Nicholas. "He likes your al dente pasta, too."

Tate placed his hand on my arm, sending a shiver down my spine. "You sure you don't want another glass of wine?"

I cleared my throat. "I can't if I'm gonna drive home."

"Well, I was gonna say..." He shifted in his seat. "You're welcome to stay here, if you don't want to drive back tonight. It's dark. And there are two bedrooms. You could stay with Nicholas in the bigger one, or you could each take one, and I can sleep on the couch."

I thought about it for a moment, but then shook my head. "I'm not sure it's a good idea for us to stay." I looked over at Nicholas. "He likes his bed."

That wasn't it. But I couldn't admit that staying overnight with Tate made me nervous. I was afraid of feeling any closer to him than I already did, and afraid of somehow feeling rejected. The more time I spent with him, the more agonizing it was to think I couldn't have him. I longed for the days when our being together didn't hurt anyone.

"Okay." He nodded, moving the food around on his plate. "Whatever you think. No pressure. I just wanted to let you know it's an option, since you're not exactly right around the corner."

We finished eating, and I was getting ready to collect our things to leave when thunder rumbled in the distance. Then came the sound of rain pelting against the roof.

I looked toward the window. "Crap. I didn't know it was going to rain."

"Let me check the forecast to see how long it will last." Tate reached for his phone. A moment later, he shook his head.

"What?" I chewed my lip.

"Looks like a heavy band of rain that will last for a bit." He made a face. "I don't want you driving in that."

Well, crap. I didn't want to drive in it, either.

"Stay," he insisted.

"I didn't bring any extra clothes, or anything for Nicholas."

He sighed worriedly. "It's up to you."

Ultimately, clothes shouldn't matter. Lord knows, I'd spent plenty of days when Nicholas was a baby wearing the same clothes for more than one day. That wasn't a good reason to put Nicholas in danger by driving home in torrential rain. I needed to do what was right.

I turned to my son. "Nicholas, since it's really raining, would you want to sleep here?"

"Yes!" he said excitedly.

I knew that would be his answer. Turning to Tate, I shrugged. "I guess we can make do with the clothes we have."

He smiled softly. "I planned to spend the weekend here, so I brought several shirts. You're welcome to wear one. I don't have anything extra to fit the little guy, but I can pick up some stuff to keep here for next time if you give me his size."

Wrapping myself in one of this man's T-shirts was not going to help my internal battle. I took another deep breath. "I'm staying here against my better judgment, because I don't like driving in the rain. I don't plan for us to spend the night here routinely. I'll drive back and forth so long as the weather isn't bad."

"Understood." Tate nodded.

Silence filled the air for a moment after that, save for the sound of the rain.

Tate helped me give Nicholas a bath in the surprisingly well-stocked bathroom. As with everything else, he had purchased a variety of soaps and shampoos. After the long ride out here and the afternoon playing outside, Nicholas was bushed. He went down within minutes of me putting him to bed.

I emerged from the bedroom, ready to freshen up and join Nicholas for sleep.

But then Tate made a request. "I was gonna stay up for a bit. Will you join me?"

Chapter 28

TATE

Blair must've sensed that something was off. She agreed to stay up with me for a bit, but the moment she sat next to me on the couch, she tilted her head as if trying to read my mind. "What's wrong, Tate?" she finally asked.

It was late, and I probably should've let it go, but I couldn't. "I'm still thinking about what you said earlier, when you were concerned that I might try to fight you for custody. It bothers me that you don't trust me not to hurt you."

Blair shook her head. "It was only a fleeting thought. I just realized he's not all mine anymore. I'm sorry if I gave you the impression I don't trust you. I've been processing this whole thing in waves. It was just a vulnerable moment. And it's passed." She looked into my eyes. "I promise."

I wanted to be sure. "I'd never do anything to hurt you, Blair. I mean, haven't I fucking done enough to ruin your life? The last thing I will ever do is make it more difficult. You're in the driver's seat here. You always will be."

She placed her hand on my leg. "You didn't ruin my life. I chose to have Nicholas. And I'd never change that."

There was so much bottled up inside me right now when it came to her. But letting it all out would be dangerous. Still, I expressed what I could. "I don't mean to sound like a broken record, but Nicholas is really lucky to have you for his mother."

"Thank you," she said softly.

We sat in silence for a bit until she reached for her phone. "You want to see some photos of him when he was a baby?"

Is she kidding? "I would love to." I beamed.

Blair scrolled through her photo library, and I leaned over her shoulder, closing my eyes as I recognized her floral scent. She smelled exactly the same. And fuck, that brought me back to those first resort nights when I'd fought with every fiber of my being to stay away from her. A lot of good that did.

Blair moved through her photos so quickly that she went too far and reached some images from when she was pregnant.

I stopped her. "Wait."

She shook her head. "You don't need to see that."

"Yes, I do," I insisted, holding out my hand for her phone. "Please."

Her face reddened as she handed it to me. I could hardly speak at the sight of Blair pregnant with my baby. Her face was a bit fuller, and she absolutely glowed. Her smooth belly peeked out from under a shirt that could hardly cover her. If there were ever a photo I wished I could jump inside, this was it. I would have bent and kissed that beautiful stomach.

Transfixed, I asked, "How many months were you here?"

"Probably right around nine, actually."

I shook my head. "You were so beautiful, Blair."

"Once again, you're a good liar, Tate."

"Are you kidding me?" I looked at her briefly before returning my eyes to the photo. "What about this isn't beautiful? Your skin. Your smile. Your curves. You're fucking luminous," I murmured. "God, it's amazing."

"Well, I felt far from luminous when that photo was taken. I was ready to burst."

I continued to stare down at it. "How *did* you feel when this photo was taken? I don't just mean physically, but overall. Tell me what was going on in your mind."

She looked at the image of herself. "I felt scared, unsure of whether I was going to be able to do it—be a mother. I knew I wanted a family someday, but not *that* soon." She turned toward me. "I also felt sad. I was still mourning losing you and wished so badly that you knew what was happening." She paused. "But I wondered how you'd handle it, too. I knew you'd had a rough time with your son, and to know you had another on the way... I wasn't sure if you'd be happy or freaked."

"I would've been happy, Blair," I assured her. "Maybe a little scared, too. But it's truly a gift to get a second chance."

"I'm glad you feel that way."

"Did you know you were having a boy?"

"I did." She grinned.

"What made you name him Nicholas?"

"It's my grandfather's name."

"Oh, sweet." I smiled. "What's his middle name?"

She grinned again and bit her bottom lip. "Tate."

My eyes went wide. "You're kidding," I whispered.

She shook her head. "I'm not."

"I can't believe you did that."

"It was a last-minute decision. I wanted him to have some connection to you, and at the time, that was all I had to give him—your name."

"Wow," I murmured. "What an honor."

"I've been waiting to tell you. I suspected you'd be happy about it."

Nicholas Tate Moynihan

Maybe one day she'd let me change his last name to Delaney. He'd be the first of my kids with my last name, since Taylor's mother had given him hers, and I hadn't fought it.

I returned my gaze to the photo of Blair pregnant. My smile faded. "At what point did you have to drop out of school?"

"I stayed until I had him. So I only missed one year."

But she'd missed the most important year—the one that would've earned her a degree in nursing.

When I went quiet, she said, "Stop feeling guilty, Tate. It is what it is. Neither of us planned it, but it was destiny anyway."

I arched a brow. "You think Taylor's gonna feel that way?"

"No." She shook her head. "But that doesn't mean it's not destiny. No matter how he feels, we have to go through the fire."

She offered me a comforting smile that made me feel good, despite the anxiety looming over me. It reminded me of the talks we'd had at the resort, where Blair, with all her nineteen years of wisdom, had somehow made me feel better about my fuckups. For a moment, it felt like no time had passed.

"I feel like I'm two different people," I admitted.

She adjusted her position on the sofa. "How so?"

"I'm Taylor's father, trying to figure out how to protect him from my actions. But sometimes, I'm also Tate… just a man who's been reunited with his dream girl."

"How come you never came looking for *me*?" she asked. "You could've gotten my name and contact info through the resort, even if yours wasn't traceable."

I'd been waiting for her to ask this. I sighed. "I had myself convinced that you'd chosen to not look back, and had maybe even thought better of your decision to sleep with me." I shrugged. "Looking you up, when the ball was in your court, felt intrusive. I didn't want to interrupt your life. Since you never reached out, I believed separation from me was what you wanted." I shook my head. "Obviously, if I'd known what was really happening, I would've made a different decision. It's hard for me to fathom that I was out there somewhere having a mediocre day while you were giving birth to my child. It seems like I should've sensed the world shifting or something."

"When I first looked into Nicholas's eyes and saw you, I felt even worse that you didn't know about him. It was hard seeing you in him each and every day."

Damn. My eyes watered. "I guess the thing that makes this situation so difficult is also a blessing, right?

Because if I wasn't Taylor's father, we might never have reconnected."

"I know," she whispered.

She then scrolled forward and showed me some of Nicholas's baby photos and videos. It was nearly too much to take: his little angelic face, his rosy cheeks, that adorable, toothless grin. One video nearly did me in: he was about a year old and wouldn't stop giggling every time Blair jumped out in front of him. She said he'd had his first real belly laugh that day. Such a happy baby, blissfully unaware that one half of him was missing.

As I checked out a Christmas photo of Blair holding Nicholas up as he sat on a shopping-mall Santa's lap, I shook my head. "I still have so many questions."

"Ask me whatever you want," she said.

"Where were you when you went into labor?"

"I was in line at Target." She chuckled. "My water broke, and I called my mom to come meet me. We drove to the hospital together. He was a week early."

"And how was the labor itself?"

"It was twelve hours. Not as bad as some women have to go through. He was born at three in the morning."

"Your mom was there the whole time?"

"Yeah. She was the only person I wanted in the room with me."

My chest ached. "I would've wanted to be there."

"I know," she whispered.

"Would you have let me come in the room?"

"Of course. You're his dad."

"I'm sorry I wasn't there to hold your hand."

"Well, giving birth was the easy part," she pointed out. "It was the weeks after when I could've used you."

"Tell me what it was like after you got home."

She played with some lint on the couch. "Those first couple of weeks took a lot of getting used to. The breast-feeding wasn't easy, but we eventually got the hang of it. As each week went by, it *did* get smoother. He was just such a good baby. Much like he is now, easygoing. I'm very lucky."

"He gets the easygoing part from you."

"How do you know?"

"Because my mother always told me I was a little tyrant."

She smiled. "Did you tell your mother the news about Nicholas?"

"Not yet," I said. "But I plan to this week. What about you?"

She shook her head. "I haven't told mine yet, either. But I still plan to."

"I hope it brings you some peace to talk about it with her." After things went quiet, I changed the subject. My mind was all over the place tonight. "Do you really not remember what you wrote in that letter to me?"

Blair smiled. "I don't remember the exact words, but I *do* remember I told you I loved you."

"Yeah," I whispered.

She'd given me exactly what I wanted to know. And I wanted to tell her I'd loved her, too, but I couldn't. I couldn't toy with her emotions like that. And I had to balance my need for free expression with what was best for *both* of my children right now.

"Taylor's friend Adam called me this week," she announced.

Talk about a buzzkill. I'd been so comfortable talking to her, all the old feelings rising to the surface. But now? I stiffened. "Really..."

Blair nodded. "He asked me to go to dinner next weekend."

I cleared my throat. "What did you tell him?"

"I said I'd let him know."

"So, you haven't ruled it out..." My cheeks burned. I couldn't fucking help it. I hated being this way.

"No, I haven't," she said.

"I thought you weren't into him." My jaw tightened.

"I'm not sure. I told him I'd think about it."

"What's holding you back?"

"I don't know if I like him that way."

My blood pressure rose. "Can I ask you something?"

She looked up at me. "Yeah..."

"If we hadn't found each other again, would you be hesitant?"

Her cheeks reddened. "You think you're the reason I'm apprehensive about dating?"

"I don't know." I shook my head. "From the moment I saw you at the wedding, I've been unable to concentrate on the idea of anyone else. It was the main reason I had to end things with Leah. So I'd understand if you felt the same."

She swallowed. "Obviously you have an effect on me, Tate. You likely always will. But I feel like now more than ever, I need to try to move on with my life. If you truly feel like we can never be together because it will hurt Taylor, the sooner I can move on from any false hope, the better."

"I thought we *both* felt that way," I countered.

I knew in my heart it was best for her to move on. Perhaps if she were with someone else, that might lessen the blow when Taylor found out about us. But the idea of seeing her move on with someone else made my insides twist like never before. I might be too old for her. I might not deserve her. But I *loved* her. I loved and respected her now more than ever, knowing what she'd sacrificed because of me. Yet I also understood that sometimes loving someone means letting them go. Hadn't I held up her life enough?

Despite the regret rising in my chest, I forced myself to speak. "If you ever want to go out, I can keep Nicholas here for the weekend, so you have some freedom."

Her expression was hard to read, and she wouldn't look at me as she said, "I appreciate the offer."

I'd indirectly given her my blessing to pursue other people, ignoring every last thing my heart and body truly desired. But I couldn't allow her to give up any more of her life than she already had.

After a moment, she stood. "I think I'm going to hit the sack."

"Okay…" I got up from the couch. "Did you want a T-shirt to sleep in?"

She shook her head. "No. I'll just sleep in my clothes."

It didn't surprise me that she'd reject wearing something of mine. It felt too intimate.

Tension lingered in her wake as she nodded and walked away. Long after she'd joined Nicholas in the bedroom, I sat in a daze, yearning to be in there with both of them.

Chapter 29

BLAIR

I'd insisted my mother sit down when she came to visit me this morning. After the intense Saturday at Tate's rental, I needed to talk to her more than ever.

Nicholas was still sleeping, so I served her coffee and recounted the entire story of how I'd figured out Tate was Taylor's father. Needless to say, she was shocked.

"What the hell are you going to do, Blair?"

"That's a fair question." I shrugged, stirring my coffee. "Basically, I'm screwed."

Her mouth hung open. "I can't believe this."

"I know. I'm still absorbing it myself."

"It was shocking enough when you came home from that trip four years ago and three months later announced that you'd gotten pregnant by an older man you met at the resort. I'd come to terms with the fact that we'd never find or know Nicholas's father. But this? I don't know how to process *this*."

I sighed. "Aside from the fact that Tate is Taylor's father, I still don't regret anything. I told you a lot about

Tate—what I remembered of him, what a good man I felt he was—before we knew his identity. None of that's changed."

My mother rubbed her temples. "Do you have a photo of him?"

Reaching for my phone, I smiled. "Yes. Finally, I do after the nightmare of having all my photos stolen from the trip. I took a couple of pictures this past weekend."

I pulled up a photo of Tate and Nicholas in the yard at the rental house. They were both smiling for the camera, and the resemblance was uncanny. And Tate looked gorgeous, of course.

Her jaw dropped all over again. "Wow. Okay. Uh..." She shook her head. "Well, I can see why you got wrapped up in him. He's an extremely handsome man."

I couldn't help but laugh because I knew she'd react that way once she got a look at him—the way *anyone* would. "Doesn't Nicholas look just like him?"

"I absolutely see that, yes." She nodded. "Tate also looks young for his age. A little different than I'd imagined." After a moment, her expression changed.

"What are you thinking, Mom?"

She looked up at me. "I just feel badly for Taylor. He's been such a good friend to you. This situation isn't fair to anyone involved."

I sighed. "There's no way to sugarcoat it. This is going to crush him, and our friendship may not survive. But I'm more scared about ruining what he's built with his dad."

My mother let out a long breath. "I don't know how to feel, because I'm so thrilled that Nicholas will get to have his father in his life."

I nodded. "I know. It's bittersweet."

"I'm also a little concerned for you," she added.

"Me?" I blinked. "Why?"

"Well, it's clear you still have feelings for this man. But I don't know that I trust him. He may be Nicholas's father, but he's much older than you—*my* age, for Christ's sake. And obviously, Taylor's had a rocky relationship with him."

"Tate's worked a long time to repair his relationship with Taylor. He understands where he went wrong, and it wasn't all his fault. Taylor's mom made things tough for him when they were younger. His relationship with her is better now, too." I sighed. "Anyway, he and I have decided we can't be together romantically. So, you don't need to worry about me."

She arched a brow. "Really, Blair? The look on your face a few moments ago when you were showing me the photo? The way you used to talk about the man you met on the trip? You're absolutely smitten."

I tried to shake it off, though I knew she was right. "It doesn't matter, Mom."

"Sure, it does. Why don't *your* feelings matter?"

Sitting up straighter, I announced, "I'm actually going on a date with someone else."

Her eyes widened. "Really?"

"Yes. I made the decision earlier this morning. Tate encouraged it. He offered to babysit. Apparently, he's already trying to pawn me off on someone else. See? There you go. Nothing to worry about."

"I find that a bit strange." My mother drew in her brows. "Who's the date with?"

"It's that guy Taylor surprised me with when we all went out to Bianco's the other night."

"Do you like him? You didn't seem all that sure when you came home from that dinner."

I shrugged. "I like him enough…"

"That's promising." She rolled her eyes. "Sounds to me like you're forcing yourself to go out with him as a distraction from your feelings for Tate."

I didn't even try to deny it. "Well, I can't pine over someone who's determined not to be with me—and rightfully so. I agree with his stance, all things considered. It wouldn't be fair to Taylor."

My mother offered a sympathetic smile. "I don't mean to antagonize you. Please never stop being honest with me. I so appreciate that you talk to me. And in return, I'll always give you my honest opinion. I want what's best for you. You were just getting your life back on track when this came about."

"None of this changes me finishing nursing school. If anything, I'll have more help with Nicholas now that he has another parent in the picture." I paused. "Tate also wants to help financially. He's insistent on it."

"Well, financial help should be a given."

"I told him I didn't need his money."

"Why not?" She glared. "Of course you do."

"I really don't. We get by just fine."

"You've been living off your savings, Blair. You should start putting money away for Nicholas's college now, and most definitely his father should be contributing."

Once again, she was right. I suppose I'd been in denial about my finances.

"Do you think Nicholas senses anything about Tate?" she asked.

"I don't know. He really likes him. But that's because Tate's been bending over backward to spoil him."

"Well, that gets old fast. It remains to be seen what kind of a father he will be."

I knew Tate had learned from his past mistakes and would be the best father to Nicholas. But it wasn't going to be easy to convince my mom. Time would just have to prove it.

"Well..." she added. "I'm glad Taylor chose to get married when he did. Because this situation would only be more complicated ten years down the line."

I nodded. "That's for damn sure. As things stand, I think Nicholas is the winner in all this. That's why I'm okay with how things have played out. If it was a choice between dealing with this situation or Nicholas never knowing his dad, I'd choose this over the alternative."

"He's not only gained a dad but a brother," she pointed out.

Chills ran through me. "As long as Taylor can accept the situation." I frowned.

"Well, he already loves Nicholas," she said. "That can only help."

"That's gonna be another thing I have to explain to my son someday. How *Uncle* Taylor is suddenly his brother."

"Taylor has one other sibling, right?"

"His mom and stepdad have a daughter. So a half-sister, Katy."

My mother leaned over to hug me. Even if she was a bit critical of Tate, talking to her had made me feel better.

"I think the important thing to remember here is that no one did anything wrong," she said. "And while Taylor is going to be distraught for a while after he finds out, it's not the same as you knowingly getting involved with his father. If he chooses never to speak to you again or to disown Tate, the punishment certainly won't fit the crime."

Ironically, that afternoon Taylor stopped by as he sometimes did on his way home from work. It rattled me a little this time.

"This is a surprise," I said as I let him in.

"Actually, don't get too excited. I have to take a piss so bad, and I know your bathroom is cleaner than the gas station."

"I feel honored."

Taylor was wearing his work clothes, a collared shirt and khakis, and he carried a small bag.

"But I haven't seen Nicholas in a while…" he added. "I got him a little something from the trip and wanted to give it to him in person. Be right back, though," he said, placing the bag on an end table and escaping to the bathroom.

I could hear him tinkling behind the door.

Nicholas had been playing in his room, and I went to get him.

"Nicholas, Uncle Taylor is here!" I announced, desperate for the distraction of my son. I feared Taylor might sense that something was wrong. This was the first time he'd come by since the wedding.

My son's eyes brightened, and he ran out of his room just as Taylor exited the bathroom.

"Hey, buddy!" Taylor opened his arms.

"Hi, Uncle Taylor," Nicholas said in his cute little voice.

"I missed you." Taylor knelt and hugged him. "I have a surprise." Taylor reached for the bag and took out a rubber iguana "I got this when I went to Aruba. I saw it, and all I could think was how much you would like it. There are lots of these iguanas there." He handed it to Nicholas.

My son took it into his palm, looking down at it intently.

"What do you say, Nicholas?" I smiled.

"Thank you, Uncle Taylor."

"You're very welcome. And know what the best part is?" Taylor took it back for a moment and squeezed the iguana, prompting a rubber tongue to pop out. "Check out that tongue."

Nicholas giggled and repeated the motion.

Taylor laughed. "Do you like it?"

Nicholas nodded.

He ruffled my son's hair. "Well, good. I love you, little buddy."

That squeezed my heart. *Oh, Taylor, I hope you love him even more when you find out he's your brother.*

As Nicholas skipped away to play with the iguana, Taylor turned to me. He placed his hands on his hips. "So..."

I blew some air up into my hair. "So?"

He smirked. "Adam told me you agreed to go out with him Saturday night."

I exhaled. "I did."

He chuckled. "You don't have to marry the guy, B. Just have some fun. You spend your days taking care of Nicholas, which is obviously the priority, but you need to get out more. You're too damn young to be cooped up the way you are."

He made himself at home, grabbing a bottled water from the fridge. "On that note, I meant to tell you Juliana and I can babysit whenever you need us. She said to make sure you knew. And that includes this Saturday night."

"She's looking for practice, huh?" I teased.

If Taylor and Juliana had a kid, Tate would be a grandfather. That was wild.

"She might be." He laughed. "But we both agreed it won't be happening anytime soon."

"Unless you get lucky, like me." I winked.

"Anyway, we're serious about the babysitting thing."

"I appreciate that, but I have it covered." *Your father is watching him.*

I was relieved that he didn't ask *who* so I didn't have to lie.

"Well, I was glad to hear you agreed to go," he continued after a moment. "I felt like you two were vibing the other night."

I cleared my throat. "He's a nice guy."

"He's *very* into you. I probably shouldn't be ratting him out like that, but he won't stop talking about how hot you are during our lunch breaks at work. It's fucking annoying."

I forced a smile, but couldn't exactly return the sentiment. Adam was a good-looking guy. When it came to looks and sexual attraction, though, nothing compared to the way I felt about Tate.

Every second Taylor stayed to chat made me more and more nervous. There was no reason Tate would show up here, but I'd been on edge about that possibility since the first time he dropped by unannounced. I reminded myself that Taylor had been away then, and Tate was smart enough not to risk dropping by now.

"The thing is, even though you shouldn't be taking anything too seriously right now, I wouldn't set you up with someone who had no potential for the future," Taylor explained. "Like, if things were to work out between you guys, I *do* think he'd be father material. It's important that you don't waste time with someone who doesn't like kids."

"Yeah, you're definitely getting ahead of yourself, my friend."

"I know. I know. Just saying, even for a casual thing, it's not worth your time if the guy's an asshole or doesn't want children. Because ultimately, you're a package deal, whether you like it or not."

"Thanks for likening me to this week's special at the supermarket."

"You know what I mean." He laughed.

"I do. I'm just kidding, and I know you mean well."

Except Nicholas already has a father and won't ever need a replacement.

Chapter 30

TATE

My mother sat across from me in tears.

Her reaction was more emotional than I'd expected, although I was probably an idiot for not realizing what was going to happen. How else do you react when you find out you have a grandchild you never knew existed? I was an only child, so any grandchildren had to come from me. Mom had likely assumed Taylor would be it for her.

"I remember you telling me you'd met that younger woman at the resort," she said, pulling herself together. "Even over the phone, you sounded very taken with her. I can't believe she was Taylor's Blair."

Taylor's Blair.

Talk about guilt. I felt those words in the pit of my stomach.

"Had you met Blair before?" I asked.

"Only one time before his wedding. I can understand why you were so enamored with her. She's absolutely beautiful."

"She is, and she's amazing inside and out. Also mature for her age."

Mom wiped her eyes. "Do you have any photos of my grandson?"

"I do." I smiled, taking out my phone.

I scrolled through and found a photo I'd taken of Nicholas playing in the sandbox. He was smiling and looking straight into the camera. Feeling almost giddy, I handed her the phone.

She covered her mouth. "Oh my God."

"I know."

"He looks so much like you at that age."

I grinned. "He does."

"I'd ask how it's possible that Taylor hasn't noticed, but I don't think he's ever seen your baby photos. At least, I've never showed him any."

"Not sure even the resemblance would lead him to the right conclusion. Taylor has no reason to believe I was at the resort the same week Blair was. He and I hadn't fully reconnected back then, so I hadn't told him about my impromptu trip."

"And, of course, he doesn't know you as Tate." She shook her head. "I didn't even know that nickname until you told me about it." She tilted her head. "What's wrong with Teddy, anyway?"

"Nothing's wrong with Teddy. I just never liked Theodore. You know that. And one of my buddies started calling me Tate when I was in the service." I shrugged. "It stuck."

"Oh my." She placed her hand on her heart as she looked down at the photo of Nicholas. "My heart hurts for Taylor." Mom frowned. "I'm sorry. The reality of this is just coming in waves."

"I know." I sighed. "Believe me, I know."

She took my hand. "My heart hurts for you, too."

"Because of Taylor?"

"Not just that. You have yourself convinced that the mother of your son is better off without you. But I can see in your eyes that you still have feelings for this girl."

"You can?"

She nodded. "You're my son, Teddy. I know you. I remember when you were younger, the way your ears would turn red when you were excited about something. The same thing happens when you talk about Blair."

If anyone could see through me, it was my mother. Gulping, I said, "It doesn't matter how I feel about her anymore."

"Of course it matters," she countered.

I hung my head. "Taylor's been trying to set her up with one of his friends."

"Well, you need to stop that."

"I encouraged it, actually." I gritted my teeth, pissed at myself.

"Why?"

"Because no matter how much I want her, I can't have her if it means hurting my son. She should also be with someone her own age. Don't you think?" I shook my head and laughed. "Her *parents* are my age."

Mom gave me a look. "I think it's a little too late to be worrying about that. She should be with the person she *wants* to be with, regardless of age or anything else. There's something to be said for making things work with the father of your child."

"That would make sense under most other circumstances. But Blair needs to experience more before settling down. I want to help take care of Nicholas so she can get some of her life back. And neither one of us wants to hurt Taylor."

My mother sighed. "I know things are still raw between you and him, but Taylor is a grown man who's married. This is going to shock him, yes. It's going to hurt him, too. And it may destroy the progress you and he have made. But he *will* get over it someday, and when he does, you'll be happy you didn't let her get away."

She was really fucking with my emotions right now, pointing out things I had tried to deny and bury. Was it worth uncovering them?

"I wish I could believe that, Mom. I really do. But how many years now has Taylor held my past mistakes against me? I don't think he'll be too excited about having more to forgive. Have you *met* my son?"

"I have, and I understand why you might think that. But you have another son to think about now, too."

"Nicholas will always have me in his life. That's a given."

She nodded. "When can I meet him?"

"Soon, hopefully. I'm actually watching him this weekend. But probably not then because he's still getting used to me and doesn't know who I am yet. I don't want to overwhelm him."

"How are you managing to watch him?"

"Blair's gonna drop him off at the house I'm renting in Western Mass." I paused. "She's going on a date with the guy Taylor set her up with, and I'm babysitting."

My mother grimaced. "That can't be easy for you."

"It's *not* easy for me. Right now, though, I want to make life easier for *her*. I owe her that. And if she wants to date this guy, I don't have a right to stop her."

She smiled sadly. "This secret is going to be really difficult to keep from your father. But I won't say anything until you give me the go ahead."

"Well, thank you in advance for your discretion because the fewer people who know, the better. At least until Taylor finds out."

"When do you plan to tell him?"

"We're giving it a few months. Taylor's adjusting to married life, and his job is stressing him out. Plus, he and I are just getting to a point where things have felt stable. It's not the right time to rock the boat."

"It's never going to be easy, Teddy. You might be better addressing it sooner rather than later."

A part of me did wonder if my delay was simply procrastination. "I hear you. But Blair has to be ready, too. We both decided to give it a little time."

"Fair enough." She exhaled. "Thank you for confiding in me."

"Thank you for listening and not judging. I appreciate your perspective."

"From everything you've told me, you weren't being irresponsible at the resort. And yet the universe allowed this to happen. We can't always control things, no matter how hard we try. This situation seems crazy, but it also feels like destiny."

Chapter 31

TATE

*N*ervous wasn't a strong enough word to describe how I felt about seeing Blair tonight.

I didn't want her to sense my jealousy. The closer it got to her date this evening, though, the more freaked out I became over the prospect of her falling for someone. I wanted her to be happy. I just didn't know if I could handle having a front-row seat to it all.

I was a wreck, which made me realize how poorly I'd been managing my feelings for her. Offering to watch Nicholas sent her the message that I was okay with her dating other men, when in reality, I wasn't okay at all. I felt ragey, to be honest. Like a fucking caveman.

Nicholas.

You need to focus on your son.

I'd worked extra hard this week to wrap up some projects at work so I could give Nicholas my undivided attention. This was big—our first time alone together. That was the only bright side of this whole date event. Getting one-on-one time with the little guy was a gift.

I'd bought more of the snacks I'd learned he loved from last time, some spare clothes in case he needed them, and a few new toys. Yes, I supposed I was trying to buy his love—whatever made it easier for him to be comfortable around me. Once he trusted me, I could slowly scale back on spoiling him.

Blair pulled up in front of the house, and I went out to help her bring Nicholas' stuff in. When I saw her, I nearly lost my breath. Her hair was down and styled into long, loose waves. Her black dress was form-fitting with tiny sequins. And it looked awfully familiar. It hugged her ass and breasts in a way that made my heart race. Her lips were painted red. The way she looked reminded me of the night at the resort where she'd dressed sexy to torture me. In fact, I was pretty sure it was the same dress. I remembered it. *Fuck.* It had worked then to drive me absolutely wild, and it was working the same way now.

It occurred to me that maybe Blair knew exactly what she was doing—just like the Blair I knew and loved back then. I cleared my throat. "You look nice."

Nice? She looked fucking hot.

I tried like hell not to look down at her chest like a creeper. But it was hard to take my eyes off her. Memories of her beautiful body beneath mine flashed through my mind. It was downright painful to remember what it'd felt like to be inside of her. There was nothing I wanted more than to feel that again, and I feared I never would.

How would I handle her getting involved with another man? Could I be cordial to him? Could I hide my pain?

I went around to open the back door of the car and forced myself to shake off the jealousy for the sake of my son. "Hey, buddy!"

"Hi, Mr. T."

His little voice hit me straight in the heart. I couldn't wait for the day when he could call me Daddy. "Are you ready to have a fun night?" I asked.

He nodded as he exited the car.

I guided him inside as Blair followed with his overnight bag.

"You didn't have to bring anything, actually," I said. "I meant to tell you that. I bought him some clothes to keep here, even though you told me not to. Just wanted to make things easier for you if you don't want to truck stuff back and forth. You'd mentioned he was wearing a size 4T now, so I kept that in mind. Got stuff in 5T, too, in case he has a random growth spurt."

She nodded. "Okay, well, I'll know for next time."

"When are you coming back?" I asked, trying like hell not to scan her body like I wanted to.

"Tomorrow morning. Is that okay?"

"Yeah. Of course." I scratched my chin. "You're going straight to meet him from here, I assume, if you're all dressed up..."

"Yeah. I won't have enough time to stop back home again."

Unable to stop myself, I gave her a once-over. "Well, be careful."

"I will," she said. "Let me know if you have any questions. Just text me if you need anything."

What I *needed* right now I'd be keeping to myself. I managed a nod. "We'll be fine. Don't worry. Just try to enjoy yourself. You deserve a night off."

She didn't seem to be looking me in the eye much,

which was strange. Was she ashamed of what she planned to do tonight? Or was that my paranoia playing with me?

"Please be a good boy for Mr. T," she said as she hugged Nicholas.

"Okay, Mommy."

Blair chewed her bottom lip. "I wish I could stay a bit, but if I don't leave now, I'll be late."

"Take your time. Don't rush. Believe me, what's-his-name won't mind if you're a few minutes late."

As if I could forget his name.

Adam.

Fucking Adam.

After she walked out the door, regret set in. Nothing about her leaving sat right with me. But I forced myself to shake it off and focus on my son. He deserved my full attention.

I turned to him and grinned. "Want a snack?"

Nicholas jumped in excitement. I laughed and got him situated in his seat in the kitchen. Then I prepared him a plate: two mozzarella cheese sticks, some Teddy Grahams, orange slices, and Cheez-Its.

"I'm making spaghetti later. How does that sound?"

"Good." He nodded with his mouth full.

I sat across from him, leaning my elbows against the table and watching him eat, and a calmness came over me. There was nowhere in the world I was meant to be besides here with my baby boy. This kid had no idea how much I loved him. What a dream it would be to share a meal with *both* of my sons someday, out in the open with no worries. A lump formed in my throat. That would be a miracle.

When Nicholas looked up and noticed me watching him, he smiled. I smiled back, amused once again to see my own eyes staring back at me. "What's your favorite thing in the whole world, Nicholas?" I asked.

"Trucks," he said as he chewed.

Yes. That was the answer I'd been hoping for. This kid was nothing if not predictable.

"I have a surprise for you after you finish your snack, okay?"

No, it wasn't his birthday. But I'd already missed three of those. I'd missed a few Christmases, too. So that's how I justified it. This was long overdue.

After he finished, I couldn't wait to bring him outside before it got dark.

Nicholas squealed as he got a look at his very own ride-on truck. I'd gotten a dark gray one, just like mine. I knew this was completely gratuitous. I hadn't even told Blair I'd purchased it, for fear that she'd tell me not to spoil him. But I couldn't help myself and hoped she wouldn't be pissed.

He got in, and I spent the next several minutes teaching him how to use it. Then I watched in satisfaction as my little man drove himself around the grass.

"What a big boy," I called out. "You're such a good driver."

The love in my heart at seeing his palpable joy felt limitless. Tears formed behind my eyes. Never again would I miss a moment of his life. What a freaking gift. Not only to have a second son, but to *have a child with Blair*. Something I would've never willingly allowed, but the universe allowed anyway. It felt like an honor I'd never deserve, nor fully repay.

I took some videos of my son riding around in his truck. In fact, my camera roll was fast becoming filled with Nicholas images and not much of anything else.

After an hour and a half of playing in the yard, followed by dinner, it was getting close to bedtime. I finally convinced Nicholas to give the truck a break, promising we'd spend more time outside tomorrow.

While he played with the train set in the living room, I drew him a bath. Once I led him into the bathroom and put him in the soapy tub, he splashed with his rubber toys while I watched him like he was the second coming of Christ.

At one point, he looked up at me and asked, "Who are you?"

I froze. That was an odd question. Cocking my head, I squinted. "What do you mean, buddy?" He sensed something. I knew it in my bones.

But rather than answer my question, he just smiled and said nothing. The urge to whisper, "I'm your daddy," nearly overwhelmed me for a moment, but this wasn't the time.

After I put Nicholas to bed, I realized how much his presence had consumed me. I'd thought of nothing else for hours. Now I checked on him periodically, and it seemed he was out like a light.

That left space for my mind to return to Blair. I sat on the couch, mindlessly flipping through channels, unable to concentrate on anything but the fact that she was out on a date.

What if she really likes this guy?

What if she has sex with him because it's been so long for her?

She said she hadn't had sex since me.

Fuck. The thought of that made me crazy.

She'd also said she was looking for the same thing as when she'd met me—and I knew what that was. She'd been starving, and she was most certainly starving now if she'd gone four fucking years without it.

Fuck.

I felt sicker with each minute that I sat here, torturing myself. So I forced myself up and went into the bedroom. I decided to work out, anything to get rid of this nervous energy. I wanted to punch the wall, but I couldn't with my sweet boy in the next room. This also wasn't my home to destroy.

As I did push-ups, I felt feral and possessive. I'd made a huge mistake in encouraging Blair to go out. I wanted to be a better man, a stronger person, but I wasn't. Because my feelings for her and my fears when it came to Taylor were mutually exclusive.

Despite the urge to text her, I couldn't allow myself to do it. The push-ups continued.

Then my phone chimed.

Blair: How did everything go?

Tate: Perfect. He's sleeping. We had an amazing time. He's getting used to me, which is cool.

Now that she'd opened the door, it was so much harder to hold back.

Don't do it.
Don't do it.
Don't do it.

Tate: I fucking miss you, though.

Tate: I thought I could do this, Blair.

Tate: I fucking can't.

I closed my eyes in shame, vowing not to type another word.

Blair: I know it's late, but can I come there tonight so I can be there when he wakes up in the morning?

My heart beat faster. If she wanted to come *here*, it meant she *wasn't* with him.

Tate: Of course.

I paced for the next two hours as I waited for Blair's arrival. The moment I saw the lights outside, I went to the door and opened it before she'd even exited the vehicle.

"Sorry if I made you wait up," she said, walking past me into the house.

"I wasn't tired anyway." I ran my hand through my hair. "How was it?" I tried to ask calmly, even though I was champing at the bit.

"I don't know." She shrugged. "It was okay, I guess. We went to dinner. That was it. He seemed very interested in me. But..." She hesitated.

"But what?" I asked as my pulse raced.

"I just wasn't...there." Blair took a couple of steps toward me. "I was *here*. My mind was here."

She'd given up her life for my child. I owed this woman the fucking truth.

"Well, it's interesting you say that because from the moment Nicholas went to bed, I couldn't get you off my mind. I've been going nuts." I inched closer. "I acted like it didn't bother me that you went out with this guy tonight, but it fucked me up, Blair." I shook my head. "I wanted to be strong. But... You look so goddamn beautiful. And I just—"

"I got dressed up for you, not him." She looked down a moment. "But you barely looked at me."

"I was *trying* not to," I murmured. "It reminded me of the time you dressed up at the resort and nearly gave me a heart attack."

"It's the same dress..."

"I know," I whispered.

"It was all for you, Tate. All I wanted was to come back here and be with you tonight. I'm sorry... I can't just shut it off. I don't want anyone else. I haven't since we were together." Her chest heaved. "I can't help it."

The last fuck I had to give evaporated upon hearing those words.

"You've been so busy these past few years, trying to build a beautiful life for that boy. You've done an incredible job. He's absolutely perfect." I ran the back of my fingers along her cheek. "But no one's been taking care of *you*." I inched even closer. "Tell me again. What do you need right now, baby?"

"I need *you*. I've always needed you. Even after I thought you were gone forever, I kept looking for you. I couldn't handle being with anyone else."

My heart leaped, and I erased the space between us. "I've been fucking pretending this whole time, Blair."

"Show me what's real then," she begged.

I dug my fingers into her hair. "*This* is real." I took her mouth in mine and never looked back.

Chapter 32

BLAIR

The moment Tate's lips touched mine, his taste was my oxygen. I hadn't realized just how much I'd needed this until it was happening.

"You've been waiting for me, haven't you?" He groaned over my skin.

"Yes..." I murmured, my legs ready to collapse under me. "You ruined me for anyone else. Don't you know that?"

"I lost my fucking mind tonight." He tugged on my hair. "I've never been so jealous. You're the only woman who can bring that out in me." He looked into my eyes. "I don't care what it fucking takes. I don't want to lose you, Blair. I can't live without you."

I threaded my fingers through his silky mane. "You already have me. You always did. You're fucking etched into my soul, Tate. I haven't been able to allow anyone else in."

"What do you need right now?" he asked.

"I need you inside of me. I need it more than I ever have."

He stepped back. "I don't have any protection here. I wasn't expecting to—"

I ran my fingers through his hair again. "I have an IUD now. Not for birth control, but because I was having some pain. So you can... It's okay if you—"

"Fuck, yes." Tate took my mouth again before I could finish that sentence.

The muscles between my legs quivered. I thought I might die if he stopped this. But I knew he wouldn't. We'd gone past the point of no return.

"I can't let you go, Blair. I fucking tried."

"I don't *want* you to let me go."

He unzipped my dress, and it fell to the floor. He slid his calloused hands down my back. A shiver ran through me. "I just want to look at you for a minute," he said. Tate traced his finger along the curves of my body, circling my nipple, grazing my belly button. "You're so damn beautiful." He knelt and placed a kiss on my stomach. "I can't believe this beautiful body carried my child. I'll never get over it, Blair. I swear. It's such a miracle."

The heat of his mouth ignited a flame inside me, which was about to erupt into a full-on fire. He went lower, and without warning, Tate pulled my panties aside and pressed his mouth to my clit. He gripped my ass and pulled me against his face. I bent my head back in ecstasy as he devoured me. His groan vibrated throughout my core, his tongue lapping at my tender flesh. Raking my fingers through his hair, I closed my eyes, falling further and further into an abyss each second. When I felt myself almost ready to come, I pulled on his hair.

"You need to stop before I—"

"Fuck," he murmured, rising to take my mouth in his.

I could taste myself on his tongue. I wrapped my arms around his neck, so hungry for him. He kissed me harder, our breaths erratic, tongues colliding. I couldn't get him inside of me fast enough.

I knew having sex with Tate was a bit reckless with our son in the next room. But I was willing to take the risk. I unsnapped my bra, tossing it aside as Tate slipped his shirt over his head. The hunger in his eyes was the same as I remembered from the first time we'd made love. It was even more intense now.

Tate lifted me and carried me to his bed. After he put me down, he whipped his belt off and stepped out of his jeans, pushing down his boxer briefs. The sight of his beautifully hard cock made my mouth water. He lowered himself over me and let out a deep growl as he pushed inside in one desperate thrust. I was so ready that it didn't even hurt, though I hadn't had sex in four years.

"Look at you, soaking wet. You feel so damn good." He rocked into me. "You're fucking mine, aren't you? You've been mine this entire time."

I tugged gently at his lip with my teeth. "From the moment I met you, and every day between then and now." I dug my nails into his back as he pounded into me. I was desperate for each and every thrust.

Squeezing his ass, I tightened my muscles around his thick cock. I'd nearly forgotten how good it felt to be pinned down and ravaged by this man. And it was even better because there was no barrier this time. "I want to feel you come inside me," I breathed.

"Now?" He panted.

"Yes," I begged.

His body shook and jerked forward. "Shit..." He gasped. "Fuck. Oh my...God, I'm..."

Feeling the heat of his load was all it took for me to spasm around his cock. It was the most intense orgasm I'd ever had. I never wanted it to end.

Tate pumped in and out of me slowly, long after he was finished. I loved feeling his hot arousal between my legs, and he lay on top of me for the longest time, our bodies still connected.

After he pulled out, we turned to face each other.

"What now?" I whispered.

"Fuck if I know, baby," he said, dragging his thumb along my chin. "But things just got a whole lot more complicated."

I looked into his eyes. "This was inevitable, wasn't it?"

"Like fucking death and taxes." He kissed my forehead. "We'll figure it out together."

I brushed my finger along his stubble. "My handsome man. I missed you so much."

Tate smiled. "From the moment we left each other at the resort, I never stopped thinking about you, Blair. I need you to know that. Never stopped hoping that phone would ring. But I never allowed myself to imagine an actual future with you, certainly not a child with you." He paused. "I will be eternally grateful for the gift you've given me. It is beyond my wildest dreams."

"I wish we could be together without having to hurt anyone," I said.

"Me, too, sweetheart. Believe me. But I'm done denying how I feel about you, which has nothing to do with

you being Nicholas's mother. This is about you and me—
the connection we have that never died. It's been there all
along, even before we found each other again."

"That's exactly how I feel."

My phone chimed, interrupting our moment.

I reached for it on the nightstand, and my stomach
dropped. "It's Taylor," I whispered.

Tate's expression grew dark, the light in his eyes fad-
ing.

I looked down at it.

Taylor: How did the date with Adam go?

"Shit," I muttered.

"What does it say?" he asked.

I faced the screen toward him.

"Well, that's a slap in the face from reality." Tate exhaled.

I put the phone aside.

"You're not going to write him back?" he asked.

"Not right away." I shook my head. "I hate lying."

"What are you going to tell him?"

"I guess I'm just gonna say I'm not feeling it for Adam
the way I should."

He nodded, and I could tell his mind had gone to a
guilty place.

I sighed. "I certainly won't be telling Taylor I can't
like Adam because I can't get over his father, no matter
how hard I try."

"I don't *want* you to get over me."

"Is this the part where you tell me you want me under
you, not over you?" I teased.

"Well, that too." He groaned. "Nothing felt worse than when you went out tonight, and I thought there was a chance you could fall for someone else." He pressed his forehead to mine.

"That was never gonna happen." We stared into each other's eyes. "God, I love looking at you. You're freaking perfect, Tate."

He ran his fingers through my hair. "I love the way you look at me. I love knowing how much you want me. I love everything about you, Blair."

He stopped short of saying he loved *me*, but it was pretty damn close.

"What's the plan for tomorrow?" I asked.

"We spend the day with our little boy, and we figure out the rest some other time." Tate reached for his phone. "I want to show you something."

"Okay..."

"I wasn't going to show this to you. But after tonight, I want you to read it."

"What is it?"

"You know how you left me that letter back at the resort..."

I nodded. "Of course."

"Well, I've always regretted not writing you something that day, too. I couldn't gather my thoughts fast enough to do it before you left, but I *did* eventually write you back."

My heart fluttered. "You did?"

His mouth curved into a smile. "I wrote an email to myself, just to get the thoughts out. I would've written on paper, but my penmanship sucks. Nicholas probably has better handwriting than I do." He scrolled through his email. "Anyway, would you want to read it?"

The butterflies in my belly came alive. "Of course."

He handed me his phone.

Dear Blair,

I don't know if this message will ever reach you. But I still feel the need to write it.

It's been one year since I've seen your beautiful face in person. One year since I've gotten lost inside of you. And one year since you walked out of the resort with my heart.

We had less than a handful of days together, but each and every one of them meant more to me than all of the other days of my life combined.

Every day for a year, I've hoped I might hear from you.

I have to believe you have a damn good reason for not contacting me. As each day passes, I've come to terms with the fact that I may never see or hear from you again.

Though you're not around physically, I want you to know that I have felt you. I've felt you when I've looked up at the moon, I've felt you on a gentle breeze or a hint of a stranger's blonde hair. Most of all, I've felt you in my dreams, where you make appearances often.

When we left each other, I didn't have the band-width to string words together in a meaningful way. I chose to spend each and every waking moment with you instead. Now I have the benefit of hindsight and lots more time to articulate things, and yet, I still struggle to put into words the way you made me feel. Except to say this: You taught me how to love in a way I didn't understand before.

While I still long for you every day, you've left me a better man, even in your absence. I just wish I could've told you how much you meant to me before we went our separate ways.

All this to say, I love you, too, Blair. So much. And I will never forget you.

Love always,

Tate

My eyes watered. "This is beautiful." I looked at the date that he'd emailed this to himself. It was indeed a year after we'd left each other. I'd made the right decision in following my gut and coming back here tonight.

"When I wrote that message, I never dreamed I'd be in this place with you. I certainly never dreamed you were out there somewhere holding my baby." His eyes glistened.

I squeezed his hand. "You said there were times you could feel me. I wonder if one of those times was the moment he was born."

"It's possible." He smiled. "You know, tonight when I was giving Nicholas his bath, he looked at me and asked,

'Who are you?' I feel like he senses something, even if he doesn't fully understand."

"Wow." I smiled. "I wouldn't doubt it. A biological bond is a real thing."

Tate nuzzled my neck. "What time does he normally wake up?"

"He's a pretty sound sleeper, but he's usually up by seven AM."

"I'll set an alarm for six, so we're up before him." He spoke over my lips. "But also, so I can have you again."

"Wanna take me again now, too?"

"I thought you'd never ask," he said, flipping me onto my back. I immediately came alive. Tate and I made love again, and that night I slept better than I had in ages, in the arms of the one man who made me feel whole.

Chapter 33

TATE

Today had been a high point right up there with the time I'd spent at the resort with Blair four years ago.

The three of us had hung out from morning till night. We didn't even leave the house much. Blair and I got up right before Nicholas, and then she made pancakes. We'd tossed a ball around the yard with our son, and as expected, Blair gave me hell for buying him that truck. All in good fun, though.

After that, we went to a local café where Blair and I sipped coffees while watching Nicholas devour a chocolate donut like it was the best thing either of us had ever witnessed. On the way home, I went to the market and bought all the ingredients to make homemade breaded chicken tenders and cheesy rice, which was apparently one of Nicholas's favorites. Blair made a big salad for us, too.

And though we were supposed to go our separate ways this evening, I'd convinced Blair to spend one more night here with me. We'd both drive back on Monday morning instead of the original plan of Sunday night. This time with them felt precious.

I'd just put away the last of the dishes and ventured out to the living room. Blair was cuddled next to Nicholas on the couch in that lazy time after dinner but before his bath. She'd fallen asleep while Nicholas was tired but awake, petting Khloe who was comfortably situated next to him. My heart felt ready to burst.

My family.

This was my family—the one I'd never known I wanted until it appeared in front of me. Now I didn't know how I'd lived without them for so long. I sat next to Blair and gently kissed her hair. Resting my arm against the back of the couch behind her, I leaned my head toward hers and closed my eyes for a moment.

I needed to find a way to be with them every day. Before we'd even separated, I was already dreading the week ahead. I loved Taylor and didn't want to hurt him. But after this weekend, I knew we couldn't wait to tell him the truth. If things were tough after doing so, at least I could be with Blair and Nicholas instead of having to hide my love for them.

She blinked her eyes open and looked up at me. "I can't believe I fell asleep."

I kissed her on the forehead. "Well, it's been a big weekend."

When Nicholas hopped off the couch to play with the train set, I took the opportunity. "What do you think about telling Taylor sooner rather than later?"

Her expression dimmed. "How soon?"

"Like in the next couple of weeks?"

Blair looked down. "I thought you wanted to give it time?"

"I don't think I can live much longer not seeing you and Nicholas during the week. Waiting to tell him isn't going to lessen the shock. I think I've just been looking for excuses. My mother said the same thing."

Her head tilted as she thought. "Okay, well, Taylor's birthday is in a week. So sometime after that. I don't want to ruin his day."

"Agreed." I nodded. "And once we get past telling him, I want you and Nicholas to live with me, either in your house or mine, and ultimately in a bigger and better place than either of those. I want to respect your boundaries, though," I added, forcing myself to breathe. "So there's no pressure. Just letting you know what *I* would love. It'll make it easier for me to watch him while you're at class or doing your thing, too. You tell me, though, if that's not something you want." I paused again. "This is your time, Blair. I want you to do all the things you've been missing out on because you've had to care for Nicholas on your own. My work schedule is flexible. You're my priority now, just as much as he is."

She smiled. "That sounds like a dream, but I don't have a desire to spend all that much time away from you. I just got you back."

My heart felt like it would burst. That was too good to be true. "Well, I'm cool with making up for lost time together—as long as that's what you want, baby. I just don't want you to feel stuck or pressured. I want you to *want* to be with me. We're still at different stages of life. I'm still old enough to be your goddamn father. If you ever feel—"

"You're the only one I want, Tate. Period. Full stop."

Her words did things to me, things I couldn't fully act on at the moment. I glanced over at Nicholas, only to have him come over and hop onto my lap. He rested his head in the crook of my arm, and I kissed the top of his head. I was so damn grateful. I closed my eyes and breathed him in. When I opened them, Blair was smiling.

"I love him so much," I mouthed to her. "And I love you."

"I love you, too," she mouthed back.

We went to bed that night feeling so peaceful, so blissfully oblivious to the nightmare that lay ahead the next day.

Blair and Nicholas left the house about ten AM on Monday morning, and I stayed behind to clean up and do a load of Nicholas's laundry so I could fold it and have his clothes ready for next weekend.

A phone call interrupted me just as I was smoothing out a pair of his jeans.

"Blair?" I answered.

Her voice shook. "Tate, we were in an accident."

My stomach sank. "What? Are you okay?"

"We're in an ambulance. We were thirty minutes from home, and someone rear-ended us." She took in a shuddering breath. "Nicholas is unconscious. He's breathing, but I think maybe he has a concussion."

"Oh my God." The jeans fell from my hands.

"He was in his car seat, but his head snapped forward and hit something. I'm so scared."

The room felt like it was spinning. Running out of the laundry area, I scrambled to locate my keys. "I'm getting in my car right now. What hospital are they taking him to?"

She didn't immediately answer, and then I heard the muffled sound of her talking to someone.

"Lincoln Memorial," she finally said.

"Try to breathe, Blair," I said as I got into my truck. "Everything's gonna be okay. You have to believe that."

"I know. I'm just scared." She exhaled. "Just get here."

"I'll be there as soon as I can. You want me to stay on the phone with you?"

"No. I need to pay attention to what's happening."

"Call me back if you need me."

She sniffled. "Okay."

My tears fell the moment I hung up with her. I could barely see through them.

I began to pray to a God I hoped was listening. I hadn't asked Him for much in my life, always fended for myself. But I needed help right now because anything happening to that little boy was unthinkable.

"Please. Please, let my baby be okay. I promise to spend the rest of my life trying to be a good person, a good father."

I had so much love for him in my heart, and I couldn't imagine not giving it to him. He didn't even know he had a dad who loved him.

The drive to the hospital was a blur, and I texted Blair the second I parked to ask where she was.

She told me they were in the pediatric ICU and instructed me to let them know I was his father; otherwise, they wouldn't let me in.

When I finally made it to the room, the overhead lights practically blinded me. I struggled to see what was happening. Nicholas was surrounded by medical staff, and Blair stood at the head of the bed, looking panicked as I rushed to her side.

But when I looked down at my son, relief washed over me. His eyes were open, though not entirely focused.

"This is his dad," Blair said to the doctor.

The doctor looked at me. "Nicholas's vitals are good, and he's stable. With small kids, there can be a loss of consciousness even in minor accidents. We're going to keep him overnight for observation. It's a good thing he was in a car seat."

"Thank you so much for taking care of him," I said, reaching for Blair's hand.

After he left, I pulled in a full breath for the first time since I'd left the house.

I took Blair in my arms. "Are you okay?"

She nodded.

I started to cry in relief. I couldn't remember the last time I'd sobbed like this. Blair, too, had tears running down her face. We sat at each side of Nicholas's bed.

"Hi, my boy," I whispered.

"Hi," he answered groggily.

I patted his hand. "You're gonna be okay, little guy."

He looked into my eyes, just like he had that night in the bathtub.

The weight of what could have happened hit me all over again. "Daddy loves you," I said. "Daddy loves you so much."

I looked up at Blair, expecting to gauge her reaction to the words that had unexpectedly come from my mouth. But instead, what I saw was my *other* son, standing behind Blair in the doorway.

Chapter 34

TATE

Blair turned to see what I was staring at. When she looked back at me, her face had turned white.

And then Taylor disappeared, gone as quickly as he'd appeared in the doorway.

"Stay here with Nicholas," I told Blair as I ran after him.

My heart pummeled against my chest as I looked around the hospital for him.

How had he vanished so damn fast?

Outside the main entrance, I finally spotted Taylor rushing through the parking lot.

I ran to catch up with him. "Taylor, please. Wait," I said, practically breathless.

He stopped, turning to look at me. The color had drained from his face. "I don't understand what's happening here," he said in a shaky voice. "But I didn't want to scare Nicholas, so I got the hell out of there before I fucking screamed or did something to upset him."

"Please don't run away." I attempted to catch my breath. "Let me explain what's happening."

Looking dazed, he shook his head. "I'm not sure how you could *ever* explain this, Theodore."

Theodore. It had been a long while since he hadn't referred to me as Dad. But I didn't blame him one bit for reverting back to the name he'd called me for most of his life. He needed some distance from me right now.

Taylor's lip trembled.

My poor boy. *I never meant to hurt you.*

And just like that, I lost my composure for the second time in a matter of minutes, tears running down my cheeks. "I know you want to run right now," I told him. "I know that's the easiest thing. But I beg you to let me explain this."

Several moments passed as we stood facing each other, cars whizzing by on a nearby highway the only sound.

He just kept shaking his head. "I don't understand."

"Taylor..."

He looked up. "You've been having an affair with her since my wedding?"

Shit. He'd drawn the wrong conclusion. He thought I'd been playing house with Blair and Nicholas. I shook my head. How could he think anything else? The truth was so far-fetched.

"Taylor, no. It's not like that." I swallowed. "It was me. *I* was the man Blair met at the resort. We...didn't know." I looked him in the eyes. "I'm Nicholas's father."

His face transformed in disbelief. "What?"

"I'm Nicholas's biological father," I said again.

"Oh my God." After a moment, he repeated it. "Oh my God."

Taylor stepped back, and I took an equal number of steps forward in an attempt not to lose him.

I forced myself to continue. "Neither one of us knew that the other had a connection to you at the time. And then, as you know, she and I lost touch. We only figured everything out at your wedding—the moment you introduced me to her in the receiving line. I hadn't seen her since the resort and had no idea Nicholas even existed."

He blinked in confusion. "She said the guy's name was Tate."

I took a deep breath and nodded. "Tate is a nickname I got in the military. It's the name I use when I meet anyone new."

"You gave her a fake name?"

"It's not a fake name," I insisted. "I've been going by Tate for several years now. Even Leah knew me as Tate. It's a—"

"I'm gonna be sick." He held his stomach, looking disgusted.

I wondered if he might actually vomit in the middle of this parking lot. "I don't blame you, son. You have every ri—"

"Don't 'son' me." He shook his head. "This is not the time."

"Okay…" I swallowed, feeling my heart slowly breaking.

A long, tense silence passed.

"How the fuck could you take advantage of her like that?" he finally spat.

"I swear to you, I didn't. She and I formed a true connection. It was unlike anything I've ever felt with anyone, despite the age difference. I know she talked to you about it. Surely she must have told you how things were with the man she met?"

"Oh yeah. She told me all about the guy she met—who manipulated her."

My brows furrowed. "She didn't say that."

"No, she didn't say that, but that was always *my* take—or any smart person's take. Blair was too disillusioned to realize she was being taken advantage of. I never wanted to make things worse by throwing my opinion at her. Especially once she found out she was pregnant. It wouldn't have helped to tell her I thought she'd been manipulated by an older guy. But now that I know it's *you*?" He exhaled. "My original opinion makes even more sense."

Every word hurt more than the last, but I had to keep trying. "I never deceived her, Taylor," I raised my voice, desperate for him to see this in a different light. "Blair and I met, and I tried to resist her initially. But then we had an amazing several days together. I thought I was being safe..." I hesitated. "I didn't want to ruin her life, so I encouraged us to go our separate ways when she left."

"You didn't want to ruin her life, and yet you did. You're pretty good at that."

I closed my eyes. Man, that fucking hurt. *But it's okay. He needs to let out his anger. I can take it.*

As horrible as this was, it was also a huge relief. Because the alternative—keeping him in the dark—had been horrible, too, and now I no longer had to keep this enormous secret. No longer had to love Nicholas in secret.

I sighed. "I don't blame you for thinking the worst of me. But over time, you'll see this situation is not what you think. I love her, Taylor. And she loves me. I know it's a shock to hear that, but it's the truth. Blair and I never got over each other. And now that I know about Nicholas, all I want to do is be the kind of dad I know I wasn't for you. I will never forgive myself for not fighting harder to be a better dad when you were little. But I still have a chance to do right by him."

He shook his head. "Were you *ever* going to tell me?"

"Of course." I looked straight into his eyes. "You need to know that. We just didn't want to drop that bomb on your wedding or honeymoon. Blair and I have been debating the best time to talk to you. We planned on telling you in a couple of weeks, after your birthday. You can ask Blair. We had just decided that before this happened. I never wanted you to find out like this."

Taylor stared off across the parking lot for a long while before he finally turned to me and muttered, "How is Nicholas? He seemed okay..."

I nodded. "He's gonna be fine. They're keeping him overnight for monitoring. How did you find out about the accident?"

"One of the EMTs is a buddy of mine. He recognized Blair, even though he'd only met her a couple of times. She probably didn't remember him. But he called me." Taylor laughed angrily. "You wanna know the insane thing? I told the hospital I was his father, so they would let me see him. I worried uncle wouldn't fly. What kind of sick irony is that?"

My chest constricted. "I'm so sorry, Taylor."

"I need to leave." He rubbed his temples. "I can't do this right now."

"Please don't get in that car if you're upset." The thought of him getting into an accident terrified me.

"I have to. I can't be here anymore."

Taylor walked to his car as I followed him in silence. He opened the door and slammed it shut before starting the engine. I took a few steps back but stood in the same spot as he sped away.

It felt like I'd lost a part of my soul as I walked back into the hospital and to the pediatric ICU.

Blair's eyes were filled with fear as I reappeared. She searched my face. "He knows?"

My lip trembled as I nodded.

She closed her eyes.

She didn't have to ask how it had gone.

All it took was one look at my face.

Chapter 35

BLAIR

A week after the accident, things had almost returned to normal, at least for Nicholas.

As for everything else? Well, it was as bad as we'd imagined.

Taylor refused to talk to me when I'd called him the day after the hospital encounter. He'd answered the phone, but said he wasn't ready yet to have what he understood was a necessary conversation. He apologized for not being stronger and asked me to tell Tate not to call him, either. He said he'd reach out to us when he was ready to talk.

So, we had no choice but to give him time and hope he'd eventually be ready to discuss and accept the situation.

Tate said he'd initially felt relief that Taylor knew, but with each day that passed when Taylor didn't call, he fell deeper into sadness. Case in point, after Nicholas went to sleep this evening, I found Tate sitting on the couch, looking at baby photos of Taylor on his phone. Tate had been sleeping over almost every night.

"Hey," I said, taking a seat next to him. "I was wondering where you went."

"Hey, beautiful…" He looked up briefly, then returned his gaze to the images of Taylor. "I've been trying for so long to get him to love me. But I think the best I can hope for is that he doesn't *hate* me. It's amazing what you'll settle for when you're desperate." Tate put his phone aside. "Do you think I should try to call him?"

It pained me, but I shook my head. "He made it clear that he wants time. I think we should give him what he's asked for and not push it."

Tate sighed. "Okay. Yeah. You're right." He shook his head. "I don't know what I was thinking."

I rubbed his arm. "You were thinking that you love your son, and you can't stand the limbo. You want to make things better. I get it."

He reached for my hand. "Well, if all else fails, I still have you and Nicholas. I'm thankful for that every day."

Tate and I still hadn't explained things to Nicholas, and it seemed unlikely that he'd processed anything we said around him in the hospital. There was really nothing stopping us anymore, though…

"I was thinking," I told Tate. "Maybe we should tell Nicholas who you are now that he's recovered from the accident."

A glimmer of hope appeared in his eyes. "You think he's ready?"

"I do."

He nodded. "All right. If it's okay with you, though, I want to play it by ear. I don't want to spring it on him at some specific time we pick. I'd like to do it spontaneously, when it feels right, depending on his mood."

"Okay. That makes sense."

He closed his eyes and bent his head back.

I wanted so badly to ease the tension in his body. "Sit down on the ground," I demanded.

"Why?"

"Just do it."

Tate moved off the couch to the carpet. I sat behind him on the couch, placing a leg on either side of him.

"What are you doing, baby?" The low rumble of his laughter vibrated against my hands as I rubbed the back of his neck.

"I'm giving you a massage."

"I thought I was supposed to be giving *you* a break."

"I told you, I don't want a break. I've spent the last four years longing for you. What I want is to enjoy being together now." I dug my fingers deeper into his muscles. "Now take a deep breath and relax."

"You're a dream come true," he hissed. "The problem is, when you touch me like this, you don't *just* make me relaxed. I want to bury myself inside you."

I felt the muscles between my legs tighten. "It's good we want the same things."

He groaned under his breath. As I massaged his shoulders, I bent to kiss the top of his head.

"I don't deserve you, Blair," he said.

"Yes, you do."

He sighed deeply, his tension seeming to dissipate a bit. "You're the best thing to ever happen to me. As tough as this is, I'm lucky to have you by my side."

I circled my palms slowly over his upper back. "No matter what Taylor thinks right now, *I* know the truth. You're a good man, Tate Delaney. I'll die on that hill. You've learned from your mistakes, and you want nothing more than to show love to the people you care about. Loving each other freely and naturally will never be a sin or something to regret. I'm trying to be hopeful that Taylor will come around. But if for any reason he doesn't, just know that *I* see you. And I'm so happy you're Nicholas's dad." I stopped massaging for a moment. "Sometimes I still wake up in the morning feeling like I've lost you. For a split second, I think it's four years ago. For so long, that feeling of dread was the first thing to hit me when I opened my eyes. But now? Euphoria sets in when I realize the truth."

He reached his hand back and placed it over mine. "I love you so much, Blair."

I moved around from behind and straddled him on the ground. "I love you, too." I kissed him, feeling his erection growing between my legs.

"I'm so glad I'm your baby daddy," he said over my lips.

"There's a funny story I never told you..." I snickered.

He looked up and grinned. "What?"

"So, you remember my ex, Daniel, the one who'd left me heartbroken when we met?"

"Of course. I'll never forget that jerk."

"Well, he actually came back to ask me for a second chance."

Tate went rigid. "Really..."

"He called one night and asked if he could come by and speak to me."

His eyes widened. "You let him come over?"

I nodded.

Tate's eyes narrowed. "What happened?"

I laughed just thinking about it. "I gleefully opened the door—with my huge, eight-months-pregnant belly."

His mouth dropped. "No fucking way."

"Yup. That's why I let him come by. I knew it would shock the crap out of him. I enjoyed every second of the look on his face."

"Holy crap. What did you tell him?"

"Oh, I told him the absolute truth: that I'd met an older man on vacation who'd knocked me up."

"He must've shit a brick."

"Looked like he might have." I chuckled.

"What happened after that?"

"He left soon after, and I never saw him again." I shrugged. "But I couldn't have orchestrated a better way of getting back at him."

Tate cackled. "You're welcome."

Chapter 36

TATE

A month later, Blair and I unexpectedly found ourselves moving into our new place.

We'd been looking for a house in our price range in the same general area as Blair's place so Nicholas didn't have to adjust to new surroundings. We also wanted to stay as close to family as we'd been before. Despite everything still being up in the air with Taylor, I didn't want to be away from him. I was still holding out hope that we could move past this and be close someday.

We hadn't been planning to move so soon, but a colonial that had everything we'd been looking for came on the market—a large, fenced-in yard for Nicholas and Khloe, a big garage for my truck and Blair's SUV in the winters, and an office for Blair, something I'd insisted on. She needed her own quiet space in the house where she could escape the madness to study or just be alone. When the property became available, we made an offer the owners couldn't refuse. And since the house was already vacant, there was no reason we couldn't move in.

Blair still had some time left on the lease for the house she'd been renting, so a lot of her stuff was still over there. We'd been just casually moving things at our own pace, though we were officially sleeping in the new house now.

Tonight, the three of us were hanging out in our new living room after dinner, with a fire blazing. That was another cool thing about this house. It had a fireplace.

Scrolling through my phone, I found an old photo of myself that my mother had sent recently. In it, I was exactly the age Nicholas was now.

I faced the phone toward my son. "Who's this?"

He looked down at the photo and back up at me. "Nicholas."

Blair and I turned to each other and smiled.

"You think so, huh?" I challenged.

He nodded.

"That's *not* Nicholas," I told him. "That's me."

He shook his head. "Nooooo."

"Yes." I pointed to myself. "It's me."

"That's not Mr. T." He shook his head again. "That's Nicholas."

"That's not me now, but that's me when I was your age."

He studied the photo for several seconds, then looked up and practically stared into my soul.

I glanced over at Blair and whispered, "Now?"

Her mouth curved into a smile as she nodded.

I took a deep breath. "You look like me because I'm your daddy, Nicholas." My heart pounded.

He blinked, his expression hard to read. For a long moment he alternated between staring at the photo and looking at me.

"Do you understand what I told you?" I asked.

He shook his head.

"It took a long time to find you. But I'm your daddy. And you're my son. Do you know what that means?"

He shook his head again.

"It means that before you were born, two people created you. One was Mommy, and one was me."

Concern crossed his face as he looked over at Blair. "Mommy is still my mommy?"

"Yes," I assured him. "Mommy is still your mommy."

Blair reached out to gently rub his head. "Of course I'm still your mommy."

Nicholas seemed to think for a moment. "Mommy is my mommy…" He turned to me. "And *you're* my daddy."

"Yes. That's why you look like me. And that's why I loved you the moment I met you, even before you knew who I was."

After a long moment of silence, he nodded. "Okay."

"Yeah? That's okay with you?" I smiled at him. "So, you don't need to call me Mr. T anymore. You can call me Daddy, if you want."

"Daddy…"

"Yes."

"Daddy," he repeated.

"Yes." I bent to kiss him. "Daddy loves you, and I'll always be here, okay?"

"Okay." He grinned.

"Can I have a hug?"

He nodded and wrapped his arms around me. I breathed him in. I realized there was another layer to this conversation, explaining that the man he knew as Uncle

Taylor was actually his brother. But that was too much for today. Also, I'd need Taylor's guidance on how he wanted to handle that.

I pulled back to look at Nicholas, and he flashed the cutest smile. "Daddy?"

"Yes?"

"Can I have Skittles?"

"Of course."

"He's manipulating you." Blair laughed. "I told him he couldn't have any more until tomorrow."

"Already playing your father, huh?"

He giggled. And for the moment, all was right with the world.

The next day, we'd invited our parents over to the new house for Sunday brunch. I'd spent time with Blair's parents before, and she'd also met mine a few times, but this was the first time our parents had met each other. We'd let them know we'd told Nicholas about me so they didn't have to awkwardly call me Mr. T.

"Nicholas, every time I look at you, I see your daddy when he was a little boy," my mother said as we were finishing our meal.

Nicholas offered a shy smile.

"Has Taylor come around at all?" Blair's mom asked.

Blair shook her head. "Not yet." She reached for my hand. "But we're holding out hope."

An awkward silence fell over the dining room, and I felt my nerves spike. As we began clearing the table, Blair's dad headed out back. I realized it was probably my only chance to speak with him.

"Hey, Mr. Moynihan," I called from behind him as I stepped outside. "Can I talk to you for a minute?"

"Isn't it a little strange to be calling a man basically your own age mister?" He raised a brow.

"Actually, it is."

"I'm just messing with you." He winked. "Call me Craig."

"Craig. Thank you."

He raised his chin. "What's up?"

I sucked in a breath.

Here goes.

"It's important to me that you approve of my relationship with Blair. I know this sounds hypocritical, but if I had a daughter, I think I'd want to kill a guy if he got her into the predicament Blair found herself in. I have a hard time reconciling the fact that this happened the way it did with the idea that I wouldn't be okay in the same situation if it were my daughter. So, I can only imagine how you feel about me."

He chuckled. "I think one thing we have in common right now is that we realize we have little control over the decisions our kids make. Just as you can't control Taylor's reaction to this situation, I've never been able to control Blair, particularly once she got to be a legal adult." Craig shrugged. "I'm not gonna lie. I had every reaction at first that you probably feared I did. I wanted to kill you. I never thought I'd be able to stand across from you and not at least want to deck you."

I swallowed and let him continue.

"But the truth is, I *don't* want to deck you. Blair seems happier than I've ever seen her. She says nothing but amazing things about you, and that was the case even when we thought you were just a phantom who'd never reappear in her life." He paused. "You're also my grandson's father. So I have to be respectful of that. I don't have any intention of standing in the way of your relationship with my daughter."

"I appreciate that so much." I let out a relieved breath. "And in that case, I want to ask you something."

He nodded once. "All right."

"I don't know when, but I plan to ask Blair to marry me. I'm hoping to have your blessing." I swallowed.

Craig stared up at the sky for a moment. "Look, if the biggest problem I have with you is your age, that's not enough of a reason to dim my daughter's happiness. If you love her as much as you claim to, and if she loves you as much as I know she does, then yes. You have my blessing."

I let out another long exhale. "Thank you. I can't tell you how much that means to me." I laughed nervously. "I've had literal nightmares about your reaction to this."

"I wouldn't say your fears are totally unfounded." He flashed me a warning look. "As long as you're alive, there's still room for you to mess up. And if that happens, you'll have to contend with me. In the meantime, if you and my daughter have another kid, I'll be hoping it's a girl." Craig smirked. "You know, so I can sit back and laugh when you get to see firsthand how little control you have over your own daughter someday."

Great. I shivered at the thought. "Appreciate the... well wishes." I gritted my teeth and smiled.

He smacked me playfully on the shoulder. "My pleasure."

Chapter 37

BLAIR

Tate had just left the house for a worksite one morning when there was a knock at the door.

Assuming he'd returned because he'd left something behind, I opened it, shaking my head. "I knew you'd forget something. I—"

But it wasn't Tate. My heart clenched. "Taylor..."

He slipped his hands into his pockets and murmured, "Hey."

I stepped aside. "Come in."

He wiped his shoes on the mat. "Thank you."

The comfort he'd once had when he stopped by to visit was nowhere to be found. This Taylor was cautious and wary.

"He's not here," I told him, assuming he'd meant to catch Tate before he left for work.

"I know. I waited for him to leave so I could talk to you alone. That's what I can handle right now."

"Okay." I smiled sympathetically. "Can I make you a coffee? I have peppermint creamer. I know you like that."

"That would be amazing." He took a seat on the couch. "Thank you."

"Be right back."

As I went to the kitchen and prepared his coffee, I agonized over the situation. Tate wanted so badly for Taylor to reach out. And now he had, but specifically avoiding him. *Agh.* At least this was a small step in the right direction.

I returned to the living room and handed him a steaming cup of coffee. I'd added a little whipped cream, too.

"This is much needed. Thank you." He took a sip, then set the cup on the coffee table. "I'm sorry it's taken me so long to get in touch."

I sat on the opposite end of the couch. "Please. There's no need for you to apologize. I'm just happy you're here."

"I needed some time before I was able to talk about it."

I had to stop myself from launching into a monologue. There was much I wanted to say, but I tried to prioritize. "You know I never meant to hurt you, right? I had no idea he was your father when I met him, and from the moment I found out the truth at your wedding, I'd been trying to protect you and determine the best time to tell you. I'm so sorry you found out the way you did. I—"

"I know you didn't mean to hurt me, Blair." He shook his head. "I wish I could just be happy for you. You deserve to enjoy your life without worrying about my reaction to anything."

"I am happy. Truly. I've never enjoyed my life more. I know that might be hard to hear because it's related to your father. But it's the truth."

He swallowed and looked around. "Where's Nicholas?"

"He's sleeping. You want me to wake him up?"

Taylor shook his head. "No, of course not."

"Okay." I rubbed my palms on my thighs. "How's Juliana?"

"She's good. She's been dealing with my mental bullshit. I don't know what I'd do without her."

"I'm happy you found her."

He nodded and looked at the floor.

"Your dad's been beating himself up about hurting you," I finally said. "I know you're not ready to talk to him, but I need you to know that more than anything, he's concerned for you. He hasn't been the same since you found out."

Taylor rubbed his temples. "I've been trying to figure out *why* I'm so hurt by this. I get that neither of you knew the other's connection to me. I believe that you wouldn't have knowingly hurt me. But I can't wrap my head around him taking advantage of you."

I shook my head. "I'm gonna be very blunt here... For most of our time together at the resort, he did everything he could to resist my advances. There was no 'taking advantage' of anyone. I explained that to you before, when neither of us realized who he was. The situation doesn't change because the man I met and fell in love with turned out to be your father."

He nodded and looked out the window for a moment, seeming to contemplate my words.

"Look, Taylor, I know I was young, and maybe somewhat naïve. But I've grown up a lot since then. I have the benefit of hindsight. And there's still nothing I would change about the situation, aside from you being hurt. I love Tate even more now than I did then. And my dream is that someday you'll accept that and be happy for us."

He turned to me. "I want to get there. Even if I have issues with my dad, I at least owe *you* that acceptance. I promise I'll try." He shook his head. "I'm just not fully there yet."

"That's okay. As long as you're open to understanding us. I don't expect a miracle right away." I sighed. "I've missed you."

He smiled sadly. "Same."

"This awkwardness between us feels...weird." I blew a breath up into my hair. "I just want to like...shake you or something." I smiled.

He chuckled, a hint of sadness still apparent.

Nicholas's bedroom door opened and he wobbled out, rubbing his eyes. "Uncle Taylor!"

"Hey, buddy." Taylor opened his arms as Nicholas walked over.

As Taylor wrapped his arms around my son, he closed his eyes tightly. When he opened them, I could see that they were red.

"I missed you," he told Nicholas.

"Did you go back to Aruba?" my son asked.

"No, bud. I just...haven't been able to come by for a while. But I didn't want to go any longer without seeing you."

"Did you bring me a present?"

"Actually, I did." Taylor reached into his pocket and pulled out a mini red truck.

Nicholas's face lit up. "A truck!"

"Did you know I saved every single one of the toy cars from when I was almost as young as you? This truck is one of a kind. You can't find it anymore. I know how much you love trucks."

Nicholas stared down at it as Taylor wiped his eyes.

I felt my own eyes watering. "What do you say, Nicholas?"

"Thank you, Uncle Taylor."

"You're welcome, buddy."

"That was a really cool gift," I told him after Nicholas ran off to play with the new toy. "I know how important your old Hot Wheels collection is."

"Yeah, well, time to pass the torch."

That warmed my heart. As an only child, I loved that Nicholas had a big brother. "Thank you for being so sweet to him."

"Well, I have even more reason to bond with him now, don't I?"

I lowered my voice. "We haven't told him about you being Tate's son, too. We wanted to make sure you were ready."

He nodded. "I do want him to know." Taylor thought for a moment. "He understands now that my father is his dad?"

"We explained it only recently. We weren't sure what he remembered from the hospital. They've gotten close. Especially after the accident, Tate just needed him to know."

Taylor looked down into his mug. "I'm happy that Nicholas will have what I didn't. He doesn't deserve anything less." He sighed. "It might not have seemed like it at first, but I'm happy he found his dad."

I smiled, though I still felt sad. "Your friendship has meant so much to me over the years. I hate to see you unhappy because of my decisions."

He stood and walked his mug into the kitchen as I followed. "It's gonna be okay. I just need more time."

"Will we ever have the same friendship again?"

"I don't know if it will be exactly the same. That just comes with the territory. But you haven't lost me as a friend. And you never will."

I nodded. "Well, if I haven't lost you as a friend, Tate shouldn't lose you as a son. He's no more guilty than I am."

Taylor exhaled. "I get that on a logical level. Just...be patient with me. I'm trying. Even if I haven't been doing the work in front of you, I'm trying."

"That's fair." I smiled sadly.

He popped back in to say goodbye to Nicholas and then headed for the door.

"Can I tell Tate you stopped by?"

Taylor opened the door and stood in the doorway. "Yeah. You can."

"Anything else you want me to relay to him?"

Taylor shook his head. "No."

"Okay," I sighed.

He took a few steps down the sidewalk, then stopped. After a moment, Taylor turned around. "Actually... Tell him he's gonna be a grandfather."

Chapter 38

TATE

"Good job, kiddo!"

Nicholas had just thrown a football toward me with pretty impressive force and direction.

"Try to hold it like this, okay?" I demonstrated how to properly position the ball in my hand.

As we continued to practice tossing it back and forth, I heard a voice behind me.

"Is there room for one more?"

I turned to find Taylor standing there and froze. It had been two whole months since Blair had told me he'd come to visit her. I hadn't been sure when I'd see him again.

I got a little choked up and hadn't found my words yet when Nicholas ran to him.

"Uncle Taylor!"

Taylor knelt. "Hey, buddy." He ruffled his hair.

Nicholas looked up at him. "You wanna play with us?"

Taylor stood. "Sure, yeah."

I managed a slight smile and threw the ball to Taylor. He then threw it to Nicholas, who attempted to throw it to me. The cycle repeated for nearly half an hour as we quietly played and a gentle breeze blew around the yard. I didn't dare say a word so as not to break the moment. I just wanted it to last.

When I looked over at the window, Blair was watching us. She flashed a smile, and I assumed she'd chosen not to come outside for the same reason I hadn't said anything. Neither of us wanted to disturb the peace.

When Nicholas grew tired of the game, I finally turned to Taylor and said, "Can you stay for a bit?"

He slipped his hands into his pockets and nodded.

"Did you bring me a present, Uncle Taylor?" Nicholas piped up.

"What do *you* think?" he asked.

"He's not spoiled at all," I teased.

Taylor reached into his jacket and took out a little red car.

"Yay!" Nicholas said, running off with it.

"I recognize that car," I said.

Taylor nodded. "You gave me that one."

"Those were your favorite things when you were younger. I struggled with a way to relate to you back then, and those were the only things I knew for sure that you liked. That's why I sent so damn many of them."

"I've decided to pass them on to Nicholas," he said. "I don't need them anymore. And he loves them. Just trying to space them out, not give them to him all at once."

Nicholas took the car inside to show his mother, leaving us alone.

"How have you been?" I asked Taylor.

"Better lately, actually."

Hope sparked to life inside me. "Really?"

"Yeah." He nodded.

"I left you a couple of messages when Blair told me about Juliana's pregnancy. Not sure if you got them. I hope you know how happy I am for you."

"I know. I got both messages. And the gift card." He smiled. "Thank you."

"You're welcome. I want to do more but—"

"It's okay."

"Was the pregnancy planned?" I asked.

"Definitely not."

"Been there..." I chuckled.

"I guess that's one thing we have in common now." He grinned.

My heart leaped again. "What brought you by today?"

"Oh, you know...just in the area," he teased.

I arched a brow. "That's it, huh?"

"No." He kicked some dirt. "I realized that if I'm gonna be the kind of father I want to be, I need to work on my own issues."

"Boy, can I relate to that feeling..."

"I've started seeing a therapist."

I nodded. "You're a better man than I am. I keep saying I'm going to go, but I never do. I'm proud of you for that."

"Good. I'm sending you the bills."

"I'd let you. I'm not even kidding."

"Well, *I'm* kidding."

He began to pace around the yard, and I followed alongside him.

"I've been working on letting go of what I can't change," he explained. "There is no other choice." Taylor looked over at me. "I was blindsided. And I've spent enough time being butthurt about the fact that I was the last to know about you and Blair." He exhaled. "The situation is what it is. It's never gonna change. I can either lament it for the rest of my life or try to let it go. Holding on to the resentment will suck too much energy out of me. I need that energy more than ever now." He paused. "And ultimately, I owe it to Nicholas to be strong about this."

"I know it's not easy for you."

"It's not. But it's not impossible, either."

We took several more steps in silence before I asked, "What does this mean for you and me?"

"It means we take it one step at a time. I still need you to be patient with me, but I want to work our way back to where we were before this happened."

"That means the world to me, son." I froze. "Can I call you that?"

He nodded.

"I waited a long time to regain a relationship with you once. I'll wait as long as it takes to get it back again," I said.

Taylor stopped walking and faced me. "How are you and Blair doing?"

I cocked my head. "You really want to know?"

He shrugged. "I'm trying here. Just go with it."

"Okay." I smiled. "We're very happy." I hesitated, but decided I was done keeping things from him. I cleared my throat. "Actually, I want you to be one of the first to know that I plan to ask her to marry me."

He nodded. "Really..."

I swallowed the lump in my throat. "Are you okay with that?"

Taylor took a deep breath in and let it out. "You seem to make her happy. That's all I've ever wanted for her. And if I can't accept this, that's my own problem. I won't make things more complicated for you or feed her negative opinions. You seem to really love each other."

Thank God. "I asked her father for his blessing," I said. "But I'd feel remiss if I didn't also ask for yours. I know how important she is to you, and you to her." I paused. "Just to clarify... Do I have your blessing?"

He looked up at the sky a moment. "Yeah."

Letting out a long breath, I nodded. "I'm so grateful, Taylor. Thank you."

Taylor nodded and then checked his phone. "Listen, I've got to get going." He scrolled through some photos. "But I want to show you something first." He turned the screen toward me.

My eyes watered the instant I saw what it was: an ultrasound photo of his baby. *My grandchild.*

"Juliana's five months along now."

I shook my head. "I can't believe you're gonna make me a grandfather."

"I want her to know you."

It took a few seconds for it to register. *Her.* He wasn't talking about Juliana. He was talking about...*her.*

My *granddaughter.*

I pried my eyes off the image to look up at him. "Her?"

His mouth curved into a smile. "Yeah."

I hadn't met this little girl yet, but I knew I'd always protect her.

It seemed the curse Blair's father had placed on me was already coming true.

Chapter 39

BLAIR

"The petition is granted. The child's last name is hereby changed to Delaney."

Nicholas clapped upon hearing those words from the judge's mouth.

This name change in family court had been a long time coming, as it had been on the back burner for several months between the move, school for me, and Tate balancing his construction business with family activities.

While I'd had a handle on raising Nicholas before Tate reentered the picture, I hadn't realized how much better life could be with him as a partner. He'd left the name change up to me, but it had always been what I wanted. I knew it was especially important to Tate because Taylor had his mother's last name, Shea. I think he'd always dreamed that Taylor would choose Delaney as well someday, but that hadn't happened.

In other ways, though, things with Taylor had been slowly returning to the way they were before Tate and I reconnected. Taylor had come by a few times to visit Nicholas, and during the last visit, we all finally sat down and explained as best we could that Taylor was also Tate's son. Nicholas was confused at first, but he seemed to be getting it now and was thrilled to have a big brother.

Taylor had reached out since then to ask Tate to teach him how to fix something on his car, and Tate had also given Taylor and Juliana some money he'd saved for them to put toward a down payment on a house. He was pleasantly surprised when Taylor actually accepted it. Maybe having a child on the way had helped him to put aside his pride and be practical. I'd done the same when I'd agreed to let Tate help me financially.

Tate, Nicholas, and I held hands as we walked outside and down the steps of the courthouse.

"You know what I was thinking, Nicholas?" Tate said.

"What?"

"I was thinking...it would be really cool if Mommy's last name could be Delaney, too." He stopped walking. "What do you think about that?"

"Yes!" our son shouted.

"Should I ask her if she'd change her name to match ours?" He winked.

Oh my God. What's happening?

"Yes! Yes!" Nicholas jumped up and down.

Tate got down on one knee.

My heart began to race. While I'd suspected a proposal might be coming, this timing was a surprise.

Tate looked up at me. "I was wondering if you'd like to be a Delaney, too?"

Tears sprang to my eyes. "I want nothing more than to be a Delaney."

His eyes sparkled. "From the moment I saw you at that kiddie pool, I knew you were..." He paused. "I wanna say *the one*, but I didn't know that then. I knew you were special, but I don't think I realized you were the one until your absence. Being separated from you left me incomplete. I didn't feel whole again until after I found you, four years later. I will thank God every day that Taylor brought you to me. I'm too old for you, and I'll never feel like I deserve you, but I love you, Blair Moynihan." He reached into his pocket and took out a small box. When he opened it, the sun reflected on the most perfect oval solitaire. "Will you be mine always?"

"Will you marry Daddy?" Nicholas added, right on cue. He was in on this, too!

"Yes!" I bounced as Tate stood to place the ring on my finger. I wrapped my arms around him as our son hugged my legs.

Tate and I fell into a long kiss, as Nicholas expressed his distaste.

After we pulled away from each other, Tate said, "I asked your dad for permission, and he cursed me. He told me he hoped we have a daughter someday, and though he didn't say it, I think he also wished that she'll run off with some old dude."

"That sounds like my dad." I laughed.

"I also asked Taylor for his blessing."

My heart fluttered. "You did?"

"Yeah. Like four months ago, when he surprised us in the yard that day. Remember?"

"I do. And he gave it to you?"

Tate smiled. "He did."

I placed my hand on my chest. "That makes me so happy."

He gestured down to our son. "And of course, this guy gave me his permission, too."

"You did, did you?" I tickled him.

"Uh-huh!" He nodded. "Can we get ice cream now, Daddy, since I didn't ruin the secret?"

Tate winked. "A deal's a deal."

Two nights after our engagement, we got a surprise phone call. Taylor reported that Juliana had gone into labor that morning and given birth to their seven-pound, six-ounce baby girl.

He indicated that they hadn't chosen a name yet, but said if we wanted to come by to meet her, visiting hours ended at eight.

So after we finished dinner, Tate, Nicholas, and I got into the car to drive to the hospital.

As we walked into the building, Tate seemed tense.

I rubbed his arm. "You nervous?"

"Anxious to meet her, I guess." He shrugged.

When we got to Juliana's room, it looked like there had been an explosion of pink balloons and flowers. I placed our own pink flowers on a table to get lost in the mix.

"Hey!" Taylor beamed as he walked over to greet us.

Juliana held the baby, who had dark hair like both of her parents and was absolutely precious.

Tate reached out. "May I?"

"Of course." Juliana lifted the swaddled baby toward him.

"Hey, sweet girl." Tate rocked her, making his way to a seat in the corner. "Oh my God. She's the most beautiful baby I've ever seen."

"I definitely think so," Taylor agreed.

"We might be biased." Juliana smiled.

Nicholas walked over to where Tate was sitting. "Baby," he cooed.

"Yeah." Tate grinned. "This is your niece, Nicholas. Can you believe it?"

Everyone chuckled.

"You can thank your dad for that, little guy," Taylor cracked. "Maybe someday we'll get lucky and have our own reality show."

Tate glared playfully at Taylor.

Relief washed over me. If Taylor was cracking jokes, we'd come a long way.

"I can't believe I'm saying this..." Tate looked down at the baby. "But I'm your grandpa."

And if that was true, then in my mid-twenties, I was a step-*grandmother*. *Only in this family.* But what a blessing.

The next time I looked over at Tate, his eyes were glistening. Then I noticed Taylor smiling, too. I realized Tate's emotion wasn't just general overwhelm. He'd been looking down at his granddaughter's hospital bracelet.

I leaned in and got my first look at her name. It was the ultimate act of forgiveness.

Taylor might not have had Tate's last name, but he'd given it to his daughter, *Delaney* Marie Shea.

Epilogue

TATE

FIVE YEARS LATER

As I stood in line at the concession stand, I dialed Blair. "Hey," she answered.

"Where are you?" I asked.

"I'm dipping my toes while she swims in the kiddie pool."

"The kiddie pool, eh? Looking for a hookup?"

"You've got my number, Theodore Delaney."

I chuckled. "We'll head over there, then. See you in a few."

After I hung up, I turned to Nicholas. "Mom and your sister are at the kiddie pool. I need you to help me carry these drinks over there, okay?" I handed him one tray as I lifted the other.

Nicholas nodded, always eager to help. Since the line was so long, I'd ordered enough drinks for an army: four iced coffees and four slushies.

Nicholas and I each carried a tray over to where Blair and our daughter, Destiny, were just stepping out of the pool. Water droplets glistened on my beautiful wife's arms.

Blair's eyes widened as Nicholas and I approached. "What's with all the drinks? We're a party of four, not eight."

"These will last us the afternoon. I didn't know what you girls would want, so I brought a variety."

Blair dried our daughter off and got up on her tippy toes to kiss me. "I want the hot dad," she whispered in my ear.

"Some things never change." I winked. "Don't you find it ironic that when you met me you assumed I was someone's dad, and now I *am* the dad to your two kids?"

"That's one of *many* ironic things about our story, but yes."

"Very true, baby." I smiled.

This was our first family vacation since Destiny—whom we called Dessy for short—had been born three years ago. Midnight Key seemed like the obvious choice, not only because it cost us next to nothing, but because Blair and I hadn't been back here since the time we'd met. Our triumphant return to the place where it all started had been long overdue.

Nicholas was now eight, and I was having the time of my life raising these kids. Blair and I had gotten into a real groove over the past few years. I'd coordinated my work schedule around the three days she worked twelve-hour shifts as a labor and delivery nurse. That way one of us was always with the kids.

About a year after we'd gotten engaged, we got married. We had a traditional church wedding and reception—the whole nine. Blair had said she didn't care about all the fanfare, but I still found myself self-conscious about having taken opportunities from her, and didn't want her to miss out on anything. So I'd insisted on the big wedding, afraid she'd regret it if we didn't. I still struggled with occasionally feeling like I didn't deserve her or this life, but nevertheless, they were both mine, and I never took that for granted.

Taylor had been my best man at our wedding. I think becoming a father to Delaney had helped him to see how imperfect we all are as parents, and my granddaughter was the glue that helped put our family back together. I'd always be thankful for Taylor's forgiveness and the true second chance he'd given me after working through his issues with Blair and me. Taylor and I hanging out in the yard with our two little girls was always a sight to see. Every day with my family felt like a gift.

I looked over as Nicholas reached for a napkin and wiped his sister's bathing suit after she spilled some of her red slushie on herself. He was a good big brother and coming into his own. Nicholas loved flying drones and building stuff, while dancing was Dessy's thing. I'd sometimes take her to toddler dance classes on the afternoons Blair had to work. That was about the last thing I'd imagined I'd be doing in my mid-forties. But Blair's father's curse had fully come true, and with every year that Dessy got older, I braced myself. Of course, she had to look just like Blair, except with my dark hair. I was gonna be in trouble someday. At least she had two older brothers to back me up.

Blair took a sip of her iced coffee and turned to Nicholas. "Did you know this is where I met your daddy?"

His eyes went wide. "Midnight Key?"

"Yup."

"How old were you when you met him?" he asked.

Oh boy.

She glanced over at me. "I was nineteen."

"Almost twenty." I cleared my throat.

Blair laughed.

"How old was Dad?" he asked.

"Thirty-six," she offered.

Nicholas's brows drew in. "Did you think he was weird, Mom?"

"Not at all." She laughed. "I was sort of the weird one back then."

"I can attest to that." I raised my hand. "But meeting your mother was the best thing that ever happened to me."

His forehead scrunched. "What did you guys do here?"

"We went kayaking and...ate a lot." Blair cleared her throat.

Right. I remembered being *very* hungry on that trip. "We explored the jellyfish a bit, too..." I smirked over at Blair.

Nicholas narrowed his eyes. "So I wouldn't be here if you'd never met?"

"That's right." She pinched his cheek. "And I couldn't imagine that."

"Me neither." He sipped his slushie.

"You know what we can do later?" I tickled my daughter.

"What?" Dessy squeaked.

"There's a dessert bar, and you know what they have?"

"What?" She kicked her legs excitedly.

"Your favorite. Strawberries dipped in chocolate!"

"My favorite, too," Blair chimed in.

"Your favorite thing to torture me with, yes," I murmured. "I'll never forget that."

"It was all part of my evil plan." She winked.

I had my own evil plan tonight and could only hope the kids would sleep soundly so I could get some action. At least we had a suite with a separate bedroom. *Wish me luck.*

After we left the pool and cleaned up, the four of us headed down to one of the resort restaurants for dinner.

"Good evening, everyone," the server said as she approached our table.

I looked up at her. *Holy shit.* She looked familiar.

"Hey... I know you people." She smirked. "Been a while..."

It was the same waitress from years back who'd caught us in Blair's lie about me being her father, celebrating my fiftieth birthday.

She turned to Blair. "I see you and your *father* have a little tribe now..."

Blair's face reddened.

"Actually, this is my *wife*, Blair," I said. "And our two kids. Sorry about that fib."

"I'm surprised you remember us," Blair said.

"Oh..." She laughed. "Your story is pretty legendary around here. How could we forget the lying father and daughter? We joke about it all the time." She turned to me. "You must be pushing sixty now." She winked.

"Still kickin'." I shrugged. "I'm a grandfather, actually. No joke."

"Not sure what to believe with you people." She laughed, turning to our son. "What's your name, young man?"

"I'm Nicholas." He beamed.

She placed a menu in front of Dessy. "And this pretty little lady?"

Our daughter *loved* when anyone gave her the opportunity to state her full name.

She flashed a huge grin and proudly proclaimed, "Destiny Doris-Delores Delaney!"

Acknowledgements

I always say the acknowledgements are the hardest part of the book to write. There are simply too many people that contribute to the success of a book, and it's impossible to properly thank each and every one.

First and foremost, I need to thank the readers all over the world who continue to support and promote my books. Your support and encouragement are my reasons for continuing this journey. And to all of the book bloggers/bookstagrammers/influencers who work tirelessly to support me book after book, please know how much I appreciate you.

To Vi – You're the best friend and partner in crime I could ask for. I couldn't navigate my life without you. Here's to the next ten-plus years of friendship and magical stories.

To Julie – Cheers to more than a decade of friendship, Rebel cheese, and Fire Island memories.

To Luna –When you read my books for the first time, it's one of the most exciting things for me. Thank you for your love and support every day and for your cherished friendship. See you at Christmas!

To Erika – It will always be an E thing. Thank you for your love, friendship and summer visits. You're a rockstar—especially this year, and you know why.

To Amy – You're such a dear friend, and I look forward to each and every moment spent with you. If it weren't for our car conversation plotting this story on the way back from Boston, Taylor's Father might never have come to be!

To Cheri – Thanks for being part of my tribe and for always looking out and never forgetting a Wednesday. You're simply the best!

To Darlene – I am very lucky to have you as a friend—and sometimes signing assistant. Thanks for making my life sweeter, both literally and figuratively. You're pretty good at making me laugh, too.

To my Facebook reader group, Penelope's Peeps – I adore you all. You are my home and favorite place to be.

To my agent Kimberly Brower –Thank you for working hard to get my books into the hands of readers around the world.

To my editor Jessica Royer Ocken – It's always a pleasure working with you. I look forward to many more experiences to come.

To Elaine of Allusion Book Formatting and Publishing – Thank you for being the best proofreader, formatter, and friend a girl could ask for.

To Julia Griffis of The Romance Bibliophile – Your eagle eye is amazing. Thank you for being so wonderful to work with.

To my assistant Brooke – Thank you for hard work in handling all of the things Vi and I can't seem to ever get to. We appreciate you so much!

To Kylie and Jo at Give Me Books – You guys are truly the best out there! Thank you for your tireless promotional work. I would be lost without you.

To Letitia Hasser of RBA Designs – My awesome cover designer. Thank you for always working with me until the finished product exactly perfect.

To my husband – Thank you for always taking on so much more than you should have to so that I am able to write. I love you so much.

To the best parents in the world – I'm so lucky to have you! Thank you for everything you have ever done for me and for always being there.

Last but not least, to my daughter and son – Mommy loves you. You are my motivation and inspiration!

Other Books by Penelope Ward

The House Guest

The Rocker's Muse

The Drummer's Heart

The Surrogate

I Could Never

Toe the Line

Moody

The Assignment

The Aristocrat

The Crush

The Anti-Boyfriend

Just One Year

The Day He Came Back

When August Ends

Love Online

Gentleman Nine

Drunk Dial

Mack Daddy

Stepbrother Dearest

Neighbor Dearest

RoomHate

Sins of Sevin

Jake Undone (Jake #1)

My Skylar (Jake #2)

Jake Understood (Jake #3)

Gemini

Other Books by Penelope Ward and Vi Keeland

Denim & Diamonds

The Rules of Dating

The Rules of Dating My Best Friend's Sister

The Rules of Dating My One-Night Stand

The Rules of Dating a Younger Man

Well Played

Not Pretending Anymore

Happily Letter After

My Favorite Souvenir

Dirty Letters

Hate Notes

Rebel Heir

Rebel Heart

Cocky Bastard

Stuck-Up Suit

Playboy Pilot

Mister Moneybags

British Bedmate

Park Avenue Player

About the Author

Penelope Ward is a *New York Times, USA Today* and *#1 Wall Street Journal* bestselling author.

She grew up in Boston with five older brothers and spent most of her twenties as a television news anchor. Penelope resides in Rhode Island with her husband, son and beautiful daughter with autism.

With millions of books sold, she is a 21-time *New York Times* bestseller and the author of over forty novels.

Penelope's books have been translated into over a dozen languages and can be found in bookstores around the world.

Subscribe to Penelope's newsletter here.
https://tinyurl.com/mwz27c6h

Social Media Links:

Facebook:
www.facebook.com/penelopewardauthor

Facebook Private Fan Group:
www.facebook.com/groups/PenelopesPeeps/

Instagram:
www.instagram.com/PenelopeWardAuthor/

TikTok:
www.tiktok.com/@penelopewardofficial